I hope you fri[...]   [...]ng
and informati[...]

D0585425

love

Tony

_____.

'Tis easy enough to be twenty-one :
'Tis easy enough to marry ;
  But when you try both at once
'Tis a bloody big load to carry.

NOBODY'S FAULT

Brian is a poet who has ceased to write poetry and withdrawn into the cultivation of failure and silence. His needs are few; he lives in a small, shabby bedsit. There, when the need overtakes her, Tamsin visits him.

Keith is an extrovert, a wheeler-dealer who has risen to the top of the pop music industry. Trendy, gregarious, he knows everyone, goes everywhere – usually with his wife, Tamsin.

Tamsin loves both of them. All three have been involved since they were students, when they edited the university magazine together. Tamsin has not only loved both, she has been married to both – to Brian, as he tried to establish himself and a life-style in a croft in the Scottish highlands, and to Keith, for whom she is a prop to his self-confidence and a highly competent and presentable aid to his social and professional life.

The love triangle Mervyn Jones describes is an unusual one. With quiet skill and sympathy he describes the progress of their relationship from the callow uncertainties of their adolescence through the dramas of their early adult life to a strange placidity and resignation in the face of a difficult human entanglement. Probably Tamsin should never have married either man but, as Brian reflects, 'Tamsin has no gift for solitude'. Neither does she possess Keith's singleness of mind. Things are as they are, and ultimately everyone accepts this; it is, after all, nobody's fault.

Also by Mervyn Jones

Fiction
No Time to be Young
The New Town
The Last Barricade
Helen Blake
On the Last Day
A Set of Wives
John and Mary
A Survivor
Joseph
Mr Armitage Isn't Back Yet*
The Revolving Door*
Holding On*
Strangers*
Lord Richard's Passion*
The Pursuit of Happiness*
Scenes from Bourgeois Life*

Non-fiction
Potbank: A Study of the Potteries
Big Two: Aspects of America and Russia
Two Ears of Corn: Oxfam in Action
Life on the Dole
The Oil Rush* (with Fay Godwin)

*Available in Quartet editions

NOBODY'S FAULT

MERVYN JONES

QUARTET BOOKS LONDON

First published by Quartet Books Limited 1977
A member of the Namara Group
27 Goodge Street, London W1P 1FD

Copyright © 1977 by Mervyn Jones

ISBN 0 7043 2135 1

Typeset by Bedford Typesetters Limited

Printed in Great Britain by litho at The Anchor Press Ltd
and bound by Wm Brendon & Son Ltd
both of Tiptree, Essex

NOBODY'S FAULT

PART ONE

I

Tamsin came yesterday. I knew she would. She's in a phase of needing to be with me, I don't know why. If it's to do with Keith, I don't want to know. I should like her to be happy with Keith; at least, I don't wish her to be unhappy.

It still seems strange to both of us that she comes here out of another life, a life on which she closes the door, of which she doesn't speak and doesn't think while she's with me. Strange: but then her coming here has a meaning that it couldn't have when she came home to me every day, when we were . . . yes, we were married. She says now that being married is wrong for her, she'd always have been better off without it. Yet she's been married, first to me and then to Keith, ever since she was twenty-one.

The truth is that Tamsin has no gift for solitude. That's where she envies me. I'm here, within the door. She has to pass through the door, escaping from the other life – the marriage – to which nevertheless she needs to return. She dashes about in her little car, cutting down the time when she must be alone, hurrying to me, hurrying back to Keith.

When we were married she used to come in every day – at exactly six o'clock, barring a delay on the tube or a halt at the corner shop – and give me her news. Her job, her office, the little successes and failures, the little intrigues and rivalries. 'Oh, Brian, I must tell you . . .' Paterson went out to lunch and never came back. Miss Fowler so horrid to Penny that she cried. I recall the names, and Tamsin probably forgotten them; but I was the listener. And I had to find

and at night until very late, it's noisier than in the day; that's why I generally go out. Sometimes I can't hear the church clock strike and I've no idea of the time.

The couple who live in the next room to me go to bed about nine o'clock. He's an enormous brawny Scotchman, a building labourer when he has a job. She's a mousy little woman, meagre and flat-chested, but somehow attractive to men. It's really her room and she's lived with three men – all unskilled labourers, one of them black – since I've been here. She works, also on and off, as an office cleaner or as a home help in the nearest middle-class neighbourhood. The Scotchman screws her every night. She always sobs and whimpers . . . 'no, please don't, oh no' . . . as though he were beating her up, but all he does is standard screwing so far as I can tell. Perhaps he's too big for her and it hurts, perhaps he's a Catholic and won't let her take precautions and she's terrified of having a child, perhaps she really hates it. Why does she have him to live with her, then? I suppose she has no gift for solitude.

I went out later, to Solly's club. It was about half full, with most of the regulars and a sprinkling of what Solly calls tourists, though they're generally Londoners. I sat down at my usual table in the far corner and Dinah brought me a coke. Solly likes people to imagine that his club is a rendezvous for poets and artists, hence the free drinks. But he won't risk his poets getting drunk and noisy, nor does he want to spend too much on them. So we – the few of us who qualify – get only soft drinks.

The group started to play. The sound seems to want to burst out of the low-ceilinged basement room, but that's part of the idea. Despite the miserable pay Solly manages to get some rather good groups, mainly because of the availability of drugs – all kinds, if Solly trusts your discretion. Some of the tourists danced, either with their girls if they'd brought girls or with the so-called hostesses. Solly employs three girls in addition to Pepita, the stripper. Only Pepita is paid at all. The others get a free meal, drinks, and the opportunity to make pick-ups. They aren't allowed to leave until two o'clock. The club closes at three, so they have an hour to clinch a deal.

Just after twelve, as usual, Clancy came on and sang. Clancy isn't his real name, of course. He pretends to be an American and he did live for a time in Galveston, Texas, where he acquired a suitable drawling accent and his repertoire of songs. He sings folksongs and Western ballads, some authentically traditional and some commercial imitations – he doesn't know the difference. He has no voice or style to speak of, but he comes across passably with his country-boy good looks and his floppy yellow hair. After he's finished his turn the regulars shout for him to sing obscene songs; he shows reluctance but lets himself be persuaded. This goes down well with the tourists, who feel that they've struck a special occasion, almost a private party. And I like Clancy's dirty songs. The charm lies in his lack of leering slyness and the impression that he doesn't understand the double meanings and puns, which is quite possible as he's very stupid. Women feel that Clancy, in bed, would offer virility and innocence, like the sort of local youth they dream of picking up on holiday. Once a girl who'd come with a tourist tried to leave with Clancy and there was a row. Solly ordered him not to let it happen again. Clancy didn't mind; he isn't very interested in women.

Finally, Pepita came on and stripped. Pepita isn't her real name, of course. She comes from Leeds but, by some quirk – her father may have been a Spanish waiter, for all she knows – she's olive-skinned and raven-haired. Men feel that Pepita would be a tremendous lay, lascivious and fiery and all that. According to Solly, who lays all his girls, doubtless to establish his authority over them, this is far from true. Pepita is under orders to reject offers from tourists unless they come to the club repeatedly and raise their bids; most of the money will go to Solly. She's a sincere, decent girl, nearly as stupid as Clancy, and still believes she'll get rich in this game. She's the eldest of nine children by assorted fathers and sends postal orders regularly to her mother, so she needs the free meal at the club almost as badly as the girls who aren't paid. Her figure isn't wonderful, but she's rather a good stripper because she still aims to put on a good performance and hasn't yet acquired the usual look of weary boredom. She smiles at the customers with an expression of anxious amiability which can be mistaken at a distance for orgiastic pleasure.

There isn't a second show except on Saturdays when the club is packed, and in summer when there are real tourists with lashings of travellers' cheques. The regulars went home, and only a few people stayed to dance, or to claim the girls after two o'clock. Dinah came and sat next to me. She's a cheerful Cockney girl – or rather woman, nearly my age probably. As usual she talked about her kids, to whom she is devoted although they have to be in care. She's actually married to their father, who is in prison. He's coming up for parole but won't get it, Dinah is certain, because the date of the hearing is in a bad conjunction. Like practically all tarts, Dinah rules her life by astrology; there are some nights when she won't come to the club and Solly has to accept this. She likes me because we're both Pisces.

'You can stay with me if I don't strike lucky by two-thirty, Brian.

Dinah said. This is an offer she makes from time to time when she's in a good mood and the stars incline her to behave generously. Solly doesn't like it – he finds it immoral for a tart to have a non-paying customer – but Dinah is a free agent any time after two, so he can't prevent it. Dinah is a friend, so it wouldn't do for me to reject her offer. Anyway, I find her moderately attractive and I enjoy gossiping through her hearty breakfasts. It occurred to me that, thanks to Tamsin, I could pay for her tonight. But if I ever did that we'd cease to be friends. She would be obliged to look at me with calculating eyes as though I were any other customer.

At two-twenty, Filthy Jack lurched across to our table and said to Dinah: 'Come on, love, how about it?' He's a local garage foreman, quite a regular at the club. He has been with all the girls and they try to dodge him because he's filthy. They're not referring to his habits – the girls put up with anything in that line – but to the fact that he doesn't wash properly, he stinks of engine-oil and grease. However, money is money and when you're a professional you're a professional. Dinah gave me a wry grin and went to fetch her coat.

Solly came over and asked: 'How's life treating you, Brian?' This means that if I'm skint I can stay on to sweep the floor and wash up the glasses. It's no worse than any other way of earning, and better than some. I like the quietness in the deserted club and the lack of pressure, for obviously I can take as long as I like. But I never work when I don't need money.

'Pretty good at present,' I said. Solly nodded, understanding that I wasn't going to clear up. His offer, and my reply, are always phrased elliptically. At one level of thinking, Solly undoubtedly despises me. At another level, he doesn't feel it right to have his floor swept by a gentleman, a man with a college degree and an educated accent, a poet.

I left soon afterwards. The street was beautiful – a thin drizzle falling, the pavements and the metal of the parked cars glistening under the lamps. Many times, Tamsin and I used to come home at this hour, walking all the way from some party or other, taking our time, looking at shop windows, kissing again and again. I thought of her: but not too long, not too hard.

2

I don't knock at Brian's door. He knows it's me coming up the stairs, holding on to the creaking banister. He never looks surprised to see me, even if I haven't been for weeks. I don't ask myself whether he's pleased or not. I have a right to come, considering everything.

As I go through the house, I prepare myself for Brian's room. It isn't a house really but an assemblage of rooms, though a hundred years ago it must have belonged to some respectable family with six children and four servants. It's a secret place, where everyone is in hiding. All the doors are closed except the front door, which has no more meaning now than the corner of the street. The lock is broken, anyway. There are several bells, six or eight of them, with names on yellowing bits of cardboard, but I'm sure most of these names belong to people who have gone away years ago. The bells don't work either.

This time, there was a man sitting on the stairs between the second floor and the third. He didn't move. I had to touch him as I went past, my leg against his arm and shoulder, but he didn't notice me. I often meet people on the stairs when I come here, but they don't recognize me and I don't recognize them. They don't look at me, even. Sometimes I fancy that, by entering the house, I become invisible. The house draws me into its own atmosphere, an atmosphere of indifference. Not hostility or suspicion, not even a cold indifference – something quite gentle and tolerant, really. But an absence of curiosity, of the normal desire to wonder about other people, their business, their lives. Normal, I say. I don't know what's normal any more.

Brian was lying on the bed, as usual. That's quite reasonable; he has

only one hard chair. It's a small room; but as Brian has very few possessions and hardly ever moves about, it doesn't feel small. There are
two curtains, one at each end. Although I know that Brian hangs his
clothes behind one curtain, and there's a sink and a gas ring behind the
other, they impart a sense of mystery, these curtains. The window is
dirty and always closed. There's always a fug and a mixture of smells,
partly smells made by Brian – cigarettes, cooking out of tins, stale
socks he hasn't got around to washing, his own body – and partly the
ancient smells of the house. It's dark, or at least dim. There's a light, a
naked bulb, but Brian doesn't put it on, even on these winter afternoons
when daylight ends early.

'Hullo,' he said.

I said 'hullo', took off my coat, and hung it on the hook – nail, rather –
on the door. I was wearing an all-purpose black dress, quite simple but
expensive. I haven't got any cheap clothes now, I can't help it. But
Brian wouldn't notice a thing like that.

I asked: 'How have you been?'

'All right,' he said, as usual.

I took off my shoes and lay down beside him. I would have taken
off my dress if it hadn't been cold – Brian always wears a sweater. But
I don't have to take off my clothes to be naked with Brian.

The bed is hard and narrow, and yet I'm at rest here as I can't be
anywhere else. I become absolutely relaxed, like being weightless. I
try to be like this at the osteopath and at the dentist. Relax, they keep
saying to me. But I can't manage it except with Brian.

I said: 'I thought of you yesterday, at just this time. I was at the
library. I met a woman I know, very-nice-very-boring, and we were
talking, in between fiction S to Z and biography. And suddenly I
thought of you and I couldn't hear a word she said. Did you think of
me then?'

'I often think of you,' he said. 'Yes, I do believe I thought of you
yesterday, about this time.'

'So that was it.'

'That must have been it.'

I don't think he was telling me the truth, but it doesn't matter.
With us, things become true when we want to believe them.

We talked for a while. I don't come here to talk, I come to be quiet;
but we keep that in store. We never talk about the past because that
would hurt. We never talk about the future because we've given up
planning and hoping and all that bother. I don't talk about my life
outside this room because that would mean talking about Keith.
Brian wouldn't mind that, I daresay, but I should. And of course I

don't talk about the things that come up when we go to parties or out to dinner (Keith and me, that is) – who's in line for a new job, who's moving house or buying a cottage in Wales, where you're going for your holidays, inflation and tax avoidance and so forth – because Brian never did care about those things, and when I'm with him I don't either. In fact I don't care when I'm with Keith, but I look as though I did.

No, we talk about the cloud that travelled right round the world, and returned full of experience and wisdom. We talk about the sounds that are heard by the deaf, who hear from the inside outward instead of from the outside inward. We talk about our next lives, in which we can scarcely expect to progress, but Brian will be a fish and I'll be a seaweed, and we might even meet. It's Brian who thinks of these things. He's still a poet although he doesn't write poetry.

We lie quite still, and while we talk we don't look at each other. Voices don't grow older, until you're very old. I look older than when I married Brian – older than when I married Keith for that matter. But Brian doesn't look at me, and when I'm here I don't have to look at myself. I can't help looking at myself at Keith's house . . . at home, I ought to say . . . because it's full of mirrors. Brian hasn't got a mirror. Keith looks at me, too, frequently and attentively. Checking up, as he checks up on scratches on the cars and bare patches on the lawn. I look middle-aged, I know that. I hate the idea; I'd rather be old. My parents were always middle-aged and they still are, incapable of the dignity of growing old. And now I'm like them, I'm middle-aged too. But not here.

Keith still looks young. It takes an effort, but he's quite up to it. 'Youthful, vigorous' – he'll be called that for a long time yet. He looks after himself, just as he looks after a car. If he could replace himself, he would.

I'm aware that Brian looks bad, much the worst of the three of us. He doesn't eat properly, he takes no exercise, he stays in this stuffy room, so what can one expect? But I don't look at him. I'm with him, which is far more important.

After a while, we stopped talking. When I'm with Brian I can stop in the middle of a sentence, like falling asleep in the middle of a sentence when I'm reading. The time had come for silence, for the peace that I can't find anywhere else, only in this small room. It got quite dark. I knew that I ought to go, not because of Keith of course, but because I had attained what I came here for. But I was so relaxed, so completely at rest, that I couldn't move a muscle. I may have fallen asleep, I don't know.

8

Eventually I got stiff, lying there on my back. I have this middle-aged spine trouble, that's why I go to the osteopath. It brought me back to the rest of my life – my real life, or my unreal life, according to how you look at it.

'Brian, I have to go,' I said.

'All right.'

I combed my hair, put on my shoes and my coat. I couldn't see a thing but it wasn't for me to put the light on. I kissed him. I kiss him when I'm going, not when I come into the room; it's to keep me going after I leave.

Before I went, I asked: 'D'you need any money?'

'Might come in handy,' he said, as usual.

I gave him two five-pound notes. I pushed them into the pocket of his jeans, so they wouldn't get lost.

'I'll come again, Brian.'

'So long, Tam.'

'So long.'

I had to feel my way down the top flight of stairs, grasping the wobbly banister. After that there were some lights, naked bulbs of course, and finally the yellow glare from the street-lamp.

Keith was at home. He used to do a lot of after-office drinking and get home about eight, or else phone me and tell me to collect him and we'd have dinner out. But now he knows that I might be seeing Brian in the afternoon, he makes sure to get in before me.

I kissed him. I made it a medium kiss, neither perfunctory nor very sexy, so that it wouldn't tell him anything. He always knows, though. He doesn't say anything. He used to, but now he doesn't. He doesn't want me to know that he knows, but I do.

Yet he doesn't exactly know. He thinks I've been committing adultery. He would die rather than utter these old-fashioned words like 'adultery' and 'unfaithful', but really that's how he thinks. However, he also thinks that people like him shouldn't make a fuss about 'situations' which should be contained within phrases like 'the elastic structure of our marriage'. So it's easier for me to let him believe that adultery is what I've been doing. What would really hurt him would be to know how much it means to me simply to be with Brian.

He was drinking this special malt whisky he's discovered, Glen Morangie. Keith drinks a lot, but he doesn't get drunk. He's one of those people on whom one or two drinks have a definite effect, but an effect that doesn't increase as he goes on. It would be true to say that he hasn't been strictly sober, except in the mornings, since the price of a bottle ceased to matter to him.

9

I poured myself a gin and tonic and sat down in a swivel chair, moving it from side to side. We've furnished our house with things that don't stay still – mobiles, swivel chairs, rocking chairs. We strew cushions all over the place. We eat or drink or make love wherever we happen to be. The house is open plan, so you don't know what room you're in, still less what it's for. And because of the patios and balconies and picture windows, and the plants which proliferate everywhere, you don't know whether you're indoors or out. The house is ridiculously big for two people, but it isn't a house so much as a habitat, where we wander about like animals in an ultra-modern zoo.

'I saw Adrian today,' Keith said. 'He's on the box tonight.'

'Oh, is he?'

'Yes, he's in this new chat show.'

'What time's that?'

'Late. I'll check.'

'D'you want something to eat?'

'Just a bite. I had a huge lunch.'

I told the maid to make cheese omelettes. We ate them in the living-room, or drinking-room or whatever it is. Dialogue area, perhaps.

'How is Adrian, then?' I asked. I couldn't care less if Adrian has cancer, but it was something to say. I don't aim at silence with Keith.

'He's fine. He's decided to come out. Join Gay Lib, and all that. He wants to get a profile published with a picture of him and his boy-friend. Only thing is, the boy-friend doesn't want to be identified.'

'As a queer, or as Adrian's boy-friend?'

Keith said: 'Oh, come on, honey.' He doesn't like me to use words like 'queer' which he considers prejudiced and, worse, outdated. Also he doesn't like me to be lacking in respect for celebrated people – 'personalities' – such as Adrian. The conversation lapsed.

I had a bath, and then I got into bed and watched an old film. We have TV sets all over the place. Rather to my surprise, Keith came and joined me. I didn't expect him to sit (or rather lie) through a film with Cary Grant and Katharine Hepburn, in black and white too, but he must have heard that Hepburn is a cult-figure among the young. The film put me in a good mood. I knew it was going to end happily and thus shield me from reality.

After the film we watched the talk show. I wasn't keen on this, just willing to concede Adrian to Keith in return for Cary Grant, but quite unexpectedly it was great fun. It had been recorded out of sync, so that Adrian and the rest of them were still moving their lips after uttering their words, and for once Adrian looked as phony as he actually is. I giggled helplessly, and Keith decided that he'd better laugh too, so we ended up on pretty good terms. Not that we're ever on bad terms. That isn't where it's at.

Then he went to sleep. We didn't make love. At one time, when Keith first found out that I was 'unfaithful', he used to make a special point of regaining possession of me by making love to me, very passionately or at least energetically ('youthful, vigorous') after I'd been with Brian. That was to tell me that he knew. But now he just goes to sleep, right over on his side of the great wide bed. This serves just as well to tell me that he knows, because we still make love most nights in the ordinary way.

I went upstairs – our bed is downstairs, handy for a morning swim in the pool – and watched TV on another set until it closed down, and then listened to foreign stations on the radio, and read a long story in the *New Yorker*. I wasn't sleepy at all. But in the end I went back to bed, because it was better to be with Keith than to be alone.

3

Tamsin finished work at half past five and was home by six. The other girls used to linger, smoking and chatting after they'd cleared their desks, in the hope of being taken to the pub across the road by the men. But Tamsin looked at her watch, said: 'Bye . . . see you tomorrow,' and hurried off. Although she was the youngest, she was the only one who was married.

Arriving home, she ran up the stairs – she ran up stairs everywhere, including escalators – and opened the door to the flat. The second door she opened more tentatively, only a few inches, to see whether Brian was sitting at his table, actually writing. But no, he was in the armchair. (They had one armchair, two upright chairs, and an old car-seat where Tamsin usually sat in the evening.)

'You didn't hear me coming,' she said.

'I don't have to hear you. I know when you're near.'

'There could be a poem about that.'

Brian said nothing. She remembered that he didn't like her to suggest ideas for poems.

'I'm going to mend your sweater.'

'Are you?'

'Yes, it's got a hole. Brian, you know it's got a hole. It'll only get bigger.'

He took off the sweater obediently, and she settled down with the darning-wool. She had chased round to buy it in her lunch-hour and was relieved to see that it matched, or nearly enough.

'How about that poem, then?'

'I'll think about it.'

'No, no – the poem you're writing now.'

'Oh, that,' he said. 'It's no good.'

'Honestly?'

'No good at all.'

'Can I see it?'

'No, I don't want you to see my no-good poems. It's bad for my reputation.'

'You did finish writing it, though?'

'I scrapped it.'

It wasn't clear from this whether he had finished it or not, but Tamsin didn't want to pin him down. She wondered whether he had started anything else. He would tell her in due course, she supposed.

'You could be wrong about it being no good,' she said.

'No, I'm not wrong.'

Tamsin said no more until she had mended the sweater. He put it on again. He wore a sweater all summer, and didn't wear a jacket over it in winter.

'Oh, I must tell you,' she said then. 'Penny read one of your poems, the one that was in *Stand*. She said she couldn't understand it. So I told her to go and read it out loud. Which she did, in the loo.'

'That's good. There could be a scheme for loo-reading, couldn't there?'

'Movement poems,' Tamsin said instantly. 'Open your bowels to art. However, I don't think it helped very much with Penny. She tries to understand poems like understanding statistics.'

'She should do well at Paterson's.'

'You'd be surprised, she doesn't. She strains herself taking it too seriously, and then she makes mistakes. Perhaps she's been there too long.'

'How long should one be there?'

'I don't know. I didn't mean . . . You mustn't think I'm fed up, Brian.'

'You're not?'

'Well, it's a job in publishing.'

In their final year at the university, Brian and Tamsin and all their friends had joked wryly about the uselessness of an English degree. 'This time next year where shall we be?' Emptying dustbins . . . selling cinema tickets . . . making hotel beds. The ideal of an 'interesting' job, the goal since the innocent days at school, was something one didn't dare to mention for fear of derisive laughter. Yet Tamsin continued to hope quietly for a job that would justify the training in appreciation of everything from Beowulf to Orwell, by which she meant precisely a job in publishing. And here she was, with a job in publishing.

13

Still more remarkably, she had landed the first job she'd applied for. She had walked out of the interview with a distinct impression of failure. Not with a feeling of despondency, since she took a cheerful and resilient view of life on principle and had reckoned on several tries before she struck lucky, but with a sense of failure all the same because the interview went so badly. Mr Paterson scarcely appeared to listen to her answers to his questions about her education, her leisure interests, and her literary tastes. She didn't in fact have any intriguing leisure interests, and as for her tastes Mr Paterson wasn't so impressed by Gerard Manley Hopkins as she'd hoped. Then he stared at his calendar, and she was afraid that he found her hopeless and was seeking an excuse to curtail the interview without seeming unfair. After going over her university career for the second time, he said: 'Well, you'll hear from us, Miss . . . um.' In the waiting-room, Tamsin glanced at the other candidates and decided that almost all of them were more suitable than she was. Two or three were obviously older and doubtless had years of experience with other firms, and they all wore seemly dresses or tweed skirts, whereas she wore jeans as (at that time of her life) she always did.

But she got the job. Later, she wondered why. Perhaps – since anyone of the most modest competence could do the work, as she soon discovered – the names were tossed in a hat and the interviews were a charade. Perhaps Mr Paterson, who was very lazy, had decided to give the job to the first girl he saw (Tamsin's surname began with an A) unless she was deaf or crippled, and thus save himself the trouble of concentration in the other interviews. Perhaps her jeans, untidy hair, and generally studentish appearance appealed to him and were not a mistake after all. Perhaps she was favoured simply because she was pretty. Tamsin was annoyed by this idea, but a girl can't very well disguise or disfigure herself in the interests of justice.

She reflected, in this connection, that she might have landed the job on false pretences. She hadn't mentioned her marriage in her letter of application or at the interview; an employer, she thought, might be wary of her rapidly getting pregnant and leaving. Office gossip informed her that Mr Paterson couldn't stand his wife and made unmistakable (though discreet and delicate) advances to the girls. One girl had been his mistress for a couple of years, but had abandoned both him and her job in favour of a TV director; Mr Paterson had not yet succeeded in replacing her, other than in the office. Once she started work Tamsin let it be known that she was married, but she felt that she owed Mr Paterson an explanation.

Mr Paterson – son of the founder, and the only link with the firm's origins – had been responsible for bringing it close to bankruptcy. It was then taken over by a large group, the result being a complete change in its character. The terms of the deal assured him of continued employment and a block of shares, but he exerted hardly any influence, let alone authority, and willingly took on chores such as interviewing candidates for junior jobs. A tall, stooping man with rimless glasses and a wispy moustache, he spoke – when necessary – in a soft voice and a style of old-fashioned courtesy. He dictated long, discursive, profusely apologetic letters to authors whose books were unsuited to the firm's new policy, and otherwise avoided the office. His lunches, often lasting from twelve to four, were a standing joke. Everyone laughed at Mr Paterson, but Tamsin liked him very much.

Editorial direction was in the hands of Miss Fowler, who by contrast was voraciously hard-working and courteous neither to the staff nor to authors. She was also – it had to be admitted, though everyone hated her – extremely capable; her decisions were swiftly made and always right, in the sense of profitable. Tamsin had applied for the job almost idealistically, remembering the firm as the publishers of some of her favourite books. Now, however, it published no novels, no poetry, and only a short general list of popular biographies and ghost-written memoirs, heavily edited in the office. The main output was of the kind of books that one doesn't see in bookshops, or not in the bookshops ('proper bookshops') that Tamsin frequented: textbooks, computer handbooks, reference books.

Tamsin's job was to go through the books at the proof stage to check the statistical tables, graphs, diagrams and maps. Crude steel production had to be in roman type, estimated production had to be in italics. A town of 100,000 population had to have a black circle, a town of 250,000 had to have a black square. The work was absurdly easy and she was never pressed for time. Although Miss Fowler chivvied the girls and alluded sternly to printers' deadlines, she had a low estimate of what a girl could do in a day, so an hour of steady work amply made way for half an hour of relaxation.

To friends who envied her this job in publishing, Tamsin confessed that it had nothing whatever to do with literature. The girls who typed invoices or sat at the phone switchboard, and hadn't been anywhere near a university, could have done her job as well as she did. But it was a start. She might, after a time, get on to the books on the general list and have a chance to put them into less excruciating prose. Better, she might – qualified now by experience – find an opening in another firm that lived up to her idea of what publishing ought to be about. She wasn't impatient nor, on the whole, discontented with her situation.

All day, she thought of Brian. She thought of him in the coffee-break, the lunch-hour and the tea-break; and when she got ahead of her work and took it easy; and indeed while she was working, once she'd acquired the knack of doing the job adequately though applying only part of her mind. At times, she had a wild desire to dash out of the office and go home. More reasonably, she had impulses to phone him, and this she occasionally did when Miss Fowler was safely occupied with a visitor. But only occasionally; it was her duty not to disturb him.

'You're very much in love, I can see that,' her mother had once remarked.

Tamsin accepted this phrase with indifference tinged by irritation. It seemed to her, like most of the things her mother said, to hit the nail not quite on the head – to reduce a truth to a slot in a familiar category instead of seeing its uniqueness, its particular quality. She hadn't, either when she agreed to marry Brian or since, thought much about being in love with him. To friends, she said: 'We're absolutely on the same wavelength' or 'We're so much the same sort of person.' Some times, when they were impelled to a sudden kiss or when they were in bed, she said: 'I love you'; but this she offered almost as a joke, as part of a sensuous game, like the kiss itself or like an arousing touch on a responsive part of his body. If Brian said: 'I love you' – but he seldom did – she took it in the same spirit and answered: 'Isn't that nice?'

As she saw it, the most ordinary people could be in love: people without sensitivity, without imagination, without the wish or the capacity to deviate from a set pattern. By loving – or rather being in love, a satisfactory condition like being in funds or being in good health – they achieved something that it would be regrettable to miss. It was the same with making love, a phrase which Tamsin (as an up-holder of clarity in language) disliked because it didn't mean what it said. Anybody could do that, or almost anybody, and it was no wonder that some people – as her mother disapprovingly said – 'thought about nothing else', since they did nothing else that provided the sensation of being fully alive. She enjoyed making love with Brian, since she was readily overcome by a sexual ardour which she considered to be some-what at odds with the rest of her character, but she attached no great importance to it. It wasn't the central part of their life together; it was, she rather felt, an entertaining diversion from the intensity of that life.

So, for that matter, was the state of being in love. Tamsin could marshal several proofs of its relative superficiality. One could be in love with someone with whom one could never share anything except love; thus, she had been in love with Keith shortly before deciding to marry Brian – even perhaps at the moment of that decision. Luckily, she hadn't married Keith. One could fall in love (the passivity of the verb was significant) at a time of disorientation or loneliness, and one could fall out of love – a truly comical phrase, this, like falling out of bed. And love could dwindle away without the fact being even noticeable. If that didn't prove its secondary status, nothing did. In this case, supposing that there had been nothing else, the two people concerned were left without any real bond. For instance, on her principle that anyone could be in love, Tamsin was ready to credit that her parents had been. Now they were not; they rather disliked each other, though inertia and convention kept them from being fully aware of it. If her father came into a room when her mother's back was turned, she didn't sense his presence. It was impossible for Tamsin to imagine that this could ever happen with herself and Brian.

No: what she felt with Brian and owed to Brian was an enlargement and enrichment of her personality. She was incomplete without him, she was complete with him. Some people, she supposed, derived this enrichment from belief in a faith or a cause, and some from devotion to a leader or teacher, which Brian certainly was not. For her, all that was needed was the awareness of Brian's presence, an awareness of which sight and hearing were merely the simplest and, by now, unnecessary means. Even his presence was not indispensable. The thought of him, when she opened herself to it in the office or in the street, was a transformation not only of her surroundings but of her grateful self.

When she was with him, she found herself attaining her full potential. Her body moved gracefully and with deft precision; she succeeded, too, in matching his perfect and characteristic stillness, though it had been said of her ever since she was a child that she couldn't sit still for two minutes. She felt herself to be a beautiful woman. 'Objectively' she was good-looking like scores of other girls in London, but objectivity meant an appraisal by men or women who had no special effect on her. It was within herself that she assumed the luxurious ease of beauty. Her mind, at the same time, worked with a smooth power that delighted her. Ideas came to her readily, and not as tentative searchings but in finished form. Problems yielded manifest solutions. She was able to talk in a way that fully expressed both reality and thought, with wit and insight, unfailingly finding the right word.

She had begun to feel this responsive expansion of herself from the time when she'd first met Brian, although at first she had ascribed it to the atmosphere of the university. In her first year she hadn't known him well; they attended some of the same lectures but were in different colleges. In the second year they had become friends and, far more important, she had been alerted to his astounding value by reading his poetry. But in the final year she had been in love with Keith and publicly recognized as Keith's girl-friend. She hadn't, so she believed now, been ready for Brian. It required a certain maturity, a certain courage and a certain humility to merge her life with his.

Tamsin and Brian were living in a furnished flat in Muswell Hill. The two rooms were on the top floor, once the servants' attic, of a house bought for conversion. They had taken it because it was cheap, because the landlady was pleasant, and because the house stood on a ridge and their windows had a view. There was only just enough furniture to comply with the law, but for Tamsin this was an advantage. She was gradually buying things in junk-shops and street-markets, as well as putting up prints and posters, and each acquisition made the flat more their own.

'D'you like it?' she would ask every time.

'Sure.' Brian was indifferent to possessions, almost indifferent to material objects.

'You don't like it. Why not say so?'

'Yes, I do.'

'It won't be wrong for you?'

'Oh no.'

Tamsin didn't really believe that the shape or colour of anything in the flat could put Brian off his writing, but she had to be reassured. The larger of the two rooms had to serve both as a living-room – they invited friends from time to time – and as Brian's work-room. Had he demanded to live with nothing but a bed, a chair and a table, within bare walls (and this would have suited him, she suspected) then she would have instantly agreed.

When she thought of Brian's work, as she did every day in the act of thinking of him, she was thinking of the essential centre not only of his life but also of hers. She had written poetry at school; her critical sense had told her that she would never achieve anything serious, but she had an abiding memory of the creative joy. Having a share in the making of Brian's poetry – by being in tune with his silence and his reveries, and by their intimacy of thought and feeling – was the true cause of the enrichment of her life. However, this reminded her of the triviality of her own work. Measured by the significance of even a single poem, it didn't matter whether the Paterson books were produced or not. Her work was impersonal, in that anyone could do it, while Brian's poetry was unique to himself. And her routine tasks didn't even engage the whole of her intelligence, let alone her deeper nature. Meanwhile Brian was embarking constantly on fresh ventures, drawing on the utmost of his perception of truth, painfully transmuting emotion into images of resolute calm.

Always, when she thought of him during the day, she pictured him seated at his table – the same scrubbed deal table at which they had meals and sometimes played cards, but essentially 'his', the work-table. (She was planning to buy him a desk when she could find one that looked right and was a good bargain.) In fact, she didn't know how long he spent at the table. She got up first, had a cup of coffee and took one to Brian, and then went off to work. He was still in bed when she left the flat, and when she came home she might find him sitting in the armchair or perhaps lying on the bed in his clothes. But obviously one couldn't sit at a table and concentrate on writing poetry for eight hours a day. Even her own work, infinitely less demanding, was relieved by spells of relaxation.

She was puzzled when he dismissed a poem as 'no good', apparently without regret. She was disappointed, even unhappy, when he went for days and even weeks without completing a poem to his satisfaction. But she had not the least doubt of his success. She tried not to think of success in terms of output . . . still less publication . . . still, still less payment. The success was in Brian's growth as a poet, as a man of a rare and wonderful kind.

All the same, in the first year after leaving university he had two poems accepted by papers that paid, and one by the BBC, as well as four by papers that didn't pay. Also, he was awarded an Arts Council grant.

They hadn't much money, for Tamsin's salary was small and Brian's grant was more of an encouragement than a serious contribution to income. His father, who was a surgeon, handed out cheques from time to time. He thought it absurd for Brian to do nothing but write poetry, but he liked Tamsin and was sorry for what she'd let herself in for. 'Buy yourself a pretty dress, my dear,' he said. Tamsin didn't want pretty dresses and didn't mind having to manage on a tight weekly budget, which seemed to her to guarantee the authenticity of the life she had chosen. Still, it was useful to have a little extra money. Brian bought books; he went to the cinema, sometimes in the afternoon if his writing wasn't going well; he liked to meet friends in pubs, and to accept invitations to parties which meant bringing a bottle. The last thing she thought of was to grudge him his pleasures. His work was so hard.

4

When Keith and Tamsin were first married, they lived in the flat which had been his home for several years. It was a penthouse, and his office was in the same building. By arrangement with the property company that owned the building, the rent was set off as a business expense. However, Keith intended to buy a house. Perhaps he wanted to move so as to dismiss the memory of the numerous girls whom he'd brought to the flat, some of whom indeed had lived in it. Tamsin didn't care, either about whether they lived in a flat or a house, or about the girls.

The door of the lift opened and she stood aside to allow a load of Keith's employees to emerge. At the end of the working day, they retained their air of compulsive brightness. Some of them smiled at her, whether because they actually knew her or because they recognized her from the big photograph in Keith's office. She had the lift to herself going up and was at once enclosed in the privileged atmosphere of the penthouse.

The maid told her that Keith had phoned to remind her that they were going out at seven o'clock. She hadn't forgotten; Keith relied on memo-pads and tape-recorded messages, but she always kept things clear in her head. They were having dinner with a film producer who lived in a manor-house in Hertfordshire. It would take a good hour to get there, even with Keith's driving.

'All right, Vesna, I know. Start a bath for me, will you?'

Vesna was from Yugoslavia. Keith had taken her on for a year, through an agency. Tamsin suspected that he didn't want servants who could follow rapid and colloquial English conversations. But as it happened, Vesna spoke pretty good English. She had a degree in literature, a fact which gave Tamsin a measure of sardonic amusement.

As usual, Tamsin lay as deep as she could in the bath, with only her nose and eyes out of the water. She had got into the habit of taking a bath twice a day, or even three times. It had become an irresistible indulgence, like drinking for some women and eating chocolates for others. Vesna also took baths – so she had admitted to Tamsin – when she was alone in the flat. She was packing as many as possible into the year, as there was no bath in her home in Mostar. Keith preferred a brisk shower, hot and then cold.

In the bath, Tamsin felt her body to be melting, inchoate, confluent with the water. She was relaxed, or as relaxed as she ever was. Yet she was alert, waiting for Keith to come up from the office. When she heard him in the bedroom, she quickly got out of the bath and began to dry herself. She disliked having him see her in the bath – a private place, more private than bed.

'Sweetie-love?' he called.

'I'll be right with you, darling.'

She went into the bedroom. Keith, stripped to his singlet and drawers, was sitting on the edge of the bed and clipping his finger-nails. He was scrupulous about his appearance, much more so than she was. He jumped up and embraced her.

'Missed you, honey-girl. Missed you all day.'

It never occurred to Keith that these endearments were impersonal, in that he had used them to the various girls. Tamsin had always called Brian by his name and Brian had called her Tamsin, or Tam; that had been more intimate.

Keith squeezed her bottom with both hands and bent his head to kiss her breasts. He was keen on bottoms and breasts. Almost every day, he assured Tamsin that she had a marvellous figure. It was true that her breasts stood out well, since she had always been slender, but she now – obliged by Keith's praise to consider the matter – saw herself as thin and bony. However, it seemed that for Keith not putting on weight was equivalent to having a good figure.

'Mm,' he said. 'Love you like this. All soft and warm and steamy. Lucky me.'

She pressed close to him and, when he released her, clung to him for a few more seconds, partly because this pleased him and partly because she really enjoyed every contact with his body (he certainly had an admirable figure). It had occurred to her that they represented to each other a kind of automatic stimulus, like the stimulus provided by erotic pictures in sex research experiments. They were always touching each other, even when they were with other people – holding hands, rubbing legs, fondling. They made love often, and not only at night. Right now would have done very nicely, except that they had only just time to dress and go out. On principle she had never considered this to be of much importance, but it was more important with Keith than it had been with Brian.

She put on her underclothes, sat down at her dressing-table, and began to brush her hair. He took out his electric razor for a shave. His beard wasn't really fast-growing, but he had convinced himself that he needed to shave twice a day.

'What are you going to wear, love?' he asked.

'I don't know. What d'you think?'

He had already decided, of course.

'How about the turquoise silk? You look smashing in that.'

'Yes, all right, the turquoise silk.'

And the white shawl, and the Persian sandals, and the gold ear-rings; and the long hair, grown in the last year, which – even as she brushed it – Tamsin didn't quite feel to be her own.

Keith often went with her to buy clothes, indeed made her go, since his enthusiasm for them far exceeded hers. She sometimes thought that he was redesigning his wife to look like the wife whom, as an ambitious boy, he had resolved to possess. But she knew that his taste was good and, considering the money at his disposal and the circles in which they moved, wasn't ostentatious. On some occasions he had stopped her when she wanted to buy something too stridently demonstrative or, in a mood of irony, to go out loaded with jewellery like an Edwardian queen of high society. After taking his advice she was always pleased with the result – given that she was going to play this game in the first place. By this time she was beginning to enjoy dressing well, because it was the right sort of game to play with Keith. And after all, she wasn't young enough to go about in a shirt and jeans.

A game: what had to be accepted, in living with Keith, was that he treated everything as a game, including his work. This created an atmosphere of fun – they certainly had fun – and of excitement but also, paradoxically, of safety; for nothing that could happen, even the collapse of his business and the loss of his money, would be taken as tragic. Money was important to him, he was frank about that, but it wasn't all-important. Still, if nothing was wholly serious, nothing was merely frivolous either. When Keith played a game, in the ordinary sense – he played a good many: poker, bridge, squash, tennis, golf – he played skilfully and he played to win.

She was amused, but also impressed, by the range of his expertise.

He really knew about a great variety of things, from investment to gourmet food and from cars to women's clothes. In each of these he could become completely absorbed, but each could be completely dismissed from his mind. Tamsin, who had always assumed a ranking of the significant and the insignificant, didn't find it easy to adjust herself. She was beginning to think, however, that it wasn't a bad way to live. Anyway it was how she was living now, with Keith.

She had first become aware of Keith's outlook when they were students. With his working-class background, Keith knew that he could have been earning good money instead of living on a grant. He could have started in his teens on the road to success, which he never imagined to depend on degrees or other bits of paper. He went to the university, all the same, because he was intrigued and pleased to find that he could – he had brains, that was proved. Having no illusions, he wasn't liable to the disillusion of middle-class students who became suddenly aware that what they were doing might turn out to be pointless. He simply played the game to win. He finished with an upper second, the same as Tamsin. Brian got a pass degree.

Although she hadn't seen Keith for years after marrying Brian, Tamsin thought now that he hadn't changed much. He was successful and rich, but that was to be expected. He had grasped his opportunity and begun to exploit it at once. It was the time – the early sixties – when pop music swept the country like a new religion. Keith saw what it meant to 'the kids', to millions half a dozen years younger than he was. Youth as he'd known it had been dull, dominated by a vague searching, a sense of something missing. Suddenly, to be young was to be transported by a collective excitement.

Keith started a pop magazine. At first he wrote every word of it himself, laid out the pages, saw it through the press, and regularly sold it outside concerts. It went like a bomb.

By now, he had four magazines. All had snappy monosyllabic titles: *Group*, *Disc*, *Rock*, *Sound*. They were supposed to be in hot competition with one another and each had its loyal supporters. To keep up this pretence of rivalry, Keith ensured that each magazine championed different heroes and heroines of the pop world. The photography and the colour-printing were superb. The achievements, future plans and private lives of pop stars were described in detail. This was possible because the groups had an interest in the magazines, or Keith in the groups – Tamsin didn't grasp the financial arrangements. The magazines sponsored concerts, tours and festivals; Keith also owned, or had a share in, a number of clubs. It had become difficult, in fact, for a new group to make headway without his aid. Over the years, as the spontaneous amateur movement had solidified into big business, Keith had become a businessman.

The curious thing was that, although of course Keith knew an enormous amount about pop music, he wasn't particularly keen on it. When he pleased himself, he went to a Mozart opera. He said that it made a change – he listened to enough pop in working hours – but Tamsin saw that he did prefer Mozart.

She had scruples (on Keith's behalf) about the process of making money from the helplessly ardent fans, who after all were in the grip of a disinterested passion like the passion for poetry or ballet. But money was inseparable from pop, was indeed an element in its glamour, as in the glamour of Hollywood a generation earlier. The stars, she supposed, made more than Keith, and the fans admired them for it. Extravagant parties, houses with swimming-pools, flashy cars – these belonged to the mystique of pop, just as authentically as seedy bars had belonged to the legendary mystique of jazz.

It was a game to Keith, the chief of those absorbing games that he played with zest and skill. But Tamsin had observed that most occupations, if they were not drudgery (and was that preferable?), were games. Take as an example the distinguished surgeon, Brian's father. 'Lost a patient today, I'm afraid,' he would remark casually as he sipped his sherry. He had done his best on a difficult course, and gone down a point. It didn't spoil his appetite for dinner, nor presumably his sleep.

And what about Tamsin? She was in Keith's game as an auxiliary; she was tested for her response to new groups, she offered advice about the styling of the magazines. But she knew far less about the business – the scene in general – than he did, and she didn't try to compete with his flair and intuition. There was a value in this role: the value of detachment. Her essential self remained apart.

She was also in the game as a beneficiary. She lived in this luxurious penthouse. She had Vesna to spare her any chores to which she was disinclined. She wore fine clothes. She was taken to expensive restaurants, to Covent Garden, to holidays on Greek islands. The only difficulty would have been to stop Keith spending money on her. She didn't try; spending money, rather than making it, gave him pleasure.

She wouldn't have married Keith if he hadn't had money. It wasn't a question of marrying him 'for his money' in the usual sense of that phrase, nor even for ease and comfort. Tamsin knew herself well enough to be free of that reproach. It was simply that money was the index of his success, and success brought to fruition all the qualities in him that had attracted her years ago and charmed her now: his vitality, his robust self-confidence, his gaiety and cheerfulness, his generosity. If

24

he lost his money now these qualities wouldn't, she believed, be much diminished. But if he'd never succeeded he would have been a less considerable, and surely a less attractive, man. For he was a self-made man, really, in the truest sense: a man who had steadily added to his endowment.

. For several months after her marriage, her sole occupation was to be Keith's wife – 'just' his wife, as one says. She was kept pretty busy meeting new friends, entertaining and party-going, adorning and displaying herself. When she was alone she did the things that she hadn't, for years, had time for; she went to lectures, she went to museums and exhibitions, she spent hours reading or listening to music, since she could buy all the books and records she wanted. Nothing involved her much, but she wasn't conscious of idleness and the days passed pleasantly. She could go on like this, she felt, for the rest of her life. Keith clearly expected her to.

However, she was afraid of a change in herself, beyond the change implicit in being married to Keith. After a phase of relaxation, her new life became distasteful to her – partly because of how she appeared to other people, principally because of her conception of herself. It didn't suit her. Rightly or wrongly (she wasn't taking a moral stand) she wasn't cut out to be a hedonist. She told Keith that she was going to look for a job.

He was amused, naturally, and made a few cracks about any help with the household expenses being welcome. But he didn't mind. It was a matter of Tamsin being Tamsin, so far as he was concerned. It distinguished her honourably from the girls he'd lived with; they'd all stayed in bed until noon and lounged about the flat while he worked.

Tamsin found a job with a housing trust. Its tenants had originally been working-class families, but with the passage of time – the trust was a venerable institution and a Victorian air pervaded its office – they were mostly old people. Her job was to inspect the houses and report on any repairs that might be needed. She was also supposed to find out whether the tenants were neglecting the property, in which case an effort was made to get them moved into old peoples' homes. If they were behind with the rent, she had to find out why. The rents were low, and anyone who failed to pay generally turned out to have a problem of a more or less intimate nature, ranging from alcoholism to meeting the debts of an improvident son or daughter. Thus, Tamsin had become an unofficial social worker.

Keith, having grown up close to poor people, wasn't sentimental about them. He warned Tamsin against being conned – 'They're out to see how much they can make you believe, love, it's only natural.' He would have liked her to get some amusement out of her work, as he did out of his. But if it made her happy, that was what counted.

Certainly, the work was not onerous. The trust couldn't pay much – somehow, Tamsin had never had a job with a good salary – and the directors were delighted to have found someone of Tamsin's integrity and intelligence. If she didn't feel well, she had only to phone and say she was taking the day off. There was no urgency about her reports; she delayed some of them on purpose, to keep the tenants out of trouble, and nobody pressed her. The office staff regarded her with a degree of awe. She didn't talk about Keith, but they guessed that she was a wealthy man's wife. Perhaps it was her clothes, though she tried to dress simply for work; perhaps it was her car. It was only a Mini, but her daily use of it indicated that it was the second car in the household. (Actually it was the third.)

Inevitably, Tamsin herself was conscious of the gulf between the social sphere in which she spent her working days and that to which she returned in the evening. If Keith took her out to dinner – nothing special, just a 'Let's eat out, sweetie' impulse – he spent more than the trust's average tenant had to live on for a week. But Keith, she reasoned, wasn't exploiting the tenants. He made his money out of teenagers, most of whom had plenty in their pockets. Anyway, Tamsin couldn't change the world. Indeed, she had always been sceptical about the possible benefits of revolution, even of social reform.

Now and again, she thought of giving up the job. It had a smell of charity, of being a sop to her conscience and a support for her tenuous self-esteem. And she didn't, to be honest, care deeply about it. Perhaps it would be more consistent to find a job – in publishing for instance, she thought wryly – that would mean spending her days with people like herself, youngish educated wives who preferred not to think themselves useless. (People like herself, except that they would buy their clothes at C & A and their husbands would have mortgages.) Or perhaps it would be more consistent, when all was said and done, to be 'just' Keith's wife. Consistent with what? With the choice she had made, presumably.

But then, the people at the trust would miss her. The tenants would miss her. It was cheering to be valued.

She had breakfast in bed and went out about an hour after Keith, who began the day with a run round Hyde Park or a swim. After going through her papers and having a chat – dignified by the name of 'conference' – with the rest of the staff, she set off on her rounds. She spent as long with each tenant as she felt like. It didn't depend on what they had to say, but on her mood. Sometimes she took pleasure in listening to long chapters of reminiscence (though her attention was likely to wander); sometimes she was brisk and business-like. She was always scrupulous in noting down the essential facts. That was because she found it natural to do a job efficiently, or doing it otherwise would have nagged at her; and also to persuade herself that she cared.

The tenants believed, she could see, that they had a friend in Tamsin. In a sense, this was true. The trust might have employed some bastard who would have got them evicted on the least justification. But a friend, really? They were imagining it, out of innate good nature or anxiety or loneliness.

Loneliness, mostly. Tamsin breathed its stale atmosphere every day. There was an old couple – in fact not very old, for the man still worked as a factory storeman – whose children for some reason had all emigrated to Canada or Australia or Rhodesia. It had been a large family and had given the parents whatever they'd found in life of significance or pride, and now it was in dispersed fragments. Echoes were picked up occasionally in the form of Christmas cards or cuttings from local papers, all of which were eagerly shown to Tamsin. But most of the sons and daughters were known only to memory.

There was an old woman, really old this time, who had never got over the death of her husband. He had been an actor, a handsome fellow to judge by photographs, and had died suddenly on tour before his wife knew he was ill. He wasn't given proper treatment, she believed. Tamsin had to look at wedding pictures, holiday pictures, postcards from provincial towns, programmes of plays by Maugham or Charles Morgan, reviews in which a mention of the actor's name was lovingly underlined. There had been no children. The death had been effectively the end of the woman's life. She had been a widow for forty-five years – had suffered longer, by a good margin, than Tamsin had been alive.

There was an old man, once a sailor, whose mind dwelt obsessively on the remembered warmth of the various women he had conquered. He carried on a pathetic kind of flirtation with Tamsin, in the guise of the man he had been long ago – 'You should have come across me then, I'd have given you a time and a half.' Tamsin pretended to be shocked by his jokes, and as a special favour sometimes sat on his lap. In the timorous slithering of his hand on her knee, and the faint hint of an erection, she felt the ghost of Keith's confident virility.

These days with lonely old people were followed by evenings with the young people of the pop world: people constantly asserting their youth even if it was vanishing into middle age, people apparently without a past, always on the move, always in a crowd, always shouting and laughing. She enjoyed being with them – why deny it? – far more than she enjoyed being with the old. Yet she also had a sense of un-reality, of existing in a moment without perspective. Watching the young people dancing in one of Keith's clubs, she seemed to see them absurdly immobilized in a photograph – the clothes and the dance movements dated, the smiles rendered as meaningless grins. And she was overcome, not by dislike or contempt for them, but simply by indifference, an inability to care whether they went on being famous and happy or not, whether they died early or had to learn to be old.

Brushing her hair, listening to the buzz of Keith's razor, she won-dered whom she would meet tonight. At least two or three celebrities, no doubt – men or women for whom fans waited for hours, standing in the rain to be rewarded by a glimpse. Tamsin still found it intriguing to compare the private face with the public mask. But she was beginning to realize that this notion was illusory; it was a matter of a change of mask, that was all. There was a mask for the restricted-audience oc-casions such as this dinner-party, and probably another mask for intimacy, for the bedroom. Was this true of everyone – of herself? It was only recently that the question had occurred to her.

It would be amusing, it would be fun, anyway. One man or another would show that he found her attractive, but she wouldn't have to respond except by smiling banter. She wasn't sure whether this was only a convention of such evenings, or whether she had actually become more attractive as her appearance came to conform with the norms of the scene. Not that she cared much about this, either.

Keith zipped up her dress and kissed her between the shoulder-blades.

'Here we go then, lovey-bunch,' he said.

'Here we go.'

PART TWO

I

When Brian was a student, he was acutely aware that he didn't know about girls. He didn't know what he could do, nor what the girls would do. Even worse, he felt that the girls knew that he didn't know. It was embarrassing and confusing.

Partly, the confusion belonged to the times. The old restraints had lost their authority – that was clear. The daring, the pioneering, had been the privilege of an earlier period (before 1939? before 1914? Brian tried to deduce this from literature, but without complete certainty). Some of his friends slept with girls and seemed to take it as a matter of course. But the disapproval of established society, of guardians whose conventions hadn't weakened though perhaps their convictions had, still exerted power. It was mocked, it was continually evaded, but it wasn't defeated. Girls who lived in halls of residence were in trouble if men were found in their rooms. Landladies, in general, required visitors to leave at ten in the evening.

Then, while some girls could be persuaded, others could not. It might be impossible to overcome a girl's obedience – passive rather than consciously admitted – to the lingering psychological force of the old rules. Or it might not . . . one could meet a rebuff by hoping for too much, or forfeit a success by expecting too little. One might have known a girl for a year and talked with her for hours, and still be in doubt.

Class was involved, as in all delicate situations in England. At Brian's university, some girls came from wealthy or even aristocratic families. But were their traditions those of formality (a ritual of courtship, 'honourable intentions') or of the raffish rich (impulses freely indulged, scorn for middle-class puritanism)? It was hard to guess, and by guessing wrong one could be put down painfully. Most of the students were middle-class, of course, but this was a broad category. Brian's father was a consultant surgeon; Tamsin's father was a gas showroom manager.

Brian's parents represented a distinctive English tradition – the tradition of keeping sex in its place. It was quite possible, he thought, that they had a very good time in bed, despite the fact that his mother was remarkably plain and had a heavy masculine figure. He had always assumed that whatever they did, they did well. It was also possible that they'd stopped making love years ago. They had married in their thirties and Brian was an only child. They gave the impression of being excellent friends, friends who didn't see enough of each other – as indeed they didn't, since they both worked tremendously hard. When they met, often late in the evening, they kissed briefly and started talking nineteen to the dozen. They were both very brainy, Brian's mother more so; she was the only woman of her rank in the Treasury. Sex came up in their conversation seldom but without inhibition. Generally it was a comment on someone who had allowed it to get out of proportion: 'He's lost his head over some bit of fluff, silly ass' or 'It's quite extraordinary, she can't think of anything else.'

Brian was fond of his parents, not least because they didn't treat him as a child. When he was ten, he was instructed to address them as Robert and Dorothy. The idea came from their background in the progressive circles of the 1930s, and also reflected their desire to finish with having a child to look after. Yet he didn't feel that he was fully admitted to their friendship. They were waiting until he was really grown-up and on the way to some achievement akin to theirs. This wouldn't include writing poetry – the only thing he cared about – which they regarded as an interesting spare-time accomplishment. Anyway, he didn't see much of them. In his teens, he lived in a limbo between childhood and the world that Robert and Dorothy had conquered, and very much alone.

He went to a boys' grammar school with a strong academic emphasis. He wasn't very good at the work and was scared of the shame, and the disappointment to his parents, of failing to get a university place. He had no real friends because the brilliant boys excluded him from their set, while he couldn't sincerely line up with those who rejected the school's values. After school, he went straight home. The house was empty, of course. He wrestled with homework, read, and wrote poetry. He knew no young people in his neighbourhood; it was a fair distance from the school, and his parents were far too busy to be friendly with local families. As for getting to know girls, he might just as well have been at a boarding-school.

He started to write poetry when he was thirteen. The study at home, in which he was allowed to do his homework, was lined with books inherited from Dorothy's father. When he began to read poems, they gave him what the sound of music or the touch of a football might have given another boy: an instant sense of recognition and self-discovery. He was soon writing poems of his own. It seemed to be his way of giving shape to his ideas and feelings – and his only way, for he had trouble writing essays and stumbled over his words when he talked. Poetry came to obsess him, to capture his mind in class and when he confronted his homework. It was an irresistible temptation, a secret necessity, like masturbation. He was mortified when Robert, unexpectedly entering the study, found out what he was doing. After this, although from time to time Robert or Dorothy asked in encouraging tones whether he'd written any poems lately, Brian replied that his homework took up all his free time. The truth was that he hurried through the homework or put it off to the end of the evening, and lost himself in poetry. It was, he knew, a cause of his mediocre exam results.

Yet the idea that he was to be a poet – that this would be his life – was daunting for Brian. It was a burden imposed on him, not an ambition. It would be very hard, much harder than being a doctor or a civil servant, for there was no certain measure of achievement; any of his poems could strike him as wretched failures when he re-read them. But no other life seemed possible. He had to march on where he was driven. Or limp and stumble on, or fall in his tracks – there was no telling.

It was daunting for another reason, too. Poets often wrote about love, and indeed about sex. Apparently that was part of being a poet. A poet ought to have a woman who would respond to his love, enrich him with her body, and also understand and inspire his art. The three concepts – love, sex, poetry – whirled in Brian's mind, elements in a mysterious new world. He wondered whether he could ever find his way in this world of passions, so unlike the common-sense world of Robert and Dorothy, without blunders and disasters.

At the university, he found life easier. To his surprise, he didn't need to worry about the work so much as at school. Most first-year students brought a poorer equipment than he did; his essays were rated as exceptionally literate. He had plenty of time to write poems. Now that he read new poems in magazines, and not only the great poems of the past, he decided that his own were quite good. He submitted one to the university magazine, and it was accepted.

Also, he had friends – not intimate friends, perhaps not 'real friends' at all, but people who included him in an evening of beer or coffee and talk. He still wasn't a good talker, but talking to girls wasn't any more difficult than talking to men. Some girls were willing to go out with him. When he ventured to kiss them he was conscious of doing it clumsily, but they seemed quite pleased. 'That was lovely,' one of them said. Startled, he asked: 'Was it?' The girl laughed: 'Well, after all, Brian, you must realize you're very good-looking.'

He hadn't realized it. If it was true, some girls would also be willing to go to bed with him. But of course, he didn't know which girls.

He was anxious to lose his virginity, but more anxious to acquire a girl-friend in the complete sense. Unfortunately, he didn't see how he was to do either. There was a girl called Tamsin, also taking an English degree. It seemed to him that she could be the girl he was looking for. She was attractive, and she was intelligent; she was quiet, but she sometimes talked in what Brian called to himself an answering way, finding words for another person's thoughts as well as her own. He felt – intuitively, as he sensed the beginnings of a poem – an affinity with her, a belief that together they could be more than two separate beings. Belief, or at least hope: the hope of living in a new dimension, of seeing his way more clearly.

He was falling in love with Tamsin, he thought. Or he was already in love with her. That would be more significant and more exciting than simply having a girl-friend. But he wasn't sure; he had no way of recognizing love. Perhaps Tamsin was simply the focus for his unsatisfied desires – desire for close friendship, and need for support, and ordinary physical desire too. And at times love also seemed to him a burden. It would complicate his life; he hadn't the right nature to take it in his stride and handle it easily. He was too young for it, probably.

Anyway, these musings had their absurd aspect, for in their first year Brian was scarcely even a friend of Tamsin's. He saw her mainly in class, sometimes over coffee or a drink in the Union bar, always in a group. She was popular, but in a subtle way reserved. He noticed that she evaded letting a man rest his hand on hers or put his arm round her shoulder. She would leave a room – the bar, especially – alone and a little before everyone else, slipping away, so that someone asked in surprise: 'Where did Tam go?' Brian lacked the boldness or the skill to press himself on her. Even to ask her out for an evening seemed more difficult than asking some other girl. No one else mentioned going out with Tamsin. It was possible that she had a boy-friend, discreetly – someone who moved in a different circle or even someone who wasn't a student. Brian really knew very little about her. The intuition of affinity could be a profound truth or a foolish delusion, and he couldn't nerve himself to put it to the test.

In Brian's second year, the professor who acted as patron of the literary magazine asked him to become an editor. The other new editors were Tamsin and Keith. Keith dealt with the printers, kept the accounts, secured advertisements and pushed the sales; he had never done any of these things before, but he picked up the knack with ready confidence. Tamsin was good at deciding what should go in the magazine and at persuading people to rewrite what didn't quite come off. Brian had been appointed, presumably, because he wrote poetry and because there had to be three editors. He didn't imagine that he was much use, but he was glad to have the position. He had two real friends now – Tamsin and Keith.

In the little office, after the work was finished, they talked about books they'd read, or more likely about films and television programmes if Keith was there. But often Keith wasn't there; he left it to Tamsin and Brian to select the contributions and he had many other friends, or other things to do with his evenings. When Brian was alone with Tamsin, his sense of affinity grew stronger than ever. She felt it too, he believed. In sudden silences, they seemed to be on the brink of finding words for something already known.

Friendship, however, offered itself as an alternative to love, even an obstacle. They shared so many ideas and tastes that they were building up an intellectual structure – not exactly impersonal, but tending to appear sufficient to itself. They ought to have started with love, Brian thought, and let it flow into their thinking and their talking; but they hadn't, and he could make no opportunity to change the mood. The silences between them were rare. Tamsin did most of the talking, finding clarity with obvious pleasure – 'it's so easy to talk to you, Brian,' she said. In the middle of a sentence, she would glance at her watch, exclaim: 'Oh, Christ, look at the time!', and dash off with a bright smile to reach her hall of residence before the doors were locked.

After she had gone, Brian asked himself angrily why he hadn't kissed her. Eventually, he did. She was surprised – with his usual clumsiness, he took hold of her abruptly while she was talking about Yeats – but she didn't object. It became usual for them to kiss at some time during the evening, and then to go on talking. Her manner implied that she wasn't ready to go any further. Perhaps, he thought, she took the kisses as a gesture of friendship, or a natural impulse – they were young, she was pretty, he was good-looking. Certainly these kisses made no commitment. He was both drawn to the commitment and wary of it, knowing that it would be absolute; so was she, he believed. Whether she held back because of her own uncertainties, or because she guessed at his, he couldn't tell. She didn't intend, evidently, to be his girl-friend in any light-hearted way. But he knew by now that she had no other boy-friend, and he had no fear of losing her. A process was working itself out, he told himself: a delicate process, not to be rushed, not without dangers.

Meanwhile, he made a deliberate decision to get rid of his virginity. He had no reason to assume that Tamsin was a virgin simply because she was emotionally unattached, after all, and indeed her calmness when she was kissed seemed to show that she knew much more about men than he did about women. He started to scan all the girls he knew, however slightly, and listen to what the men said about them. He had noticed that a man didn't talk about a girl with whom he was having a steady affair, but did talk about a girl who could be had for a one-night stand. That was Brian's limited, but at the moment essential, aim.

Conveniently, there were no practical problems. Brian had a landlady – a widow, but not old – who had uttered no warnings about late visitors, and who was moreover in the habit of going away for a week or so to visit her mother. Besides, if he succeeded in getting Amabel to sleep with him he wouldn't need to bring her to his room. Amabel had wealthy parents, and they had bought a flat for her.

Amabel was notorious as an easy lay, with the carefree amorality of the raffish rich, and even more notorious for doing practically no work. She was taking a degree in modern languages – French and Spanish, which she already spoke fluently, having lived abroad for years. In her ample spare time, she was involved in everything: athletics, the dramatic society, student politics. Therefore, everybody knew her. Brian knew her because they were both in the film society.

It was easier than he had dared to hope. She arrived at the next film show after it had started; he went out, came in again, and sat down next to her. Her hand moved, as though automatically, to the arm-rest. A few minutes later, she said into his ear: 'Boring flick, right?'

'Right,' Brian said, although it was an early Eisenstein that he'd particularly wanted to see.

They went to a pub in a country village. Amabel had a car of her own. 'I've been wondering why you never take any notice of me,' she said. 'I never expected you to take notice of me.'

She ruffled his hair. 'A certain amount of time has been wasted, hasn't it?'

While making love to her – actually doing it – Brian felt that he was acting out a fantasy, the fantasy he had imagined since adolescence. He couldn't have said whether he enjoyed it. The flat was too warm, he was rather drunk on four gins, he sweated profusely. His satisfaction was chiefly in achieving what he had planned. He hadn't done very well, he supposed. Amabel, however, seemed to be delighted.

In the morning, she expected to drive him to the university. She didn't care who knew, obviously. He said that he had to shave and get his books, so she left him at his digs.

'Seeing you tonight, lover-man?'

It was impossible to say no. And he was elated by her eager smile; she really had enjoyed it.

'If you like.'

'Sure I like. I like very much. Only I've got a rehearsal. Where will you be?'

'Here, working.'

'I'll come by for you.'

By the end of his second night with Amabel, Brian realized that he was having an affair with her. They talked for hours after making love. 'We'll have to get used to each other, darling,' she said. 'It's great now, but it's going to be fantastic.'

'I thought perhaps you just wanted one night with me.'

'Hell no, that's no good. They might say that about me, but it isn't true. When I start something I always hope it's going to last, anyway for a time. Could be a good long time with you, darling.'

It lasted two months. Soon, Brian decided that he was lucky to be getting a sexual education. Although Amabel was just his age, he always had the feeling that he was with an older woman. Her breasts and thighs were mature and opulent, and she was a bit overweight despite the athletics – probably she weighed at least a stone more than Tamsin. Of course, she was very experienced. She had been screwing since the age of fourteen, she told him. She was on the pill; he found this impressive, having read about it as a new discovery not long ago.

'All the girls are on the pill these days, didn't you know that?'

There was a lot he didn't know. He hadn't realized that a man and a woman could 'get used to each other' physically; that a subtle code of signals and responses guided them to an enjoyment beyond their reach at the outset. Being Amabel's lover was far beyond his original intention, but he found it absorbing as well as exciting.

He could talk to her, too, more freely than he had ever talked to anyone else, including Tamsin. Lying beside her in the wide, comfortable bed, he had the ease of complete intimacy without the tension of love. Amabel liked to hear him talk about his writing and what it meant to him. 'I'm not stupid, you know, just a bit scatter-brained,' she said. He gave her his poems to read. Tamsin had read most of them, had

35

made comments full of insight and understanding, but had also put questions that he couldn't answer. Amabel was simply and generously appreciative; he couldn't help being gratified.

He was grateful to her, altogether; she was giving him much more than he had sought. He liked her – one was bound to like someone so cheerful, warm and candid. But that was all. He asked himself whether he could imagine being in love with Amabel, if Tamsin hadn't existed, and knew that it was impossible. So the pleasure that he got from being with her gave him recurrent twinges of guilt. He had been dishonest with her, really. Wanting nothing but sex, he had blundered into a situation that suggested love, to her if not to him. He didn't know what women said when they were in love, but it must be rather like what Amabel said in bed. Probably Amabel didn't distinguish between love and sexual enthusiasm, and her words were impulses like the movements of her body. Still, it was beyond Brian's power not to take words seriously, and he was worried.

And, by leading him into this new region of pleasure, she had changed him in ways that he hadn't expected. He enjoyed things that he could never have enjoyed before, such as silly games, Amabel's reckless driving, and drinking until his head whirled. She noted her effect on him approvingly – 'You're not nearly so uptight as you used to be, darling.' He was sure that other people could see it and were wondering what had come over him, or what he was playing at.

He had no idea how many people knew about their affair. He seldom saw Amabel during the day, at the university. They met in pubs, or he went to her flat, or she came to his digs. She liked his room, for some reason – perhaps being there gave her an added sense of establishing herself in his life – and sometimes she stayed there for hours; when the landlady was away she even chose to spend the night there, though he had only a single bed. This meant that Keith knew, for he happened to live in the same street and wasn't likely to miss noticing Amabel's car – a distinctive car, painted with a flower pattern – parked there. Anyway, whatever Amabel did was soon public property.

Did Tamsin know? This was the most important question, and the hardest to answer. She behaved to Brian exactly as she had before. She scarcely knew Amabel, except in the sense that everybody knew Amabel. It wasn't, on the surface, any of her business – though Brian didn't like to think that it could be a matter of indifference to her. If she saw that he had changed, that was bad; if she didn't notice, that was bad too. He would have liked to explain to her how shallow his feelings for Amabel were, but this was absurd if she didn't know about the affair anyway, and moreover it meant portraying himself as cold and insincere. He didn't kiss Tamsin now; he was embarrassed by being alone with her, by meeting her eyes. He couldn't tell her, if the right moment came, that he loved her . . . wanted her, needed her, whatever the truth was . . . so long as there was a risk that she saw him as Amabel's boy-friend. He had ruined everything, he thought gloomily, by his false and selfish action.

Unexpectedly, Amabel released him. He didn't at first take it in when she said, in a quiet voice that was unusual for her: 'Brian, I want to tell you this is our last time.'

He was sitting on the edge of the bed, dressed and about to leave, and as usual she was still in bed. She contrived to have very few early lectures, and didn't mind skipping those that she did have.

'What d'you mean?' he asked.

'Oh well, all good things come to an end. I'm getting too fond of you, darling. It's sort of out of control.'

'But I'm fond of you . . . darling.'

'Not so much, though, are you?'

'I can't think where you've got that idea.'

'Oh, come on, a girl can tell. Especially with you. It's the big thing with you or it absolutely isn't, you're that type. So if I get too fond of you, and you don't feel the same way, it's no fun any more. It'll end in tears, as Nanny used to say. We don't want that, do we?'

'You seem to have made up your mind.'

'Yes, I have. Not without regrets, you know that.'

'Well.' Brian glanced at his watch. 'That's it, I suppose. It's been good, Amabel.'

'It has been super, hasn't it? Now I want you to give me a big kiss, and then I'll shut my eyes and you'll be gone. It works like that.'

About a week later, Brian met Amabel in a bookshop. She was with a student called John Harding; while John looked at a book, she moved her hand on his waist and rubbed her leg against his. Keeping this up, she gave Brian a friendly smile.

The Easter vacation, coming at the right time, enabled him to adjust himself and get used to a quiet life again. He had got behind with work; he had gone short of sleep, too, and the drinking hadn't really agreed with him. When the new term began, he decided to keep out of pubs, even out of the Union bar so far as possible. It was a genuine pleasure to shut himself in his room, work on an essay or a poem undisturbed, and go to bed early. It was a pleasure to be alone – he had always been used to it, it suited him.

But he did see Tamsin, as usual. They were preparing the summer number of the magazine, and she was insisting on putting in one of his poems although he wasn't entirely satisfied with it. Now that he didn't have Amabel on his mind, he was able to talk to Tamsin as easily as he had before. One evening, he told her something about his home and his parents.

'Where d'you live?' she asked.

'In Highgate.'

'Oh, I live in Barnet. We can see each other in the summer.'

'Yes, I hope so.'

She was impressed by his description of Robert and Dorothy.

'I wish I had parents like that. I mean, interesting people.'

'Aren't yours interesting?'

'They're nothing. One nothing married to another nothing.'

She had one sister, several years older. 'I quite like her, really. But she just left school and typed, and got married to a nothing, so she's turning into a nothing too.'

'You won't be a nothing, Tam.'

'I could have been. I'm still scared of it – it's so easy. I'm only here because somebody started me reading books. A boy at my school.'

'Your first boy-friend?'

'Oh, he wasn't a boy-friend, not in that sense,' Tamsin said, blushing faintly. She had very pale skin; the blush was like a fire seen through a mist.

Another time, Brian said: 'I see that John's taken up with Amabel.'

'Has he?' Tamsin didn't sound interested. But a little later, for no apparent reason, she said: 'I couldn't find John attractive, you know.'

'Girls do.'

'It depends what you want. I couldn't take him seriously, I suppose that's what I should have said.'

'Would you need to?'

'Yes, I should.'

A few weeks from the end of term, they were both invited to a party, given by a young lecturer who liked to let his hair down with students.

'Are you going?' Brian asked.

'I might. Keith's going. He says it ought to be a good party.'

'I might go, then.'

But at the last moment he decided not to. He didn't shine at parties, except small parties where one could sit and talk; at this kind of party he would be shy and clumsy. And he found himself, as usual these days, perfectly happy to spend the evening alone.

As he was leaving the university, he met Tamsin at the gate. She was smartly dressed – or quite smartly for Tamsin – with a trim black sweater above her jeans.

'Coming to the party?'

'No, I'm not actually.'

'Oh. Well, I don't think I will either.'

'Why not? You're on your way.'

'I don't care about it, honestly. Where are you going, Brian?'

'Home. Well . . . we could go for a walk.'

'Yes, it's a lovely evening.'

They walked into the town, along a main street, and then across a small, tidy park. It was still broad daylight, the sun hovering in the western sky as though halted.

They didn't talk. This long silence was something new between them; each of them searched vainly for a way to break it.

'I don't like this park,' Brian said abruptly. 'It's like a garden that doesn't belong to anybody.'

'We could have gone the other way, out into the country.'

'Yes . . . I wasn't thinking, I always walk this way. I live just over there.'

She stopped and looked at him with an expression that he couldn't decipher – somehow, at the same time confident and submissive. For no reason that could be named, he had a strange and almost fearful sense of crisis.

He said: 'Will you come in with me, Tamsin?' And he was startled by having said it – by the sound of his voice, unnaturally loud as it often was when he didn't have time to think.

'Yes,' she said simply.

The room was empty; the house was empty. Brian had known that it would be, and yet the quietness seemed to have a special quality, a quality of this moment apart from all others. The curtains were drawn. He didn't switch on the light. They could see well enough by the sunlight that penetrated the thin, cheap material.

'Do you always have your curtains drawn?' she asked.

'Yes. Especially in summer.'

She looked along the bookshelf, then touched the table.

'Is this where you write your poems?'

'Yes.'

'I thought so. One can feel it. I'm glad to be here, Brian.'

They stood looking at each other, hesitating on either side of the small distance that still separated them. Tamsin smiled timidly; he could just make out her slow, subdued blush.

'I'm so glad,' she said again.

They crossed the small distance, held each other, and kissed. When she rested her head on his shoulder, he didn't dare to let her go. She was

39

leaning against him, unsteadily. It seemed literally true that if he had moved away she would have fallen. He had always known her poised and firm; this sudden helplessness imposed a responsibility on him, something he hadn't reckoned with.

A long uncertainty had resolved itself into a certainty: he was going to make love with Tamsin. It should have been a time for triumph, for desire moving proudly to fulfilment. But, although he had imagined it many times, now that it had come he was unprepared for it. It had an accidental tinge – an absence of decision. He hadn't planned to walk into town with her, nor to bring her to his room. When he'd asked her, he had felt himself to be accepting a necessity, not seizing an opportunity. He had been prepared for being alone tonight. And the value of solitude came to his mind, a value that he wasn't ready to abandon . . . decisively, perhaps for ever.

Guiltily, he remembered that he'd felt quite different the first time with Amabel. But then, he had been carrying out a deliberate purpose. They had both been entirely clear about it, making an avowed compact, catching a note of eager candour; and yet there had been a tacit reservation in the compact, with the easy knowledge that they need not commit their ultimate selves. But with Tamsin the commitment must be unlimited, irrevocable. To think of that in advance and in the abstract was one thing; to be plunged into it was something else.

They moved, with the mystifying inevitability of a movement in a dream, to the bed and lay down, still clutching each other. She was breathing in short gasps, mumbling incoherent sounds. Her eyes – mobile when she talked – were staring and dilated. Amabel had never yielded so much of herself in the first few minutes . . . they were still in their clothes, even. He was dazed by this discovery of a passionate, wild, secret Tamsin. Discovery, or emergence? She was herself bewildered, he guessed, as much as he was astonished.

Suddenly she was still, except for a queer rapid trembling.

'I didn't know this would happen tonight,' she said.

'Nor did I.'

'It was bound to happen, though, wasn't it, Brian?'

'I wasn't sure.'

'Oh, I was sure. But I was afraid, too. It's so tremendous. I'm . . . not exactly afraid, I think awed. It is so tremendous.'

He said nothing. She asked: 'Are we going to do . . . you know, everything?'

'Do you want to?'

'Yes, if you do. You'll always be able to do whatever you want with me, Brian.'

40

She sat up and pulled her sweater over her head. Her hands fumbled with her bra; he undid the hooks for her. The veins in her breasts were clear under the pale skin. He had the feeling, not only of seeing her naked, but of seeing within and through her.

She began to slip her jeans down.

'You've got . . . you know, precautions, haven't you?' she asked.

He didn't answer for a few seconds. He hadn't thought of it. It seemed irrelevant – but of course it wasn't.

'I'm sorry,' he said. 'I haven't.'

'Oh, Christ,' she said. 'You really haven't?'

'Well, we didn't know this was going to happen, did we?'

She was holding her jeans halfway down her legs, trapped in dismayed confusion.

'I thought men usually had things.'

'Well, I thought girls were usually on the pill.'

'Oh no, Brian, it makes you ill.'

'It doesn't.'

'I've read an article . . .'

'Well, anyway, I thought you would be. I mean, when you said you wanted to make love.'

'Brian,' she said, 'I couldn't be on the pill. I was going to tell you. It's my first time.'

He was appalled by the extent, suddenly revealed, of Tamsin's trust in him. Being without contraceptives was an apt symbol of his unreadiness, when she was offering herself with total sincerity. However, in itself it was acutely embarrassing. As a matter of fact, he had never bought contraceptives in his life. With Amabel, although he hadn't actually known that she was on the pill, he must have assumed without thinking that he could leave the precautions to her experience. And if this had happened with Amabel, she would have made a joke of it. But for Tamsin, it was indeed no joke.

Brian was ashamed of himself, and miserably sorry for Tamsin; yet he was aware too of a resentment toward her. She had offered herself to him at a time that he hadn't chosen. He had felt that something would go wrong. What should have been steadily nurtured had been hurried and spoiled.

He tried to think of something he could do. There must be a late ꞓhemist not far away. No, late chemists were allowed to deal only in ꞏꞏdicines. He could borrow from Keith – Keith was experienced with ꞏꞏ, Brian imagined, he was always practical and in command of the ꞏꞏion, and he lived just down the street. But Keith must have gone ꞏꞏparty; he wouldn't be back for hours.

'I'm sorry, I'm sorry,' he said.

She attempted a smile.

'I'll take a chance.'

'I couldn't let you.'

'I want to stay with you, anyway.'

'Sure,' he said in a flat tone.

'I'm taking my clothes off. I want to be naked with you. That's something, isn't it?'

They undressed, got between the sheets, and began to kiss and fondle each other. But now there was a constraint. Two or three times, Tamsin became aroused as she had before, and calmed herself with a painful, bitter effort.

When it was quite dark, she fell asleep – suddenly, like an exhausted child, and as deeply as a child. Brian couldn't sleep for hours. Tamsin was slim, but the bed wasn't made for two and he couldn't get into a comfortable position. At last he slept for a short time, to be woken by a shaking, violent wet dream – not about Tamsin, nor yet Amabel, but simply the inchoate mystery of woman as it had entered his dreams when he was a schoolboy. He got out of bed and washed his legs, then got in again. Tamsin didn't stir.

He must have slept again, for he thought he was dreaming when he felt her grasping him, pulling his body on to hers. What told him that he was awake was her voice – a strained, hoarse voice, but still Tamsin's.

'Take me, Brian. Do it. Do it now. Do it, please.'

'I can't,' he muttered.

'You've got to, Brian. I don't care, I don't care about anything.'

His position was embarrassing – his actual bodily position. He was lying on her like an actor simulating intercourse in a blue film. She had thrown the sheets off, and he felt both the coldness of the room and the feverish heat of her body. It was light again – a grey light, the light of dawn, revealing no colour.

'I can't,' he said. 'I don't want to now. It's got to feel right.'

Her arms, and then her whole body, went slowly limp in a way that frightened him – a kind of death. He freed himself from her, crossed the room, and sat down in a chair.

'Anyway, it's crazy,' he said.

'I'll chance it. It's only once. If I have a baby I don't care about tha either. It would be yours.'

'Well, I don't want a baby,' he said harshly.

She began to cry, shuddering and heaving, turning away from hi shame and despair, hiding her face in the pillow. He knew that he to take her in his arms and comfort her, but he couldn't. In stark, ugly honesty, he didn't want to.

After a time – still hiding her face – she said: 'I'm sorry. You're right, of course. I was being irrational.'

'It's my fault. But there it is.'

'Yes, there it is. It's a bad start, isn't it?'

'Don't think about that. Try and go to sleep again, Tam.'

'Yes, I'll try.'

He covered her with the sheet and the blankets. She reached her hand uncertainly toward him, and he sat by the bed holding it and watching her. He didn't expect her to sleep again; but she did, as deeply as before, almost as one might sleep in recovering from an illness. He dressed, went back to his chair, and read a book.

At eight o'clock Tamsin woke up, smiled at him, and asked: 'Have you been reading all this time?'

'I often read when it gets light.'

'What is it?'

He handed her the book; she made an accurate, intelligent comment on it. She didn't refer to what had happened in the night except to say: 'I hope we didn't wake your landlady up.'

'She's away.'

'Oh, that's good. Can I have a bath?'

'Sure. I'll show you where it is. I'll be downstairs, I'll make some breakfast.'

Over breakfast, they talked about summer plans. Tamsin had signed up for a student trip to France – a drama festival, a music festival, and a week on the coast. Brian was going to Austria with his parents.

'It might be not too bad. We don't see much of each other when we're at home.'

'Lucky you. I wouldn't go anywhere with my parents. But they only go to Clacton, anyway.'

She washed up the dishes, while he dried them and put them away. When they were finished, he felt that something had to be said, but he couldn't think what except, once again, that he was sorry. They stood for a moment facing each other across the kitchen table. Then she said: 'Well – shall we go?'

'Right.'

'It's another nice day,' she said, walking quickly to the front door nd opening it.

Keith was just passing the house.

'Hullo, Tam,' he said cheerfully. 'Hi, Brian.'

They walked along together; it was impossible not to.

43

'How was the party?' Brian asked.

'Pretty good. Hundreds of people there – hadn't been asked, half of them.'

Tamsin said: 'I've got to do some shopping. I'll see you later.'

Walking across the park, Keith said: 'Well, nice work.'

'I should have thought you'd have clicked at that party,' Brian said.

'I got into a poker school. You have to make choices.'

2

'I've got to do some shopping. I'll see you later,' she said.

It was at that moment, Keith thought afterwards, that he fell in love with Tamsin. The phrase was shorthand, of course. A need grew over a period. You formed a picture of the sort of girl who would answer this need. Then you realized that the girl had been there all along, waiting for you to get the lens into focus, so to speak. Not the sort of girl but the only possible girl, unique, ideal, perfect. You knew, with exulting certainty, what you ought to have known long before. 'Of course!' you said, just as when the right and precise fact came to your groping mind during an exam. That was the moment.

It was the smile that did it, perhaps. A quick flash of a smile, half for Keith and half for Brian, a sign of trust and also an appeal. It was an awkward moment for her, naturally. Keith's impulse was to reassure her, to place her beyond hurt. But she was quite composed. He was aware of an inner strength, not easily assumed but mustered when it was needed.

He wondered, during the next few days, whether he was thinking of Tamsin in a new way because Brian had unbalanced the straightforward three-way friendship. Or because he now knew that she wasn't a virgin – as she had been until lately, he was ready to bet. On the whole, this encouraged him. She was ready, not merely to give herself, but to love. It was to be assumed that she loved Brian, or believed she loved Brian, or she wasn't the sort of girl who would sleep with a man on impulse, in a spirit of fun or curiosity – not for the first time, especially. Very, then: he would have to make her love him as much as she loved

45

Brian, indeed more so. He welcomed the challenge, the chance to prove his sincerity and determination.

It was a pity that he would have to take Tamsin away from Brian – his friend – but he didn't feel guilty about it. He didn't believe that Brian was serious about her. After all, he'd been screwing Amabel not long ago, and that was no great sign of seriousness. Amabel had moved on and Tamsin had filled the gap, as well as providing a refreshing contrast – she was more Brian's type, clearly. What mattered was that he, Keith, would love Tamsin more devotedly and more single-mindedly than Brian ever could. Brian's poetry would always mean more to him than anything else in the world. But Keith, though as interested in making a success of his life as the next man, could imagine no triumph that would be as dear to him as Tamsin's love.

And when he did achieve success, Keith thought, he would be doing it for Tamsin as much as for himself. He was conscious that Brian and Tamsin both came from a background that he didn't share. It wasn't a question of money – Tamsin's parents were far from wealthy, he had gathered – but of living in the part of London, and going to the kind of school, where a university place was a natural aim.

It was the first time that Keith had bothered his head about this kind of thing. He was neither ashamed of coming from the working-class nor proud of it. He had merely found it odd, in his first year at the university, to be in a world in which working-class people were a minority: odd, in the same way as an Englishman who takes a job abroad might find it odd to be exceptional by nationality. But he took people as he found them and got along pretty well with almost everyone. The fact that most students had to live on the grant and did some vacation work made for equality, too. Anyway, Keith wouldn't have been at a disadvantage in terms of money. Being working-class wasn't the same as being poor, not by a long chalk. In his home, and the homes of his various uncles and cousins, there was always money coming in from car repair and house repair and transport and removal and doing up old furniture to sell, mostly cash down and no tax. This didn't stop Keith's family from being working-class, living in Deptford and eating in the kitchen. They were used to that; they were also used to buying what took their fancy, betting heavily, and drinking champagne at weddings.

They enjoyed life more than Tamsin's family, he imagined. Still Deptford wouldn't suit Tamsin. Again, it wasn't a question of being rich or poor, nor of class in the obvious sense, but of the intrusi density of the family. He had taken it for granted until he was a stude Anyone – one of his two brothers and two sisters, or a cousin from next street – had a right to invade his thoughts and expose his life, for instance to demand to know where he'd been last night and where he was going tonight. It had struck him lately that his parents had never been alone together since he could remember, except in bed. Long ago, his mother had lost all uniqueness; his married sister was losing it now. It was impossible to think of drawing Tamsin into the network without diminishing her. And now Keith wanted Tamsin – no one but Tamsin.

All the same, he was glad to have grown up in Deptford. It had given him a handy shrewdness in dealing with people and an irreducible self-confidence. Not least with girls. Ever since he'd known that you didn't grow it to piss through, as they said in Deptford, he'd always been able to get a girl when he fancied one.

At the university, it wasn't so easy. He found it difficult to guess which girls were available and which weren't – not from inexperience with girls, like Brian, but from inexperience with middle-class girls. Besides, he had a strict and vigilant landlady. He made the grade with a few girls in his college who gave him clear come-on signals, but he preferred to find girls in the town, the kind of girls who spoke his native language (often it helped to conceal the fact that he was a student). In his second year, he changed his digs. He managed to get a top-floor room in a big house, where he could smuggle in a girl by using the garden gate and the back stairs. The landlady was usually out playing bingo or had the television on full blast, and was inclined to ignore him anyway. Still, he continued to find girls in the town rather than at the university.

Gradually, during that second year, Keith decided that he didn't want to go on like this. In boyhood it had seemed splendid to be continually scoring with a new girl: to discover, to explore, to compare. But if the conquest was exciting, the satisfaction was shallow. The girl allowed him, after some ritual squirming and struggling, to have his way: that was all. She was never genuinely with him, unless for a moment of instinctive physical response. Soon she was freeing herself from him, putting on – or more likely rearranging – her clothes, asking the time and declaring that people would wonder where she was, retreating from and denying her submission. He began to long for a fuller possession, derived from open willingness and equality of desire, from trust and candour. He imagined pleasures still beyond him: gazing on a woman's calmly displayed body, sleeping and waking beside her, exchanging smiles of cherished memory. Perhaps, after all, he could claim very little sexual experience – the kind that mattered.

You had to be in love to get the best of it, he thought. You had to love the girl – one girl, steadily and contentedly – and be loved by her.

When he realized that he was in love with Tamsin, it was as though

47

he had solved a vital problem. That he had yet to win her seemed relatively unimportant. He didn't doubt for a moment that he would succeed – because he had to, because he would throw in all his energy and persistence. All that remained was to devise ways and means.

It was almost the end of term. That could be turned into an advantage, however, if he could meet her in London away from the communal student atmosphere. A few casual questions told him when she would be back from her trip to France. She would be seeing Brian in London, that had to be reckoned with; but she would find out who really loved her.

Keith got a vacation job as a postman, working in north London. He took a furnished room, explaining to his parents that he would have to be at work at the crack of dawn. The room, a large one with pleasant modern furniture and a double bed, took a thick slice out of his pay-packet, but he didn't grudge the investment. The job was right for his purposes, too; he was free all afternoon and evening.

He rang Tamsin up on the evening when she came back. She had just had time to unpack and confront the boredom of home. Yes, she would like to see him, she said. Tomorrow – OK, why not?

They had dinner at a small restaurant in Hampstead – good Italian food, wine, dim lights (another investment). He told her about his job. When it was raining postmen missed detached houses with garden paths and put the letters into a pillar-box to make the rounds again – did she know that? She laughed, and told him in return about her holiday: it had been really interesting, she'd taken lots of photographs, she would show them to him when they were developed. They decided to go on to a film, but over the second cup of coffee they realized that it had started, so they went on talking.

Taking a risk, he kissed her in a more than friendly way when they said goodnight. She liked it, apparently.

'When do I see you again, Tam?'

'I don't know. Ring me up.'

She went out with him again, and then again. He could count on it about twice a week. She was almost always free. Astonished, he grasped that she wasn't seeing Brian.

One afternoon, they went swimming in the Serpentine. It was an average English summer, with odd hot days to be seized and prized.

'Golden girl,' he said, resting his hand on the warm smoothness of her suntanned back as they lay on a rug.

'Am I? I had a week just idling on the beach.'

'That bikini didn't help the textile industry much. Did you get it in France?'

'No, it's last year's.' She smiled, her face close to his. 'Actually we found a topless beach.'

'More lovely tan? Let's see.'

'This is London. You'll get me arrested.'

'I was thinking of a private showing.'

Her smile gave way to a thoughtful, uncertain look. She sat up and rummaged in her bag for her purse. 'Could you get me an ice-cream, Keith?'

As he stood in the queue, she stared at him and thought: he does look splendid. The firm touch of his hand seemed to remain on her back; the exact spot gave her a distinct feeling, like a bruise. When he touched her like this, and when he kissed her, she moved toward a response that took an effort to control. Am I highly sexed, she wondered? That night in Brian's room, she had been consumed by urgent desire; but she hadn't thought of it as narrowly sexual. It was still difficult to think coherently about Brian. When she tried, she was carried into the unknown. About Keith, however, she could be entirely coherent, fixing in her mind a simple fact: he attracted her. She could think of being Keith's girl-friend, as a chosen course of action, and envisage clearly what it would be like.

In the traditional sense, as understood by her mother, she was already Keith's girl-friend, she supposed. She hadn't intended this. She had simply wanted to avail herself of his company because he was a friend and because she was bored and lonely. Or so she'd told herself – no doubt she hadn't been quite honest. At all events, they both knew now that he attracted her, and she attracted him, in this direct and unmistakable way. He didn't intend just to take her out and kiss her goodnight . . . of course not.

Brian had scarcely spoken to her in the last few weeks of term, and since then he hadn't phoned her. She still believed that they had given each other an irrevocable pledge. It couldn't have been erased, surely, by an absurd mischance. Yet she remembered now that – at least in words, perhaps in more than words – she had pledged herself and Brian hadn't. She was the one who had said: 'It was bound to happen' and 'I was sure'. All he'd done was to ask her to his room, and in the circumstances any young man would have seized his chance with any reasonably attractive and obviously willing girl. He had wanted her, but not to the point of recklessness. It was her recklessness – by which she had revealed her unreserved dedication – that had alarmed him, perhaps fatally.

Anyway, Brian hadn't phoned her. She made a deliberate resolution not to think about him: made it calmly, there by the Serpentine, while

Keith was buying ice-creams. She wasn't renouncing her pledge, but she was leaving it in abeyance – on the table, so to speak. After all, there were only two possibilities. If what she had believed that night had been profoundly true, she had only to wait. If she'd been mistaken, she would have to cut her losses.

And what about Keith? She couldn't offer him what she had offered Brian – the absolute commitment, the deepest part of herself. Honesty would compel her sooner or later to make that clear to him. But not just yet, she hoped.

'I'll have to go soon,' she said. 'We've got my sister and her husband coming over tonight.'

'I was going to take you to that place in Hampstead.'

'You know I'd rather.'

'Make it tomorrow night instead.'

'Fine.'

As she dressed, she thought: how pleasant it would be if we could go on just like this.

As he dressed, still seeing her golden body, he thought: tomorrow night will be the night.

He filled the next day with cheerful anticipation. Having formed his resolution, he didn't allow himself any doubts. If it had been a fine warm evening he would have been delighted. As it was pouring with rain, he turned that into good luck. Tamsin wouldn't want to see a film or do anything else with the evening. Besides, the restaurant would be empty.

She looked entrancing as she hurried in, a little breathless, drops gleaming on her hair. He guided her to a corner table and sat beside her on the comfortable bench-seat.

Selecting his moment, after they had finished eating, he said: 'I'll never forget that afternoon, you know. You looked so beautiful in your bikini.'

'I can't swim very well. I'm lazy about it.'

'Don't swim, another time. Just look beautiful.'

'Are you a good swimmer, Keith?'

'Yes, I am. But you're beautiful. I don't mind repeating myself. It would be nice to get a reaction, though.'

'I could say: "Yes, I am." '

'That's better. You ought to know it.'

'Only I'm not.'

'I'm telling you you are. I've given more thought to it than you have.'

'Well, it's nice to hear it, I admit that.'

'Now we're getting on. This is going to be our best evening. Let's have another carafe.'

'You're trying to make me drunk.'

'Yes, I think it's good for you to be a bit drunk. You start slightly under par, sweetie.'

When the waiter had left the carafe, Keith filled the glasses and raised his.

'To us.'

She sat quite still, looking across the room, for a few seconds. Then she raised her glass too and let him touch it with his. They drank slowly, gazing at each other, until the glasses were empty.

He put his arms round her and kissed her, taking his time, easing and renewing the pressure.

'I'm so much in love with you,' he said. 'So very much. I can't tell you how much, you'll just have to believe it.'

'It's nice to hear, too,' she said. 'It doesn't have to be true.'

'It's the truest thing I've ever said.'

She looked across the room again, beginning to be troubled. It really was true, she thought. It gave him an advantage – a purposeful certainty, a source of strength.

'I'm not in love with you, Keith.'

'You wanted me to kiss you like that.'

'That's not the same thing. Look, Keith, if I was in love with you I'd say so.'

'Perhaps you don't know if you are. It doesn't matter. You will be.'

'You think so.'

'I know. But we won't argue, I love you too much. What d'you want right now, another kiss or some more wine?'

'They're both risky.'

'They're both good for your health.'

She drank the wine resting in his arms. It wasn't easy to use her hands, nor to keep steady at all. He kept kissing her, tangling her hair, pressing her breasts, touching her here, there and everywhere. He kept talking, too – about how much he loved her, how beautiful she was, how happy they would be. What he said didn't vary, and it certainly wasn't highly original, but she felt that he could make it all come true through sheer persistence. She did feel happy, in a reckless and yet a relaxed way. She remembered that she'd meant, at this point, to make something important clear to him, but it was difficult now, and perhaps it wasn't a vital obligation. She had said that she wasn't in love with him – that would have to do. It was all out of her control now, she wasn't responsible, she had given herself up to his force and his certainty.

'I'll get the bill,' he said. 'They want to close.'

'I suppose they do. It's nice here.'

'It'll be nicer. You're staying with me, beautiful, you know that.'

'I never said . . .'

'You don't have to say. It's all understood.'

Yes, she thought, it was understood. And she wanted it, and it seemed perfectly right. Against her principles – the principle that it would have to be more serious than this. But since she was so glad to be loved and desired by him, since he had this compelling power over her, that did make it serious in a way, or at least significant. She couldn't work it out . . . it wasn't the same as with Brian, and yet it was also integral to her life, something that had been bound to happen.

The rain had stopped. They could walk, Keith said; it wasn't far. She found that she wasn't drunk, or at least she could compensate for it with a deliberate calmness like a driver remembering to be extra careful after drinking. Really she was quite calm altogether, sustained by no longer needing to think. It turned out to be quite a long walk, but she enjoyed it. It was new to her, walking with a man who held her round the waist with the firmness of possession.

And it was all a single process, she found. He was fondling her in the street, on the stairs of the house, moving across the room, on the bed. Clothes came off gradually; she was surprised, yet not surprised, to find herself naked.

He asked: 'D'you have anything you use, sweetheart?'

'No, I . . .'

'OK, I'll take care of it.'

She didn't see how she could tell him that it was her first time without betraying the essential truth of her night with Brian, nor without making Brian look ridiculous. And she wanted no more talk, no more complications.

Keith was astonished by her eagerness, her swift and demanding arousal. It's true what they say about these quiet girls, he thought. Then he went beyond thought into a storm of excitement and triumph. Once she cried out – almost screamed. He saw her face tense and contorted. 'All right, love?' he muttered. She panted: 'Go on – go on – don't stop!'

He couldn't have stopped, but afterwards he was afraid that he'd hurt her – torn her somehow. He was big, he knew, and she was delicately built.

'You sure you're all right?'

'Yes, don't worry. You were a bit rough, but that's good. It was marvellous.'

She wanted him again, and then again. He tried to be gentler, but she wouldn't let him. He felt that she was challenging him, making him prove the full strength of his love. Meeting the challenge gladly, he reinforced passion with pride.

In the morning, when he had to go to work, she was tranquilly asleep. He hoped to find her still in his room when he came back, but she had gone. When he phoned her, she resisted his urging to come to him that night. 'I'm going to bed early. I want to unwind, I think.'

'Everything's OK, sweetie, is it?'

'Everything's fine. See you soon.'

They continued to meet about twice a week. He couldn't imagine what she did with the other evenings, for he knew she was bored at home and he was reasonably sure that she wasn't seeing Brian. But twice a week was about right, she said firmly. Nor was it a foregone conclusion that she would go to his room after they had been out together. Sometimes she said that she was tired, or frankly not in the mood. No amount of persuasion, no kissing and fondling, could change her mind. But when they went to bed, she always rewarded him with the same passionate abandonment as the first time. He realized that she was controlling the course of the affair. She had her own kind of strength, and he must come to terms with it.

He did press her to spend Saturday nights with him. He valued the easy Sunday mornings, when they lay in bed together and talked, when he could relish the new dimension of his life. She was giving herself to him then as truly as when they made love. She mused about herself – allowing him, he felt, to overhear her thoughts.

'It's very strange, I seem to be quite a sexual person.'

'Christ, has that just struck you?'

'Don't laugh, Keith. It is strange. I still don't know if it's really me.'

'I help a bit, I hope.'

'Yes . . . it does seem to come from outside me, in a way. To take hold of me. Perhaps it's a phase. My big thing, this year.'

'Don't kid yourself, honey-bunch, it's not a phase. We'll be giving each other a great time when we're both seventy.'

Her body, pressed to his, went taut.

'Don't say things like that, Keith.'

'Why not? I fancy myself as a dirty old man. There's a lot of them in my family.'

'I can't think about being old. Even older than now, like middle-aged. I haven't the courage.'

She was reluctant to speak of the future, even the near future. He assumed that she would be his girl-friend at the university, but he saw that it would still be on her terms. The spells of passion would be distinct from her calm, serious daily life. She wouldn't want other students to know; he hadn't known about her and Brian until he found out by chance. It would cost him something to be discreet. He was proud of being Tamsin's man.

Sometimes he could almost convince himself that he was her first man. It was with him, surely, that she had realized herself as 'a sexual person'. But of course her first man must have been Brian. (Without quite knowing why, Keith was sure there had been no one else.) He resented it, like an injustice. No matter what he shared with Tamsin, no matter what happiness he gave her, there was something that he must always envy Brian.

He concentrated his thoughts on the future. He had only one guarantee, and therefore one necessary aim. That was to make Tamsin love him – and say that she loved him. He spoke of it constantly and persistently when she was with him, not only because it was his purpose but because he couldn't help it. His love surged and swelled in him, almost physically, reaching out for her.

But she said: 'I can't make myself be in love, can I?' Or: 'Don't keep on at me, Keith, please.' Or: 'We're having such a good time, isn't that enough?'

He was puzzled, but he wasn't despondent. She was holding back for some reason – perhaps to assert her independence, perhaps remembering a painful disappointment with Brian. But it wasn't in her nature, Keith believed, to give so much of herself to a man without loving him. That would be to flaw the truth of what he loved in her.

'It isn't that you can't love me,' he said one Sunday morning. 'You're refusing to.'

'Oh, that's not true. I wish I did. It would make things simpler.'

'It would make you really happy. Me, too. But you're the one who matters.'

'Perhaps I'm not cut out to be really happy.'

'That's nonsense, love.'

She was silent for a while. Then she said: 'You think love and happiness are the same, don't you?'

'Of course they are.'

'I'm not so sure.'

'Well, I am. There's nothing bigger than love, is there? It's the answer to everything.'

'It's the end, is it?'

'It's the whole meaning of what we've got together. This isn't one-sided, honey, I know it isn't. The way we are now, what you feel for me can't be any less than what I feel for you. The truth is, you do love me but you won't admit it.'

'Maybe.'

'Try saying it.'

'I love you, Keith.'

He threw himself on her.

'Say it again.'

'I love you.'

He kissed her triumphantly, then thrust into her. He had never done it before like this, without prelude, as a conqueror.

'Say it again.'

'I love you. Keith, you're hurting me.'

'You enjoy it.'

'Yes . . . I do.'

'That's because you love me.'

He could have stayed in bed with her for ever, but he had promised to have Sunday dinner at home, in Deptford.

'I hate leaving you now, true love.'

'I'm sorry, too.'

'You can come with me if you like. They'd be glad.'

'No, I don't think I want to.'

'I don't think I want to, either. I want you all to myself. I want you here tonight. You must, Tamsin.'

'We're living together now, are we?'

'We love each other. It makes a difference – you'll see that.'

She had lunch at home too (her family had lunch, while Keith's had dinner) and then went for a long walk by herself. Yes, she decided, she was in love with him. One had to go forward or back; he had understood that, better than she had. She no longer wanted to make conditions, to deny him anything. If that wasn't love, what was it?

It did make things simpler, this being in love. It hadn't the mysterious, awesome quality – the dissolution of herself – of what she had felt with Brian. But she didn't let herself think of that. She had found simplicity and contentment; that was the whole point of loving Keith.

She went to his room almost every night – they were living together, more or less. She didn't give a damn what her parents thought, she assured him. However, they had only a couple of weeks before term began.

'I won't go back to the hall of residence,' she said. 'I'll find digs near you.'

'Right, that'll be handy.'

She was amused by the strategy of the garden gate and the back stairs. As a rule, they made love in the evening and she went back to her digs before midnight. But she stayed with him all Saturday night and most of Sunday, telling her landlady that she was going home for the weekend. It worked out well.

To Keith's surprise, she chose to show herself at the university as his girl – to have his arm round her in the Union bar, to kiss him in a busy hallway between lectures. It ensured that other men didn't make passes at her; perhaps, he thought, it also warned other girls away from him. Perhaps it was a message to Brian. Perhaps she simply liked the normal situation, the straightforwardness of having a boy-friend. But mostly, he believed, being in love had made the difference.

What Brian was thinking, Keith couldn't guess. It had always been hard to make out what Brian was thinking. They met – the three of them – at editorial meetings; Keith always came along and stayed to the end, not because he was unsure of Tamsin but to spare her embarrassment.

Brian didn't seem to have another girl. Keith began to feel rather sorry for him. He hadn't felt guilty when he set out to take Tamsin away from Brian, but he was made guilty by the completeness of his success.

He said to her one night: 'We're so happy, love-girl, I don't like to think of Brian feeling bad.'

She didn't answer at once. Then she said: 'I've talked to Brian.'

'What did he say?'

'Not much. Skip it.'

Keith blurted out, though he knew it was a mistake: 'Were you in love with Brian?'

'I don't know. I can't quite explain. Skip it, Keith, d'you mind? I'm in love with you now, anyway.'

The talk with Brian – though it wasn't a talk, merely a brief and confused exchange of words – had disturbed her. She had met him in the little park, late on a foggy autumn night; he was on his way home from the film society, probably, and of course she had been with Keith. Thrown off balance – they practically bumped into each other in the fog – she said inanely: 'Brian – fancy meeting you!'

'I still live round here, you know.'

'Yes . . . Brian, I'm sorry about what's happened.'

He avoided her eyes and said: 'Don't let it worry you.'

'You didn't get in touch. I mean, in the holidays. I didn't know what . . . that is, where I stood.'

'We can't go over that now, Tamsin.'

'It could have been different, though.'

'It could. But I'm glad you're enjoying yourself.'

'I'm not exactly . . .'

'Aren't you?'

'All right, I am. I have a right . . . haven't I?'

'That's fine, then.'

She touched his arm, tentatively and clumsily. He said: 'I don't want to share you, you know.'

'No, that isn't . . .'

'Or to compete for you, either.'

She said in a pleading voice: 'I have to work things out in my own way, I can't help it.'

'Do that, by all means.'

'I hate fog,' she said suddenly. 'I can't see you properly.'

'No. But this isn't the time. Goodnight, Tam.'

'Goodnight, Brian.'

Gradually, the memory of this encounter receded. But nothing to do with Brian was ever obliterated, she felt. It was held in reserve, like a detail in an early chapter of a book whose significance is to be understood only later . . . perhaps much later.

All that year, she was Keith's girl.

3

On the boat from Dover to Ostend, the girls got talking to Mr and Mrs Butler. These amiable people – towing a four-berth caravan but travelling without their children for the first time, and not really liking it – offered them a lift all the way to Austria. It was a real stroke of luck; as well as the tremendous hitch, they slept in the caravan for free. True, they could have got along faster without the Butlers. Mr Butler never exceeded forty miles an hour, followed the road up the Rhine valley instead of the autobahn, and stopped to look at castles and cathedrals. But it was nice to potter along like this, Amabel said. They had the whole summer ahead of them.

Tamsin was eager to get to Greece, the goal of the trip, but anxious to have no disagreements with Amabel. They had never been friends in spite of having vaguely known each other for three years. Tamsin had planned the trip with Keith, but he had overspent in his final year – partly on giving her presents – and decided to spend the summer working on a construction site. She was therefore obliged to spread the word that she needed a hitch-hiking companion. When Amabel came forward, she was surprised; she would have expected Amabel to travel with a man, and anyway Amabel had a car. However, Amabel explained that she'd wrecked the car. And she remarked over a beer in Munich (they were pretty good friends by this time) that there must be men in Greece who were more fun than John Harding.

Outside Ljubljana the girls were picked up by a Yugoslav couple who wouldn't hear of their going straight through the historic and beautifu city of Zagreb. The Yugoslav lady, who was taking English lessons an delighted to supplement them by conversation, said that her childr were away at a camp and she had plenty of spare beds. Tamsin wondered if she'd ever get to Greece, but Amabel pointed out that if you stuck to a timetable you never got the best out of travelling. Their hosts were desolated when they left after five days in Zagreb.

After difficult hitch-hiking beyond Belgrade, an unplanned side-trip to Salonica, and a good look at Athens, the girls took the boat to Mykonos. It was delightful there, but extremely hot. They slept most of the day, swam as the sun was going down, and had a dinner at a friendly taverna which lasted until after midnight. Amabel then disappeared with Jean-Luc, a French student. Tamsin declined the propositions that came her way, not precisely out of loyalty to Keith but because she was quite contented; there was always a lively crowd at the taverna and she didn't mind being alone in the room which she theoretically shared with Amabel.

'Would you believe it, Amabel? – we've been here for a month.'

'I know. I'd lost track, but Jean-Luc says he's got to go home.'

'Ought we to do that, d'you think?'

'Oh, let's stay a bit longer, it's so lovely here.'

Tamsin herself was enjoying the freedom from the constraints of time, and in the heat she didn't look forward to the crowded boat, the baking streets of Athens, or the hitch-hiking on the shadeless highways. But shortly afterwards they met Demetrios, who said that Mykonos was a tourist island and not at all the real Greece, and urged them to come on his cabin-cruiser to Skiros. Tamsin grasped that he had replaced Jean-Luc and that she was earmarked for some friend of his. She said that she would meet Amabel in Athens. She was a little anxious about this – Amabel seemed really keen on Demetrios. However, Amabel turned up only three days after the agreed date.

Amabel carried an apparently limitless bundle of traveller's cheques, and when she was in the mood she would drag Tamsin into a first-class hotel for dinner and pay for it, saying vaguely: 'We'll settle up when we get home if you insist.' But on the whole she enjoyed keeping to the rules of cheap travel; she had been firm about hitch-hiking all the way through Yugoslavia when Tamsin suggested taking a bus. Also, like most rich people, she couldn't resist a bargain. Back in Athens, she told Tamsin enthusiastically that by using a student card you could fly to Beirut and back for five pounds. 'All right,' Tamsin said, 'but we're only staying a couple of nights, mind.'

In Beirut the girls met the captain of a merchant ship who offered them a trip to Valencia. It was even better than a bargain – it was free. Besides, as Amabel said, it would be easier to hitch home from Spain than through Yugoslavia again.

The ship travelled very slowly, calling at ports all along the North African coast. But they had a roomy cabin, or rather Tamsin had since Amabel was sleeping with the captain. Tamsin had to bolt the door to fend off the first mate, an unsavoury character with a pot belly and bad breath. While they were in port at Tangier she forgot about the bolt, was almost raped, and had to yell for Amabel. The girls left the ship in the morning.

In Tangier, Tamsin was taken ill. It was, she realized later, an acute attack of food poisoning. Amabel rushed her from their cheap *pension* to a hospital. It was airless and stifling, bugs crawled on the sheets, she had to stagger to a filthy toilet and passed out on the way. A woman in the next bed dripped blood on to the floor and moaned incessantly; Tamsin didn't know whether she was bleeding from a back-alley abortion or a knife-wound. Nor did she know why she herself was ill. A doctor looked at her casually and said something in bad French which she didn't understand; the nurses spoke only Arabic. In the middle of the night, she felt that she was getting worse – she couldn't bear any more, she couldn't survive, she was going to die. Lying in the darkness, too weak to call out or to brush away the bugs, she lost all hope. She could remember afterwards what seemed to be the moment of death, which was in fact the moment when she fell into an exhausted sleep. When Amabel came to see her, she was already a little better. Amabel took her to a good hotel.

When Tamsin recovered and they moved back to cheap quarters, time passed as languidly as on Mykonos. More languidly: on Mykonos one felt that summer would end sooner or later and the place would be different, but Tangier seemed likely to be the same for ever. Instead of visitors, there were exiles of various nationalities, left over from some past era when it had been in fashion. It was October by now, but in the unvarying sunlight one day was just like another.

Amabel was ready to go home – she said that Tangier was boring and the men were unattractive or homosexual or both – but she declared that she wouldn't think of making the journey until Tamsin was quite fit.

'I'm OK, really I am,' Tamsin said.

'You don't look it.'

'I'm always skin and bones.'

Time passed. Tamsin was no longer ill, that was true. But the illness had done something to her; she was everlastingly tired, she slept without feeling refreshed, she was 'not herself'. Not herself – no, she did mysteriously seem to be a different person, or something in her had come uppermost that had been contained hitherto by youth and optimism. She wondered whether it was because of the illness, or the horror of the hospital, or her resignation to death. That was the unforgettable part of the experience; she felt as though she had actually died and returned to life. After that, one couldn't expect to resume one's life just as it had been before.

˗She no longer felt certain of anything. When she left England everything had been quite clear: she would have a summer trip, then she would come back and get a job, and she would continue to be Keith's girl-friend. Now, she couldn't make up her mind to go home. She was afraid that she was succumbing to the inertia of Tangier – it was a good thing she had Amabel to save her from staying there for ever. When she thought of London she was afraid of it, afraid of what it demanded of her. She didn't believe that she would be able to get a job, or do it adequately if she did get one.

And Keith? She longed for Keith, for his vigour and strength, but she was also afraid of seeing him again. He would be disappointed by what she had become, and she wouldn't be able to explain to him a change that she herself only dimly understood. He would puzzle his head for a time and then cut his losses. Perhaps he had another girl already, or at least a girl in reserve. There was no reason why he shouldn't. She had been away a long time and hadn't told him why, nor let him know when she would be back. She had sent a postcard from Mykonos . . . it had said: 'See you soon.' In Tangier, her lassitude and her state of uncertainty prevented her from writing.

'I do think you need to see Keith again,' Amabel said.

'Maybe. I don't know if it's still on.'

'Don't feel the same?'

'I do, but . . . I don't know if I can take it up again. It's all at a distance.'

Eventually, the police came round and asked about their residence permits. The English people whom Amabel had met said that permits involved laborious red tape and, more likely than not, bribery. 'We must go, it's ridiculous,' Tamsin said.

Faithful to the original spirit of the trip, they hitch-hiked. They could get only short lifts from local people and probably spent more on hotels than the train fare would have cost. North of the Pyrenees, it was cold and generally raining. Amabel arrived in Paris with a streaming cold and said that she'd like to stay for a week; she had friends who would put her up. Tamsin decided to go on to London by train and boat. She sent two telegrams, one to her parents and one to Keith. The former said simply: 'Home soon.' The latter gave the time of the train.

As the train from Dover rattled through the suburbs, she felt that her whole future depended on whether she saw him at Victoria. It wasn't only a question of whether she was still his girl-friend, but of whether she had a place in the world, whether she existed outside her own troubled and tenuous consciousness.

He was there. They kissed before they spoke: a long kiss, warm and rich, filling her with reassurance and promise. She was exalted, and yet joyfully restored to reality, proudly aware of people looking at them. Keith drew his face gently away, keeping his arm round her.

'You're so beautiful.'

She smiled, feeling that she hadn't smiled for weeks.

'Are you hungry? Feel like a drink? What?'

'Oh . . . no. Just want to be with you.'

'Won't you have to go home?'

'It can wait.'

'I live miles away. I'll tell you about that. Still . . . I'll make a phone call. Hold on, don't vanish again.'

She waited. This was like Keith: he would always know of a place to take a girl.

'Luck's in, honey-love. He was just going out. We'll take a taxi, it isn't far.'

It was a flat in Chelsea. The key was under the mat; she was merely amused by the thought that Keith might have used the flat before. They made love luxuriously in a high old-fashioned bed.

'What are you thinking of, sweetie?'

'Just you. How good it was.'

'It's just begun. We can stay here all night, you know.'

'Won't your friend be coming back?'

'No, he's staying with his girl-friend.'

'Who is he?'

'Ted Goldman – he's an antique-dealer. Nice bloke, you must meet him some time. I've got quite a few new friends. Lots to tell you, love.'

Ted had furnished the flat, evidently, in the course of his business. Ornamental clocks whirred and chimed but didn't tell the right time; the lights were electrified candlesticks and oil-lamps; the telephone was the old kind with a separate receiver. Keith showed her round as proudly as though everything belonged to him.

'I can see you'd like to have a flat like this, Keith.'

'Yes, I would. Might not be too far off, either.'

Things were going well for him. He had a job on the advertising side of a local paper. The advertising manager was an elderly man in poor health; Keith was supposed to be learning, but in fact did most of the work. Tamsin remembered how effectively he had persuaded businesses of all kinds to advertise in the university magazine.

'I don't suppose I'll stick with it. Maybe a year or two. I'm looking round to see what I really want to do. And building up contacts – it's amazing the people you meet when you're scouting for ads. Such as Ted, for instance.'

The pay was quite good and Keith was saving most of it. He had the use of a car and charged his meals to expenses. The advertising manager, a widower and the owner of a big house, let him have two rooms at a token rent. It was no fun living miles out – the paper was in Bromley – but he worked long hours and it was handy to be close to the job.

'Right, what's your news? Where did you get to after Greece? You've had time to go to New Zealand.'

'I'm so sorry I didn't write, Keith. It was awful of me.'

'Never mind, love. You're here now, that's the main thing.'

'You see, I was ill.'

He was deeply concerned. No, she thought later, not deeply; he found it hard to imagine ill-health or suffering, and he lived so much in the present that the assurance of her being well again was what counted for him. But strongly, lovingly concerned.

It was a bug, she told him, a nasty stomach upset – nothing serious. But it had left her weak, so that she kept expecting to start for home and then not feeling up to it, and that was why she hadn't written. She said nothing about the ghastly hospital, nor about her vision of death. That experience, that knowledge, had to remain her own.

In the morning, he went off early. She slept half the day. When she finally got home, she said that she'd just come from Paris.

'Well,' her mother said, 'you've had a holiday and no mistake. We thought you were never coming back.'

'It was nice weather,' Tamsin said. It didn't seem necessary to mention that she had been ill and to be pestered with check-ups and tonics.

Amabel, not much to Tamsin's surprise, didn't turn up in London for another three weeks.

'Oh, you know, it's so decisive crossing the Channel,' she said on the phone. 'Like shutting a door, isn't it? I saw Jean-Luc again, too. Oh, I say, Tam, how's it with Keith?'

'Fine. I just needed to see him again, as you said.'

'I'm so glad. Well, we must meet. What are you doing with yourself?'

'Being Keith's girl-friend, mostly.'

'It sounds absorbing.'

'It is, rather.'

It was certainly time-consuming. An annoying amount of the time ⁓t in travelling between Barnet and Bromley. She spent most of her ⁓noons helping Keith with his job, sitting beside him in the car and making notes on his space-sheet. After he finished work they went to a pub, and then to his lodgings; but the advertising manager was a Methodist lay preacher and it wasn't possible for her to stay the night. If she didn't go to Bromley they usually met in town and wound up at Ted Goldman's flat, sometimes to spend the evening with Ted and his girl-friend, sometimes to borrow the flat. At weekends they went to a hotel in Kent which had been recommended to Keith by the news editor.

Tamsin knew that she had intended to find a job by the early autumn. But she kept putting it off; she still didn't feel strong enough to face rejection, she didn't need money, and anyway her time was fully occupied. Helping Keith was a kind of job and gave her some assurance that her thinking mind was getting back to normal. When they were out in the car, and not too rushed, he gave her driving lessons. She made a resolution to pass the test as a symbol of coping with reality. When the date came round – in January – she did pass it.

She would have to find a job all the same, she told herself. The trouble was that it would mean seeing less of Keith. Days when she didn't see him were blanks in her life, plunging her back into the aimless languor and the anxious introspection of Tangier. Being with him seemed to be a vital maintenance dose, a protection from the uncertainties which she hadn't really overcome.

If she were living with him, she thought, things would be easier. She could get a job in Bromley, or commute from there, and look forward tranquilly to the evening. She was never at ease making love in his room, where they had to be careful to be quiet and the old man was downstairs taking note of how late she stayed. As Keith's student girl-friend she hadn't minded tiptoeing down the back stairs before twelve o'clock; the Saturday nights had been more precious to him. Well, she felt differently now. Making love in three different places during a week – in his room, at Ted's flat, and at the hotel – added to her sense of insecurity. When she was at home and went to bed alone, she slept badly.

Really, she decided, she couldn't go on living with her parents. They were of course aware that Keith was her steady boy-friend and that she slept with him. They had met Keith on visits to the university; they approved of him, especially now that he had a good job, and they didn't venture to disapprove of Tamsin's behaviour. But they didn't like it, doubtless because they didn't like any evidence that things around ther were changing, and from a sour resentment at having missed somethir in their young days. They expressed their opposition circuitously method that Tamsin had always despised. Her father said that he ne

64

knew whether to bolt the front door, and her mother said that all these late nights were unhealthy.

On a Sunday morning in December, she woke up at the hotel in Kent and saw that it had snowed heavily in the night. The countryside looked enchanted, transformed from the sodden dullness of the day before into a dazzling gleam. The sun was shining, the sky was blue. Everything was fresh and clean and beautiful.

'Look, darling!'

Keith looked, and jumped out of bed.

'Isn't that great! Come on, let's get up. We'll go out while it's still fresh. We could make a snowman.'

The hotel was almost empty; no one else got up and went out. Their footprints explored – created – a new epoch.

'Happy, sweetheart?'

Held in the sustaining strength of his arm, Tamsin smiled up at him. She was happy, yes. The knowledge gave her a sense of wonder; it was an unexpected gift, like the beauty on which her eyes had opened.

'I'll tell you what we're going to do,' he said in a firm, confident voice.

He had formed some sort of plan, she saw, in his usual decisive way.

'Make a snowman?'

'Yes, we'll do that. But that's not what I mean. We're going to make this the greatest day in our lives, the day we'll never forget.'

'That sounds good.'

He put his hand on her cheek to turn her face toward him.

'My precious girl, you do realize I've just asked you to marry me?'

'Oh,' she said, 'you have?'

'Is that all you're going to say?'

'No. I mean, yes.' She started to laugh, absurdly, at the swiftness with which this was happening and at the discovery that it could be so simple. 'Of course. Yes, yes, yes.'

They kissed. She closed her eyes, and opened them again on the pure, cleansed spaces of snow and sky. She was ready to believe that Keith had arranged for it to snow in the night and clear by morning.

'I didn't think you'd be so surprised,' he said.

'I wasn't thinking. I suppose just being with you, and with everything so beautiful . . . it seemed to be enough.'

'You couldn't imagine a better time and place, could you?'

That's true. I'll never forget it, I know that.'

was just waiting for the perfect occasion. But we've known it along, haven't we?'

remembered the evening at the little restaurant, when his plan to become her lover, and of course his timing had been perfect –

taking her by surprise, but making her admit her readiness. She had felt the same sense of entrusting herself with relief to his certainty. 'It's all understood . . .' This time she'd been given a chance to say 'yes', but she had merely confirmed what he knew.

He was saying: 'We'll have a home, won't that be great? It's only the two rooms, but it'll do till we find something else. You can move in as soon as we're married.'

'You had it all figured out, didn't you?'

'It didn't take any figuring out to know I love you and I've just got to spend my life with you. The rest follows.'

Tamsin was tempted to say nothing to her parents, at least until a few days before the wedding – which, she and Keith agreed, would be as soon as possible. She detested the thought of arrangements being made by her mother, invitations to relatives who meant nothing to her, new clothes, fuss in general. There was an aspect of marriage that didn't appeal to her at all: the securing of social and official approval for what she wanted to do, which was simply to live with Keith. But what he'd asked her was to marry him, and she had responded with an immediate gladness that she knew to be authentic. As for telling her parents, that couldn't be avoided. Keith was doubtless telling his parents – the machine was in motion.

She managed, however, to give the news as casually as possible, on the Tuesday morning just as she was about to go out.

'When will you be back, dear?' her mother asked.

'I don't know. I've got some things to see to. I'm getting married.'

'Well! When did you decide on this?'

It was like her mother, Tamsin thought, to fix on the least important aspect of the matter. She said: 'Over the weekend.'

'It is Keith, I suppose?'

'Of course it's Keith, who else?'

'Well, I hope you'll be very happy.' This came out as a formal statement, at once followed by a complaint: 'You are a funny girl, you never tell us anything.'

'I've just told you, haven't I?'

'I mean, it's so sudden. You're not having a baby by any chance?'

'No, I'm not. Accidents don't happen with Keith.' While her mother was finding a reply to this, Tamsin left the house.

Remarkably, the weather was still cold and clear. Keith did expect her at Bromley until the afternoon, so she took a bu Hampstead and went for a walk on the Heath. She was in a st entranced, almost dazed happiness, a happiness that still surpris Getting married was more than simply living together, she tho

66

the first time. Keith had understood that, too. Its magnitude and permanence gave her a sense of peace, as though she had been given the keys of a solid and ample house in which she would always be sure of who she was and where she belonged. Already, calmness had returned to her. She felt healthy and strong, delighted by the cold crisp air, capable of walking for miles. Last night she had slept soundly, although alone. She didn't even feel the same anxious need to see Keith today or to be with him tonight. Soon, there would be no worries about that.

They were to be married in Bromley, to make it more difficult for Tamsin's mother to get involved. Keith said that it couldn't be quite so soon as they'd hoped; registrars, like other people, took an ample break over Christmas. So it would be in the new year – 'our new year', Keith said.

4

The phone rang half an hour after Tamsin had gone to bed. It must be next door, she said to herself. She was forced to admit, however, that the sound came clearly from the front hall (her parents were not the sort of people who had a phone in the living-room). She had to admit, too, that it was more likely to be for her than for anyone else. It couldn't very well be Keith, since she had just spent the evening with him. Possibly it was Amabel. More likely, it was a wrong number. It was her father's house, anyway, so it was up to him to go downstairs in the cold. As usual, it was quite cold enough in her bedroom. She pulled the blankets resolutely over her head.

But the phone went on ringing and, as a phone bell can, instilled by sheer persistence the belief that it had something of importance to tell. Grudgingly, Tamsin went downstairs. She stood by the phone and stared at it, requiring it to ring three more times if it was really serious. Then she picked it up and said: 'Hello.'

'Tamsin, is that you?'

'Who's this?' But she knew who it was.

'Brian. I rang earlier. I talked to your mother.'

'She never thinks to leave messages.'

'She says you're getting married.'

'Yes. I'm marrying Keith.'

'How is that?'

'What d'you mean, how is that?' But Tamsin felt immediately the need to justify herself, even defend herself.

Brian said nothing.

'Hello . . . Brian, are you there?'

68

'Sure.'

'Look, Brian, I can't talk now. I was in bed. I'm standing in the hall, it's cold.' *What are you doing to me?* she wanted to say.

'Can I see you tomorrow?'

'D'you mean today? It's twelve forty-five a.m.'

'Yes, today.'

Brian – so Tamsin learned later – had been ringing up at intervals since September. At first, Tamsin's mother said: 'She's still abroad.' Later, the formula: 'She isn't here' gave the same impression. Presumably she could just tolerate Tamsin's involvement with Keith but not another male pursuer. Scenting an evasion, Brian continued to phone. Now, triumphantly, Tamsin's mother had been able to say: 'She's hardly ever in, she's got a lot to do these days. She's getting married in the new year.'

Tamsin went back to bed and dropped into a troubled sleep, full of dreams which she didn't remember but which churned beneath her consciousness after she woke. She met Brian for lunch at a small café in Kentish Town. He had a furnished room, ironically quite near the room in which she had first spent the night with Keith. Kentish Town was on her tube line, so she could go on to Charing Cross to get the train to Bromley.

Brian looked pale, she thought, as though he didn't often go out or eat proper meals. Of course she was pale too, as usual. There was a mirror by their table. These were not faces of easy good health, like Keith's face. She had noticed before now that she looked rather like Brian, not strikingly, but enough for a stranger to guess that they might be brother and sister. It seemed to her that they looked more alike . . . they both looked older, no doubt.

He had worked in the summer, teaching English to foreign students, and saved money. Now he was writing poetry – doing nothing else, to the mild but evident disapproval of his parents. There had been no arguments, but he had moved out to avoid depending on them.

Tamsin began to tell him about her travels. She kept the narrative on the level of a funny story, describing the various delays, the people she'd met, and Amabel's sequence of affairs. She sensed that Brian wanted more than this from her. But he listened patiently, in silence.

She had only got as far as Mykonos when two men sat down at their table and began to talk loudly about football.

'We could go to my room,' Brian said.

'All right.' They were friends – it was ridiculous to demur. Or it admitted a possibility that he hadn't seemed to suggest, even to be aware of.

It was snowing again – this time a thin, damp urban snow dripping from a grey sky. They walked fast. Brian had a basement room; one got there without going through the front door of the house. It was dim, almost dark in this weather, but he didn't turn on the light. There was a divan-bed, a stained deal table and one chair. She felt, as she had felt eighteen months ago in his other room, that she had made her way into the small intense centre of his life. But she didn't feel at all that she was intruding; no, it was somehow natural for her to be here.

He turned the chair, which had faced the table, and sat down. Tamsin sat on the edge of the bed – there was nowhere else. The room was so small that they were closer together than in the café.

She resumed: 'Then, when we met up in Athens, Amabel said she'd heard about a cheap flight to Beirut . . .'

On she went, leaving nothing out. But, without any conscious intention, she found herself talking in quite a different way. She told Brian – what she had told no one else – about the night in the hospital, in full and stark detail. She told him of her helpless misery, her despair and her abandonment to death. All this time she spoke quite steadily, although in a very quiet voice, even shaping her sentences well and effortlessly finding the right words. Somehow, she was able to evoke the whole terrible reality of what she had endured and yet to remain calm, indeed to become calmer as she went on.

When she had finished, she felt exhausted: exhausted and yet re-covered, rather as she'd felt in the hotel when she knew that she had come through the illness. She leaned back against the wall. Brian got up from his chair and stood looking down at her. He smiled, and she felt herself rewarded – both for the completeness of her self-revelation and for having overcome her experience. Their eyes met and she smiled back. Then he sat down beside her, leaning back too.

There they stayed, neither moving nor speaking – perhaps for a few minutes, perhaps longer; afterwards, she had no idea. She was absolved from the need to say any more, or to think. Yet something was happening. She didn't know what, and didn't wish to define it.

At last she said: 'I think I died and came back again. Is that possible, d'you believe?'

'If you believe it, it's the real truth.'

'Yes . . . it is what one believes, isn't it?'

'And after that, you decided to marry Keith?'

'Well,' she said, attempting a laugh, 'the two things aren't connected.' He said nothing.

'Do you want me to tell you about me and Keith?'

'No, never mind.'

'But you did want to know, when you rang up. You asked me why.'

'Not why – how.'

'All right, how.' Tamsin didn't quite see the distinction. 'I'm perfectly willing to tell you.'

'Not now.'

'Well, I ought to be going, anyway.'

'Tamsin, I wish I'd been able to talk to you when you came home.'

'But it wouldn't . . .' She was about to say: it wouldn't have made any difference to loving Keith and wanting to marry him. Was this true? she wondered. She shied away from the question.

'Can I make a phone call?'

'It's upstairs, by the front door.'

She rang Keith's office and was told that he'd gone out. He had left the message that he would be in the pub at six o'clock.

'Did you get through?' Brian asked.

'Yes.'

'Well . . . so long, Tam. Thank you for coming.'

'Oh, that's all right.'

She walked quickly away, shivering in the nasty weather and wondering what to do next. She could have stayed with Brian all afternoon; she tested and rejected the idea that she had been afraid to. He hadn't pressed her to stay. Did that mean that he counted on seeing her again? Probably it meant that he wanted to write.

She decided to go to the Tate and spend the afternoon with the Turners. It was several months since she'd last seen them; a lot had happened to her, she ought to be able to get more out of them now. But, instead of giving her the positive refreshment and the clarity that she recalled, Turner left her puzzled. All those impenetrable masses of light and colour seemed to conceal . . . what was he concealing? She was aware of Turner eluding her, rebuking the insistence of her approach. She needed him today, too. She was in danger of slipping into her Tangier mood – adrift, not certain of anything.

She reached the pub in Bromley before Keith and had to wait. At this hour the pub was almost empty, but two boys who were playing bar-football – just kids really, hardly old enough to be allowed in pubs – stared at her and made sniggering remarks about her. She was angry and embarrassed, almost enough to go out and walk about until she saw Keith's car, if the weather had been better. But being stared at had left her indifferent, even amused her, as recently as this summer on the beach at Mykonos. By growing older one became more vulnerable, apparently.

Keith arrived on the dot, as usual.

'Hello, beautiful. I waited for you till past three o'clock. What happened to you?'

'I met a friend.'

They had two drinks, and then went to an Indian restaurant for dinner. She wondered whether Keith was going to take her to his room – that is, to their future home. Probably not; when he did, he usually suggested buying take-away food. The service at this restaurant was slow. Keith enjoyed the ceremonial of an Indian or Chinese meal, entering into long discussions with the waiter. She was seized – suddenly, just after he had finished ordering – by a passionate, a truly desperate desire to strip off her clothes and make love. It was strange; she hadn't felt this in the same urgent way since she had known that they were to be married. Well, she had a right to her impulses. But the impulse evidently didn't transmit itself to Keith, so she said nothing about it.

She heard him, as though from a long way off, saying: 'Hey, darling, you're not with me.'

'What? Sorry.'

'I was talking to you. You're miles away.'

'Oh . . . I am sorry.'

He leaned forward and scrutinized her.

'You don't look quite up to the mark. I hope you're not getting this 'flu that's going round.'

'Oh no, I don't think so.'

'Have an early night, anyway. I tell you what, I'll drive you home. It's lousy weather.'

'No, that's silly, Keith. It's miles.'

'Well, I'll drive you to the Elephant and Castle and then you'll only have to take the tube.'

In the car, he said: 'You'll be all right tomorrow. Hope so, anyway. We can have Ted's place, he'll be away.'

'Fine.'

'Right. Shall I meet you there? Seven o'clock?'

'Right. Looking forward.'

But somehow she couldn't look forward. She wanted to make love with Keith tonight; how could she know what she would feel like tomorrow?

He stopped the car outside the tube station. She pulled him into an embrace and a tense, searching kiss. A car behind them hooted.

Tamsin went home, surprising her parents by coming in so early, said that she was tired, and got into bed. She wasn't sleepy, really; she had to be alone, and to think. Something had happened – it was not to be denied, it had to be examined and understood. It had happened in stillness and in silence, while she was sitting on the bed with Brian. She realized that if he had made the slightest movement, even touched her hand, she would have given herself to him. That was bad – hadn't Keith given her any control over herself? But what was more mysterious and frightening was that Brian had been content with knowing (as he must have known, she was sure) what he had achieved. Something had happened while 'nothing happened' . . . something incalculably formidable. They had entered, in that zone of suspended time, into an extraordinary and unforgettable state of intimacy.

She could see now why Brian hadn't made her explain why she was marrying Keith. She had bared herself sufficiently by telling him what she had been through in Tangier. Evidently he had decided that, once he knew about that, he knew everything. He believed that, after being scared to death, after voyaging to the extremes of loneliness and helplessness, after losing all confidence in herself, she had come home seeking a rescue. She had been in need of care and protection, as they said of deserted children. So she had fallen into Keith's arms, like a castaway finding rest on the shore.

Was it true? If she had come home from Athens, found a job, established a balance in her life, would the student love-affair have lasted? Perhaps. Would she have committed herself utterly to Keith? Perhaps; more doubtful. She was genuinely in love with Keith, had been in love with him for more than a year. Yet that could be taken to prove the opposite of what she wanted to believe, for it was a different Tamsin who had loved him then. Tangier had made a change in her, a change that she had revealed to Brian and not to Keith.

She couldn't rid herself of the idea that Brian had an insight into her nature and her actions that was greater than her own. What he believed about her . . . no, what he knew about her was true, because he knew it. He had penetrated within her, in the true sense, more completely than Keith ever could. She understood why Brian had remained impassive while she was Keith's girl. He had counted on what lay deeper than eager attraction, deeper even than love. He had waited, knowing that she hadn't renounced and couldn't renounce her pledge to him. Now – as he was now, as she was now – he meant more to her than ever. And this was not by choice on her part, nor on his, but by necessity.

What was she to do, then, after she became Keith's wife? How was she to live? By giving to Keith only so much of herself as Brian allowed? Was that what Brian wanted? Or what did he want?

Through this long winter night, Tamsin didn't sleep at all. She dressed and went downstairs before seven o'clock, and made herself some coffee. While she was drinking it, her father came down.

'Fancy seeing you at this hour.'

'I thought I'd see what it's like.'

'Mm – yes.' He looked at her distrustfully; then he drew the curtain aside a few inches and peered out. 'Still dark,' he announced, as though this was surprising.

'I'll make your breakfast, shall I?'

'Wonders will never cease.'

She put on the radio in lieu of conversation. He ate his boiled egg solemnly to the accompaniment of news of wars, plane crashes, roads blocked by snow. Then she watched him clear out the grate and polish his shoes. He breathed heavily with every small effort; he wasn't old or in poor health, it was simply a habit. His movements had an air of laconic resignation. But without daily obligations, he would have been lost.

'You going out today?' he asked.

'Yes.'

'Be late tonight?' This had become a euphemism for Tamsin's staying the night elsewhere.

'I daresay.'

When Tamsin heard her mother stirring, she returned to her room. It was still barely light, so she lay down under a blanket, but she didn't sleep. She was in the state of extreme alertness that lies on the far side of tiredness, just as when she'd worked all night before an exam. This thought amused her. She was certainly heading for a test. Moving, really, toward a point of resolution which was still clouded, but which she would recognize with absolute sureness when she reached it. She was no longer thinking about it – you have to clear your mind before an exam. But she wasn't afraid.

The front door closed . . . her father had gone to work. Later it closed again . . . her mother had gone to the shops. Tamsin waited a little longer and set out for Brian's room.

Going down the basement steps, she could see him sitting at his table. She tapped on the window and he looked up. They stared at each other for several seconds; the window was dirty and she couldn't be sure of his expression. Then he went to open the door.

'Hello, Tam.'

'Hello, Brian. Am I disturbing you?'

'No, I've finished what I was working on. At least, I think it's all right. Would you like to see?'

She sat down on the edge of the bed, as before, and read the poem.

Reading it like this, in the room where he'd written it, gave her a sense of complete understanding. She saw at once that it was on a higher plane of achievement than anything he had written as a student. It had an even and unforced beauty, a perfect union of thought and form. To make sure that she wasn't merely thinking what she wanted to think, she read it again slowly, testing it, searching for flaws. It was as good as the first time.

She handed it back to him.

'It's very fine, Brian.'

'It is? You do think it is?'

He was elated, she saw. She was surprised; he had never cared much about any estimate of his work except his own. What he welcomed, she realized, wasn't her opinion so much as her response to the value of writing poetry, to the life he was leading. He had been lonely, striving in this small room.

'It's very fine,' she said again. 'You know it is.'

'Yes, I do know.'

'When did you write it?'

'Yesterday.'

'Oh . . . did you?'

The poem – its content – had nothing to do with her. But the knowledge that he had written it after being with her filled her with happiness.

'I'd like to have it,' she said.

'I'll make you a copy.'

'I'd like this – the original.'

'All right.'

'You know, after I was here yesterday I went to the Tate. I was looking at the Turners while you were writing this. I mean . . . I just thought you'd like to know.'

'I see.'

'Then I had dinner with Keith. In Bromley, where he works. Then he drove me back as far as the tube and I went home.'

'I see,' Brian said again. Obviously it wasn't important to him that she hadn't slept with Keith. But it had been necessary for her to tell him.

She said: 'You don't want me to marry Keith, do you?'

'Do you want me to answer that?'

'Yes.'

'Well then, I don't believe it.'

'You don't accept it?'

'If you like, I don't accept it. I don't accept that you should diminish yourself.'

'Diminish,' Tamsin said slowly, 'diminish. I do know what that

75

means. But it isn't with Keith that I'm diminished. I'm very diminished when I'm alone. That's me, I suppose.'

'It hasn't struck you that Keith might not be much good at being alone. You're the one who is desired, Tam.'

'Oh well, as to that . . . It's nice being desired, of course. But I also desire him, very much so. I can be happy with him. We've been lovers for more than a year.'

'That doesn't mean you should marry him.'

'But suppose you and I had been lovers for the last year?'

'That would be different.'

She saw what he meant. To have Keith as a lover – even to be in love with him – had been a stage in her emotional growth, a preparation for the real necessities of her life. That was true, she believed or was being drawn to believe. Yet it was less than the full truth.

She said: 'It goes deeper than you think – what I have with Keith, I mean. He calls on something in me that I couldn't be mistaken about. I think I need him, honestly I do.'

'Are you trying to convince me or yourself?'

'Oh, hell,' she said. 'I was all right until you came along. I felt quite sure about this until you made me doubt myself.'

'But I haven't said much, have I?'

'You disturb me, that's what you do. I'd rather not be disturbed just at this time. I've got everything settled. We're getting married on the fourth of January, let me tell you.'

'I can see it might be a nuisance to cancel a lot of arrangements.'

'Don't talk to me like that, Brian.'

'Like what?'

'Sarcastic. Cruel. Don't do it to me, please.'

Tamsin began to cry, leaning forward and hiding her face, letting the tears run through her fingers. She wasn't sure whether she wanted Brian to comfort her, or whether that was just the danger to which she laid herself open. He stood and watched her, at all events. She felt the penetration of his eyes, like needles under her skin.

'I'm sorry,' she said, finding a tissue and wiping her face.

He said: 'I wasn't trying to hurt you.'

'You can do it, though, can't you?'

'That isn't it. You're crying because you've got yourself into this . . . into what you don't believe in.'

'I don't believe in marrying Keith?'

'No.'

'Well . . . I don't know where that leaves us. Perhaps you think I should marry you.'

76

'Yes. That's what you should do.'

She stared at him as though she hadn't quite understood what he'd said. He made a blundering movement, not toward her but away from her; he came up against the table and leaned against it, gripping it with both hands. The little room was perfectly silent.

An immense joy surged in her, but she fought it down. She couldn't trust it yet.

'So I've got an option, anyway,' she said.

'I mean it, Tam.'

'I'll have to see where I am. I don't know where I am now, not at all. I don't think I'd better stay here with you, Brian. It's too much.'

Out in the street, she looked at her watch. She hadn't been long with Brian, but it was time for lunch and she was glad to find (something was normal) that she was hungry. She went to the café where she'd met Brian the day before. The waitress greeted her in a friendly way, probably assuming that she had come to live in the neighbourhood.

Uppermost in her mind, just now, was a sense of the absurdity of life . . . not its absurdity exactly, for she might be on the verge of making sense of it, but its wealth of surprises. She started to giggle, suddenly and spontaneously, while she was drinking coffee and waiting for the bill. The waitress grinned at her. I must be getting light-headed, Tamsin thought. It was the sleepless night, probably. She decided to see a film, a funny film if possible, and remembered that there was a Marx Brothers season at the Hampstead Everyman.

She came in after the start of *Duck Soup* and was soon giggling again. But then she fell asleep, and when she was woken by the house-lights she grasped that the film was over. Feeling cheated, she decided to see it again, or rather see it.

By the time she came out, it was past seven o'clock. Keith was waiting for her. But no, she thought, she wouldn't see either Keith or Brian tonight. She had to sort things out. She found a phone and rang Ted's number.

'Keith? It's Tam. Listen, I'm not feeling well. I do seem to be going down with 'flu or something. I'm sorry . . . Right, I'll see you soon.'

It was strange how easy it was to lie to Keith. She had thought of herself as a truthful person, aside from lying to her parents, of course. Perhaps Keith's trust in her supplied a temptation.

It was early to go home; she couldn't face a whole evening with her parents. She wasn't hungry now. But she couldn't just drift about London in the cold.

All of a sudden, as she stood irresolutely in the street, she was seized overpowering urge to be with Brian. She dashed through moving traffic and into the tube station. The journey seemed endless, and the resigned patience of the other passengers seemed contemptible. She had a long wait for a train to begin with and again when she changed. She wished that she'd taken a taxi . . . it hadn't occurred to her, she hardly ever took taxis.

On the way, she tried to convince herself that she wasn't making a decision. She was in the mood to be with Brian, that was all. It was only fair, considering all the time she'd spent with Keith. Then she started to laugh at herself. People stared at her, the crazy girl.

As she walked toward Brian's house, she was suddenly afraid that he had gone out. He couldn't sit in his little room all the evening as well as all day, surely. She started to run, illogically but compulsively, and reached the house breathless. The curtains were drawn so tight that she couldn't see whether there was a light in his room or not. She rapped frantically on the window. He opened the door.

'Brian,' she said. 'Brian, I can't live without you.'

In the morning, Tamsin decided to move in with Brian right away. Life with her parents would be impossible, clearly, once they knew that she wasn't marrying Keith. Brian's room was tiny, but they could find a flat. Her only anxiety was that she would be in his way while he worked. But of course she would be getting a job, she would be out all day. She was filled, this morning, with complete confidence in finding a job, finding a flat, doing whatever she wanted.

Luckily, it was her mother's day for going to lunch with Sheila, Tamsin's sister. Tamsin approached the house with every intention of packing a suitcase, leaving a note, and taking the tube straight back to Kentish Town. But unluckily, Sheila had 'flu and had cancelled lunch. Still more unluckily, Keith had already phoned to ask how Tamsin was.

'I didn't know what to say, dear. You haven't got 'flu, have you?' Tamsin's mother stressed the *you*, as though the identities of her daughters had become confused.

'No, no, I'm fine.'

With this, Tamsin edged toward the stairs. Her mother was ironing with an air of concentration; she ironed everything, including things that would immediately get crumpled – sheets, pillow-cases, pyjamas. The achievement of a neutral smoothness, Tamsin supposed, gave her a pale kind of satisfaction.

'I was quite surprised when he phoned. Just after breakfast, it was. I thought you might be with him.'

'No, I wasn't.' Trapped, Tamsin continued firmly: 'As a mat-

fact I don't expect to see Keith again.'

'Oh, you silly girl, have you had a row?'

'I don't believe in rows. But I'm not marrying him. The whole thing was a mistake.'

'Oh, is that so?'

'That is so.'

'Well, it'll be a real mistake if you break it off just because of a tiff. Keith's a very nice steady young man. He's got a good job. You might wait a long time before you find anybody else like that.'

'No, that's taken care of. I'm marrying Brian.'

Tamsin's mother put the iron down on its rest (Tamsin had been hoping to see her burn a hole in a sheet) and asked: 'And who's Brian when he's at home?'

'The man I'm marrying.'

'Tamsin, you weren't with this Brian last night, were you?'

'Certainly.'

'I really don't know what your father's going to say.'

'It's all the same to him so long as I marry somebody, and so it is to you. I can't stop now, I've got to pack. Brian's taking me to Paris for a week.'

The reproving expression on her mother's face began to dissolve with the thought of Brian's probable financial position. Tamsin went upstairs and packed.

In the evening, she wrote a letter to Keith. It was a cold and perhaps a cowardly way of telling him; but she thought that she had a right to spare herself a scene that, she was perfectly certain, wouldn't alter anything. She had always expressed herself easily on paper and the letter – quite long and entirely clear – gave her the feeling of a necessary job well done.

Looking back on her year with Keith, she saw it as an experience whose significance would become clear in time. She would see its causes, its logic and its value; it had a meaning for her, more than Brian granted. But she couldn't reflect on it now. She could only hope that Keith's strong character would close the wound. He would marry someone else soon, very likely, perhaps even on the rebound. Tamsin envisaged friendly, reminiscent foursome dinners. Amabel might suit him, possibly? Just at present, she was surprised – though naturally relieved – that he didn't pursue her and insist on speaking to her.

She was guarded against this, however. Thanks to her impromptu but inspired lie, she and Brian were believed to be in Paris. The phone at Brian's home wouldn't answer; Dorothy was in Washington for a monetary conference and Robert was joining her for a Christmas break in the Bahamas. Tamsin used the time thus gained to find a flat. Brian had been invited to spend Christmas with his uncle, a pathologist (Robert's family was strongly medical) in Southampton. There was no difficulty about his bringing his fiancée.

In a spirit of reconciliation, and feeling her future to be secure, Tamsin allowed her parents to come to the wedding.

PART THREE

I

Tamsin went to Portobello Road in the hope of buying two soup plates. She and Brian had soup quite often; some of their meals consisted of soup and nothing else. They had started married life with six soup plates, which had got broken in the course of time, mostly because she washed up when she'd been drinking or when she was very tired. She had broken the last two a couple of nights ago, both together, letting them drop from her hands for no reason except an obscure resentment as she carried them from the table to the sink.

You could buy just two plates in the market, or one plate for that matter, whereas in a shop you had to buy six. Tamsin was going to the far end of the market, the cheap end, where junk is junk and makes no claim to be antiques. But, having got off the bus at the expensive end, she walked slowly down the road and looked at the stalls loaded with things that she couldn't possibly buy – not that she had ever wanted to possess things whose loss or breakage would be a disaster. It was curious, to her mind, how valuable these nineteenth-century– occasionally eighteenth-century – plates and cups and glasses had become. They has been cheap enough to begin with, most of them: ordinary products which their owners might have liked but hadn't prized any more than she had prized her soup plates. Time had made the difference, obviously. But not only time; there was also rarity. To make that thing valuable – she reflected, stopping to look at a plate decorated with arching race-horses – it had been necessary for thousands like it to be broken. Well, she was doing her bit for the antique trade of the twenty-first century.

'Nice, isn't it?' said the dealer.

Tamsin looked up, preparing an amiable but non-committal smile.

81

'Nice to see you again, too,' he said. 'Remember me?'

She let the smile become apologetic and said: 'I'm sorry, I'm awful about faces.' Such chance encounters – they happened now and again – confronted her with figures from the far side of a gulf: fellow-students generally, though the antique-dealer looked too old to be that.

'Saw you with Keith. You used to come to my flat. Can't say I recall your name, though. It's names I'm bad at.'

'Ah.' She remembered now, quite clearly. The flat, furnished with a bizarre clustering of antiques, reappeared to her like a hotel room in which she'd once spent a holiday, distant but real.

'Of course, that's it,' she said. 'I can manage all right once I'm given a clue. Ted . . . Ted Goldman?'

'Right. Clever girl. Now then, I ought to be able to think of your name. Unusual name, isn't it?'

'Tamsin.'

'There we are. Tamsin. Well, Keith will be chuffed when I tell him. Hold on, though. I'm expecting Keith down here today. Any minute, in fact.'

'You're expecting Keith?'

'Oh yes, he's quite a collector. I've got something for him. This is it, see.'

It was a large bowl with an ornate design of creeping plants. Originally it must have been a tureen, but nowadays probably one would put flowers in it. The thing was broad, squat, and almost too heavy to lift as Ted took it from its crate and put it on his table. Tamsin thought it remarkably ugly.

'There. Don't see many of these on the market, I can tell you. Had to hunt all over the place for it.'

'How much are you selling it for?'

'Two hundred. To a friend, that is.'

'Well, that's interesting. I must be going along. I want to buy some soup plates – just ordinary ones, to use.'

'Aren't you going to wait for Keith?'

'I'll come back.'

Tamsin didn't intend to come back, or she believed later that she hadn't intended to. But at this moment Keith appeared, driving a small but expensive-looking car. She gazed at him, testing herself, trying to define what she felt. Occupied in skilfully parking the car in the narrow space between Ted's stall and the next, he hadn't seen her yet.

When he got out of the car, she held herself perfectly still and looked straight at him.

'Tamsin,' he said. 'It's really Tamsin.'

He was surprised and he was delighted, but she saw that he wasn't altogether astonished. He would have counted on his luck to produce her for him sooner or later, just as Ted had found the bowl he wanted.

He kissed her. Presumably a kiss (on the cheek) was the proper greeting for a former girl-friend. But something about the kiss – duration? pressure? – seemed to convey an additional message. Or did she imagine that?

'You must have set this up, Ted,' he said.

'Think so?' Ted asked. 'Like *This is Your Life*?'

Keith was still very close to Tamsin, one hand on her arm. He said: 'Right. This is my life.'

She freed herself from him, rather clumsily, and took a step back.

'If you want to know,' she said, 'I'm on my way to buy two soup plates.'

'Right. Let's go and buy two soup plates.'

He held her arm as they walked along the street, and grasped her closer whenever the crowd was thick. This had always been like him, this insistence on physical contact. Like the kiss, it had a certain ambiguity. She didn't know what was meant for her, Tamsin, and what was his habitual impulse toward any woman who might be with him – toward woman as an element in his existence.

'Look, there are some pretty plates,' he said.

'I'm going to buy plain white plates.'

'You're positive about that?'

'Yes. The fact is, we're poor.'

Keith received this without comment. The information it conveyed, really, was that she was still married to Brian.

She found the kind of stall she wanted and bought two plain plates, one of them cracked round the edge. She half-expected Keith to pay for them, but he didn't. Later, she learned that he did all his shopping with cheques or credit cards.

'Anything else?' he asked.

'No, nothing else.'

'I've got my car.'

'Thanks, but I can get home from here.'

'I don't think that's very friendly, Tam.'

'I know. But you must see this isn't easy for me.'

'Don't go now, Tam. Please don't.'

'This is a lousy place to talk,' she said.

They walked on some distance, beyond the last stalls to the hollow space under the concrete bulk of the motorway. On one of the pillars someone had chalked *Doris Fry fucks anybody*. On another pillar someone had sprayed in aerosol *Armed Struggal Now*. Tamsin stared at the words, absurdly but acutely irritated by the spelling mistake. They were in a worse place now, she thought. Rather often lately, she had been overcome by a sense of living amid scenes of desolation.

She said: 'I'm sorry for what I did to you, Keith. It's very late to say it, and I'm afraid it doesn't do any good, but I am sorry.'

He was still holding her arm. He made her move until she was against a pillar, with her back to *Doris Fry fucks anybody* and facing *Armed Struggal Now*. Then he kissed her again, this time on the lips.

'That won't do any good either,' she said.

'It might. But that's not the point.'

'What is the point, then?'

'Just that I love you. Exactly the same.'

Tamsin gave a little shrug, a gesture of acceptance and resignation.

'Let's go back to the car,' Keith said.

People looked at them, she noticed as they walked through the market again. She remembered that from the past: people had looked at her and Keith. He looked splendid now just as he had then, and he was very well dressed in the modern style, casual and yet with a frank assertion of careful choice – not the old unobtrusive ideal of male dress, but clothes that were meant to attract attention. He'd done very well for himself in one way or another, that was clear. But then, she had always known that he would.

And what do I look like, Tamsin wondered? She wasn't in the habit of thinking about this, but the excuse for doing so gave her pleasure. A frivolous, half-guilty and half-sardonic pleasure, yet pleasure all the same. She didn't look up to much, doubtless, with her cheap clothes and her two soup plates in a string bag (which Keith was carrying, but which identified themselves clearly with her). But if people, seeing her with Keith, assumed a deliberate avoidance of display, that could be intriguing, even mysterious. She was pale, she knew that; and it was late summer, when everyone who had been away – she never went away nowadays – was brown. Pale and interesting? She treated herself to a secret smile.

'Are you really paying two hundred pounds for that object?' she asked.

'Am I? I must be, if that's what Ted says.'

'I think it's hideous.'

'I daresay you're right, sweetie. It looked good in the catalogue. I'll have to see how it shapes up when I get it home.'

Ted loaded the bowl into the back of the car and said: 'See you around, Keith. See you, Tamsin.'

'See you, Ted.'

She got in beside Keith and he drove off.

'I still have your letter,' he said. 'Your card from Mykonos, and a book you left behind at Bromley, and your letter. It's not much, but I still have them.'

'I suppose it was a horrible letter.'

'I wouldn't say that. It was the sort of letter that gets written in the circumstances. Did you marry Brian right away?'

'Yes, right away. Actually . . . I thought you'd come chasing after me.'

'I decided it was safer not to.'

'Safer?'

'Right. I was very wild, really out of control. I might have killed you.'

He looked straight at her as he said this (the car had stopped at a traffic light) and to her surprise he was smiling broadly. Evidently she was meant to take his wildness, the fact that he might have killed her, as an entry in the record of love.

'Where are we going?' she asked.

'To my place, if you've no other ideas. We'll have a good talk. I deserve that after all this time, don't you think?'

'All right,' she said. It was dangerous, but she was plunged into the danger already. Besides, she couldn't resist the desire to see his place —how he lived.

Unexpectedly, just near Knightsbridge, he drove down a ramp into the basement garage of a big modern building. She looked round at something like a clean, opulent version of the space under the motorway. They took the lift – also clean, opulent and quiet – to the top floor.

She found herself in a large room, suitable for giving a party, and in which apparently Keith had given a party last night, to judge by a scattering of used glasses and full ashtrays. Perhaps because of this, it made the impression of being a public place, like a hotel lounge. All the objects that caught her eye were either antique, in the Ted Goldman manner, or very modern. They did add up to a collection, though a disparate one.

'It's a hell of a mess, I'm afraid,' Keith said. 'I'll clear up a bit.'

'It doesn't matter.'

'Well, what would you like to drink?'

'Whatever you're having. Can I use the bathroom?'

'It's along there, second on the left.'

The bathroom had its own collection: an array of creams, lotions and sprays, several of them male but for the most part female.

'Are you married, Keith?' Tamsin asked when she came back.

He said: 'I made you a dry martini.'

'Thank you. Cheers.'

'Cheers.'

She sat down at one end of an extremely comfortable couch. The material was soft and warm – antelope-hide, could that be it?

'You are married, then? I'm glad.'

'No, of course I'm not.'

'How d'you mean, of course? You used to be very marriage-minded.'

'I couldn't marry anyone except you.'

This came out as a plain statement of fact, something she should have known. She found nothing to say.

'I have girls, naturally. There's a girl living here just at present. But when I said I love you exactly the same as I've always loved you, it was absolutely true.'

'Well, tell me about this girl. Am I going to meet her?'

'No. Not today, anyhow. She's gone to Cornwall, her mother's ill. She's just a girl, that's all. She does her stuff.'

'I wonder what it's like to be just a girl.'

'She takes life as it comes.'

'That's quite a gift.'

Keith sat down beside her. She had known that he would, but the room was mostly furnished with couches, and if she'd chosen a chair he would have sat on the arm. His nearness, the weight and shape of his body, began to work on her as they always had. She finished her drink.

'I've never given you up,' he said. 'I didn't try to. It would be giving up all hope. A man must have hope, in order to live. I didn't try to find you because I was sure that hope would win out in the end – hope and love. I couldn't guess how long it would take. Time isn't what counts. All that time without you – it's wiped out now. We're back where we were. I drove you from Bromley to the Elephant and we kissed goodnight in the car. That was last night. It's tomorrow now, my sweetheart.'

'Oh, Keith,' she said, 'you know how to kid yourself, don't you? You make everything the way you want it to be. How can we be back where we were? D'you imagine nothing's happened except in your mind?'

But he had his arms round her, he was pressing down on her, his hands moved over her, he kissed her where she remembered his kisses. She had never been able to check or to deny the answer of her body to his, nor could she now. It was from within herself, from what he knew of her.

'I suppose you want to make love to me,' she said.

'Of course I do. And you want to, you know you do.'

She grasped both his wrists, halting his hands. They stared at each other as antagonists, declaring a challenge.

'I'm not afraid to, anyway,' she said.

In the bedroom, she pulled her clothes off as though stripping for a quick swim. The bed wasn't made; she was glad about that, it was reassuringly casual and sordid. The room was rather dim, the curtains still drawn. She switched on all the lights.

She allowed herself to become what he remembered, what she remembered of herself – his eager, passionate girl. She didn't want him to think that she couldn't risk any degree of intimacy and arousal. There was something else she remembered, something he had never known: even in giving him all that he sought of her, she retained a proud and secret part of herself that was indestructibly her own. There she was calm; there she had her refuge.

Afterwards, she said in a level voice: 'I'd like a shower.'

'Good idea.'

They had a shower together. He kept touching her and holding her; she felt a gay delight in the way he couldn't have enough of her. He dried her, and she put on a robe – the girl's, no doubt. She turned toward the large room, but he said: 'Let's go back to the bedroom.'

'That was a oncer, Keith.'

'It's cosy in the bedroom. We'll just talk.'

'Oh, all right.'

She picked her clothes up from the floor and put them on a chair, concealing her knickers which were dirty and had a hole. There were other things on the floor – a pop-music magazine, a black lace bra, and a charm bracelet.

'Your girl's very untidy,' she said, sitting down on the bed.

'That's true. But I'll be getting rid of her.'

'Oh, not on my account.'

Keith collected the girl's things and put them in a closet. He was still naked. He hadn't walked about naked in the past.

'She leaves things lying around to establish her presence,' he remarked. 'They often do that.'

'Do they?'

'Mm.' Keith yawned and lay down, of course close to Tamsin. 'You know, honey-love, I was sure it would be like this. The moment I saw you standing there, I was sure.'

She gratified him with a smile. He stroked her thigh – almost unconsciously, like a man stroking a dog, she thought – and said: 'We've never missed out together, have we?'

'Not that I remember.'

'We haven't. Never ever. It's always fantastic, like this. Don't you think that's wonderful?'

'I'm glad you weren't disappointed.'

'I don't think you were, sweetie.'

'No, I could see that you've kept in training.'

He smiled – no, grinned. She remembered this too: the complacent male self-satisfaction. It was absent in Brian; he would sit up in bed ruminating, frowning sometimes, regretting an impossible perfection, just as he had after finishing a poem.

'Well,' she said, 'we're all square now, aren't we? I've made up for my horrid letter. At least, I hope you think so.'

'That never happened, my darling. We'll just start from here.'

She wanted to laugh. Faced with such extraordinary assurance, one could only laugh or be more solemn than, at the moment, she wished. However, Keith seldom accepted the idea that anyone was laughing at him rather than with him. She looked at him as gravely as she could (even sternly, she hoped) and said: 'Look, Keith, let's get things straight. It's pure chance we've met again. It doesn't mean anything – I don't run my life by chance. We've made love, and it was very nice, but I let you do it the way I let you kiss me.'

Still grinning, he said: 'You know how to kid yourself, don't you?'

'No, you're the one . . . Oh, don't be ridiculous, Keith. Don't complicate things. Don't make me wish I hadn't done this.'

'You won't wish that, Tam.'

'I hope not.'

'You said it, you know.'

'I said what?'

'You said: "I love you.".'

'I did? When?'

'When you had to say it.'

'Oh . . . maybe I did . . . one says all kinds of things, surely you know that.'

But she was shaken. There must have been a moment when she lost herself, when he possessed her entirely.

'Stop doing that,' she said irritably, and pushed his hand away from her leg.

'Relax, darling,' he said. 'There's no sense in having an attack of conscience, it isn't logical. Things are going right for us.'

'No, Keith, it isn't so. I went wild, that's all. I had a bit of a holiday. A woman's got a right to do that sometimes, so don't think I've got any conscience about it. That's all, it's really all. If you want to be my friend I'm grateful -- I don't have many friends. But you can't be my lover. There's no space in my life for that.'

'I am your lover.'

'Well, I can see where I went wrong. I should have said all this before instead of after.'

'Why didn't you, then?'

'It would have sounded rather cold, don't you think? And I thought you'd understand.'

'I didn't notice you thinking very much, the way you jumped out of your clothes.'

That was true, unfortunately. She couldn't deny that Keith had a sort of insight into her, not deep but sharp and practical.

'I'm telling you now, anyway,' she said.

'It's what you told me then that counts, love.'

'No, it isn't. Of course it isn't.'

'Ah well, we won't argue. I'm much too happy.' He reached for her hand. 'Come on, just lie down and take it easy.'

'I'll have to go. What time is it?'

'No idea.'

'I had a watch. I must have had a watch.'

'Yes, you dropped it on the floor. I put it on that table.'

She got up and looked at it.

'It's nearly six. I do have to go.'

'I'll take you out to dinner. There's a good place just round the corner. Or we'll have something here, there's plenty of food.'

'No, thanks a lot, but I can't.'

'You might as well, considering.'

He was right about this. She hadn't thought yet about whether to tell Brian. If she was convinced of what she said – that what she'd done didn't mean anything, that there was no space in her life for a lover – then there was no harm in telling Brian; indeed, not telling him was creating a conspiracy with Keith. And if that was so, staying with Keith for the evening, or the night for that matter, made no difference.

Still, having said that she must go, it seemed best to be firm. Keith knew nothing about her life. She might have children waiting for her, for all he could tell. The idea that she could tell Keith any lies that came in handy was reassuring. But she merely said: 'I'm going. You said you wouldn't argue.'

'OK. I'll drive you.'

'I'll take a bus, I think. I'd like to be alone for a bit.'

'Well, I'll come downstairs with you.'

They dressed in silence, rather as though they were getting up in the morning. Tamsin had to wait for him. He put on fresh clothes, including ew shirt that still had pins in it. Presumably he didn't wear the same es twice running nowadays.

He kissed her in the lift, in the entrance-hall of the building – which appeared surprisingly to be an office building rather than a block of flats – and at the bus stop. All this kissing was ridiculous, she thought; surely he couldn't imagine that it left her in a different frame of mind. But, taken for its own sake, it was pleasant. From the platform of the bus as it carried her away, she couldn't resist smiling at him.

The bus was quite crowded. Tamsin had to share a seat with a fat woman carrying two packages from Harrod's. But she didn't mind; she had a light-headed feeling, a feeling that no external nuisance could affect her. The feeling, she supposed, of a married woman after a couple of hours with another man.

It occurred to her that Keith hadn't asked where she lived, nor suggested any arrangement for meeting again. But this didn't imply any acceptance of what she'd told him – what he had blandly declined to argue about. On the contrary, it revealed a rather frightening confidence. She reflected that he must have acquired plenty of skill in dealing with women.

Also, he had asked no questions whatever about how she was living, about her state of happiness or unhappiness, about Brian. All that simply didn't exist for him. He didn't seek even to offer an alternative to discontent and deprivation. He scorned that advantage – he assumed that he had regained her. This was frightening, too.

To anchor her thoughts to an irrelevance, Tamsin tried to guess from the shape of the packages what the fat woman had bought at Harrod's. It was then that she realized that she had left her soup plates in Keith's flat.

2

After Keith and Tamsin were married, he produced the soup plates from the back of a cupboard as a surprise for her. This kind of sentimentality, this cherishing of symbols and memories, was typical of him; it led them at times to the little restaurant where he had made himself her lover, and to the hotel in Kent where (as he saw it) their marriage had begun, to be resumed after an unfortunate but forgettable aberration on her part. The reappearance of the plates made her laugh, but really charmed her. As Keith's mistress and Brian's unfaithful wife, she hadn't ventured to ask for them – indeed, she assumed that they'd been thrown away – and had been obliged to buy two more. Now they were put up on the wall, in metal frames, and Keith unfailingly explained their significance to dinner guests. He liked everyone to know that Tamsin had been his first real girl-friend, that he had never ceased to love her, and that he had been rightly confident of regaining her. The whole story even appeared in a magazine profile, soup plates and all.

Content that her second marriage should resemble her first as little as possible, Tamsin accepted its public character without protest. She had imagined that the actual wedding would be a mere legal ritual – of course, they'd been living together for months while her divorce was ~ing through – but Keith's ideas were very different. He staged a -scale production, organizing it like an Albert Hall concert. There an enormous guest-list, to which Tamsin contributed only her ~ts, her sister and her brother-in-law – 'my parents always like to married,' she remarked. Keith invited about thirty relatives and ; of friends or acquaintances. She had met some of them since she'd been living with him, but by no means all. Some of the men kissed her as if they'd been on familiar terms for years, others as though testing her to judge her acceptability, and yet others with an embarrassed politeness which conceded that they didn't know her and didn't even know Keith very well. She remembered the silly story about the man who kissed the bride and, on being asked by her who he was, replied: 'I thought this queue was for the Cup Final.' For several minutes, she had to battle against giggles.

During the hours consumed by the occasion – smiling, laughing, eating, drinking, being kissed – she was photographed repeatedly, more often than in the rest of her life. She felt that the camera, instead of reflecting her appearance, was imposing a new appearance on her. Her dress felt like a costume hired for the day. However, she found that she had to go on wearing expensive and unfamiliar clothes as Keith's wife. He liked to introduce her as 'my wife, Tamsin' . . . perhaps this refuted any notion that she was just one of his girls. Ratified less by law than by publicity, the marriage thus took a rank with other marriages, with the institution of marriage. Whereas her life with Brian had been . . . what? . . . an intense and unique personal experience but not, in this generalized sense, a marriage.

A twenty-one-year-old husband, Tamsin thought, would get exactly this pleasure from presenting 'my wife' instead of 'my girl'. She often felt that she was older than Keith; more accurately, that she had lived more. He had – laudably no doubt and, one might say, innocently – done nothing but love her (it was clearly true that the various girls hadn't mattered). She was willing to believe that she had loved him for years too, not even intermittently but, with a recognizable and now surfacing part of herself, continuously. But meanwhile another part of herself had lived another life whose meaning for her was – whatever Keith chose to think – ineradicable.

She didn't conceive of time as a straight or even a winding road. It was more like a cage in which she was doomed to pace about, sometimes along one track and sometimes another. Her footprints, on ground long covered in dust, were nevertheless familiar as she trod in them again.

But for Keith there was only one direction. His road of time led straight from Tamsin's promise to him to its fulfilment. That was the point of these nostalgic visits to staging-places along the road. He ha purpose: to persuade her of his conception of time, a time wholly f by their love.

To be fair . . . Tamsin wondered why she kept remembering fair to Keith; it was a dangerous sign of detachment. Howeve

fair: the purpose derived naturally from his outlook, it wasn't a coldly devised strategy. He wasn't deliberately trying to make her forget her life with Brian. He blotted it out, just as he had ignored it and never asked her about it while it continued – while she was his mistress – partly from tact (to be fair!) and partly from confidence that she was moving into his possession without needing to be pried loose and dragged. These re-creations of youth simply showed that, for him, the past was of a piece with the present. And indeed, he hadn't changed. He was still full of boyish zest, cheerful good humour and unclouded optimism. That was why he still looked so young, she decided.

As her boy-friend, his hopes and efforts had been all for Tamsin's sake. As her husband, this was still true. His love for her had all the most admirable features, such as a sincere concern for her happiness and a willingness to defer to her moods and desires. An ideal husband, indeed. She would have liked to do something for him that rewarded his devotion adequately, but it wasn't possible. He had no wishes that required any sacrifice on her part. Now that he was married to her as well as successful and rich, he was perfectly happy.

And she was happy too; or determined to be happy, since she had no reason not to be; or at all events as happy as she was capable of being. She was still introspective, compelled incessantly to observe and analyse her life, secretive in her deeper thoughts. She couldn't help that. Loving Keith made no difference.

It seemed to her that love was, when calmly observed . . . she searched for a word . . . an attitude on his part toward her, and on her part toward him. This word, *attitude,* was cold and weak for an emotion that could rouse her to genuine and ecstatic passion. But it had, she believed, a basic accuracy. Keith liked some people, disliked others, admired some, despised others, and loved Tamsin. She liked some people, and so forth, and loved Keith. They took up these attitudes from a position of independence, he retaining his own character, and she hers.

Keith had a phrase he was fond of: 'a good marriage'. There were good marriages and bad marriages, as well as what he called rocky marriages, and blatantly mistaken or incomprehensible marriages. The quality of a marriage was visibly established; he could state positively which of his friends had good marriages and which did not. That he and Tamsin had, he took for granted. She was sure of it, too. It was what she had decided on, her consciously chosen future.

They were a popular couple, flooded with invitations, joyously greeted when they entered a room. She could see that this was important to Keith. She herself found it welcome and reassuring; she hadn't been part of a popular couple before, except in her last year at the university, as Keith's girl-friend. So this also bore out the continuity.

They went to a lot of parties. They could have gone to a party practically every night, and it was Keith rather than Tamsin who wanted to stay at home sometimes. She was intrigued by these parties, so different from any that she'd ever been to. It was like arriving suddenly in a foreign country where something curious and exciting was going on – Mardi Gras, Chinese New Year, whatever.

She was aware that in time she would get bored with parties of this kind. Their main feature was that one never talked to anybody. There was an incessant furore of delighted shouting and yelling, but that wasn't what Tamsin called talking. Often she couldn't make out the words, for Keith's friends found it normal to have pop music going at full blast, not only when they met in clubs and discos but in their homes as well. Tamsin found this absurd but funny. Whenever she observed herself in these surroundings (and inevitably she didn't cease to observe herself) she started to laugh, which reassured Keith and everyone else that she was having a good time. She played a private game of throwing into the din some such remark as 'Experimental literature is its own justification' or 'Alienation is intrinsic to an industrial economy.' Invariably, the man at whom she was smiling at the moment responded with enthusiastic agreement.

The sense of living in a foreign country was heightened because many of the people she met were famous in their sphere, although she had never heard of them. It was like spending an evening with the Prime Minister, the Commander-in-Chief and the Archbishop, who were naturally conscious of their own importance, but who happened to be the Prime Minister, Commander-in-Chief and Archbishop of Ecuador. Tamsin conscientiously tried to sort them out. On the way home, she would ask Keith who was the man with the big ginger moustache or the tall blonde girl – much to his amusement, since their country was also his and Tamsin was the only person he knew who hadn't seen them on television or in photographs, who didn't even recognize the names when she was told them.

What struck her about these famous pop stars, as she got to know them, was that they had no private lives. Certainly they had personal lives: they fell in love, quarrelled, lived together and moved out, got married and divorced. But whatever they did might be made public and they were aware of it – aware of it, Tamsin guessed, at the very moment when they passionately kissed or angrily slammed a door. This didn't make them more cautious; on the contrary, she noticed, it tended to make their behaviour more dramatic, as though driven toward the headlines. They were not even cautious in front of Keith and Tamsin, although Keith through his magazines was a crucial channel of publicity. The calculation might have been that it was wise to put Keith on the inside track, much as a government finds it more prudent to brief important editors than to leave them in the dark. But generally, Tamsin was inclined to think, there was no calculation. Whatever they did was comprehensible to Keith since, however unpremeditated the action and however white-hot the emotion, it was also part of a performance. Discretion was the style of another world or another generation; spontaneity was their style.

And Keith himself was a figure in this public scene. His role was to be in love with Tamsin, to have a good marriage. Thus, Tamsin also had no private life.

They were all very liberated; there was no imposed conformity. One could be married or not, have affairs or grab sleeping partners for a single night, make love in groups, be bisexual or homosexual. What one couldn't do was to leave other people in doubt; one couldn't evade a recognized role. In that sense, the 'permissive society' (the label of the period) was entirely traditional. In Victorian times, for instance, a man had the option of being a Loving Husband, a Dissolute Rake, or a Confirmed Bachelor, while a woman had scarcely any options; but the principle was the same.

The scene was traditional in another respect – Tamsin found herself talking with the women and not with the men. With the men she danced, ritualistically flirted, and laughed and yelled amid the pop music, but with the women she reached occasional intimacies. This was new to her. Hitherto her friends – not that she'd had many – had mostly been men. Some of these women (or girls – they were always called girls and often they were younger than she was) were stars, or on their way to being stars. But there are more starring parts for men than for women in the pop scene, as on the stage. Mostly they had been picked up by the men, plucked from a throng of devotees, and installed as girl-friends or possibly wives, simply because of their looks, their sexy gaiety, their desirability as acquisitions. They were giving a performance, presenting their personal lives for approval, just as much as the men: indeed more so, because they could easily be replaced and dismissed from the scene altogether. It was only apart from the men that they attained individuality and could escape from the levelling and relentless duty of appearing attractive.

During the big parties, which were held in hotels or clubs, they used to gather in what Tamsin had to call the ladies' room, or powder room, or rest room. It didn't seem like a good setting for social purposes, although it was often spacious and well-lighted. But they were away from the men; that was the point. The ladies' room gave them the same paradoxical kind of freedom as the women's quarters in a harem. They could be tired or bad-tempered or simply quiet if they chose. Or they could talk.

There was a girl called Josie, who lived with the drummer of a quite celebrated group. Tamsin had met her several times at the club where this group played. She used to sit at Keith's table, gazing at her man and vibrating – not really moving in rhythm, but involuntarily shaking – to the noise of the music; the drums, obviously, had a directly sexual effect on her. Whenever Tamsin glanced at her, she immediately and hastily smiled. She was pretty, of course – they were all pretty – but she had a mouth which gave her a discontented pouting expression unless she remembered to smile. She must have learned this by being caught unawares by Mike, the drummer, and asked: 'What's biting you, honey?'

Once, in the ladies' room of a luxury hotel, Tamsin saw Josie staring intently at her face in a mirror and certainly not smiling. She caught sight of Tamsin's reflection, turned round abruptly, and said: 'I've put too much on my eyes, I know I have.'

Tamsin couldn't deny it, but said: 'You can get away with it.'

'Oh, well . . .' Josie attempted a smile, apparently decided that it wasn't necessary, and confided: 'I always do something wrong at these big do's. I hate them, honest I do. It's different at the club, sort of friendly.'

'But you know lots of people here, Josie. You must.'

'Yes, I do, only . . . I can't get used to these places. I didn't want to come.'

'I didn't much want to come either,' Tamsin said helpfully.

'Mike won't go anywhere without me.'

Tamsin nodded; this was characteristic of a man like Mike. He would need a girl as an accessory, even when he went out for a short stroll or had a quick drink at a pub.

'My Dad wanted me to do something for myself,' Josie said suddenly. 'I was training for physiotherapy. It seems ages ago. I couldn't go back to it, not now I couldn't.'

'You could. I'm thinking of getting a job.'

'I suppose I could . . . it's just . . .' Josie made a vague gesture with both hands, which seemed to indicate the vast distance between a physiotherapy clinic and the world she inhabited. Failing to find words for this, she said: 'I couldn't get up early in the morning. We always go to bed so late.'

'That's a problem, I agree.'

'And you know . . . they can say what they like, you've got to have a man, haven't you?'

'So I've always found.'

'Well, I have too. Some of them are right bastards, aren't they, but you couldn't have nobody.'

'No.'

'Mind you,' Josie said hastily, 'it's great with Mike.'

'Count your blessings.'

'I do, don't you? It's great with Keith, obviously.'

'Why, were you with Keith at one time?' Tamsin asked.

But this flustered Josie. She gave a hunted look round the room and said: 'I didn't mean . . . I just meant it's great for you, anybody can see that.' They returned to the party, to their obligations.

Tamsin was amused; she couldn't be expected, surely, not to know that Keith had had a succession of girls and Josie a succession of men. Perhaps Josie imagined that marriage was supposed to wipe the slate clean. Perhaps she didn't like to recall being dismissed by Keith, which brought to mind the possibility of being dismissed by Mike. A man would easily get bored with Josie, Tamsin thought – precisely with her dependence. It struck her that Josie might have been her immediate predecessor, the untidy girl. She didn't ask Keith. He preferred those unimportant girls of his to be nameless.

Tamsin had always cared far more about how she judged herself than about what other people thought of her. But she couldn't help seeing at this time that she was envied by many people: women in particular. Envied by her sister, and by Keith's sisters. Envied by her foreign maids, who could scarcely imagine what it was like to be attractive, educated, surrounded by luxury, and loved by a man like Keith, all at the same time. Envied by girls like Josie, with their perpetual insecurity.

She regarded this envy with a degree of irony, almost with incredulity. To have achieved contentment – which was essentially what people envied – didn't appear as a plausible event in her life. It simply wasn't like her. Nevertheless, it seemed to be true. Let it last, she prayed: only let it last.

3

Keith's sister Linda came to tea on Sunday, bringing her three children. It was Keith who suggested inviting her, but Tamsin liked her – better, at least, than the other sister, Ann. While Ann openly envied Tamsin's fashionable clothes and household possessions, to which Tamsin attached no importance, Linda envied the richness of Tamsin's life: that is, the socially useful job combined with the exciting evenings out. Getting to know Linda over the year since her marriage, Tamsin decided that envy wasn't the right word so much as disinterested fascination. Certainly, Linda wouldn't have changed places. She was happy with her home and her children. Her husband, owner of a timber yard, had lately provided her with a house and garden in Eltham..

Linda was tall, strongly built and good-looking, like all the family; at times, Tamsin found her beautiful. It was the stately, placid beauty of a contented woman. The children, one on her lap and the others beside her on the large couch, reinforced it. Perhaps not very striking as a girl (Tamsin guessed), Linda had achieved – one might say, earned – her beauty with motherhood. She took the children everywhere. She didn't feel complete without them, no doubt; it was a true instinct.

She was pregnant again – that, Tamsin thought, was why she looked unquestionably beautiful on this occasion. Keith put on a show brotherly chaffing.

'Can't help yourself, Lin, can you? Family planning – you've heard of it.'

'They're all planned,' Linda said calmly.

'What's the plan, then? Any limit?'

'Well, they're spaced.' So they were, at intervals of three or four years. The eldest, a girl of ten, listened to the conversation attentively. 'I like having a baby around. When one starts growing up, I get to thinking about it again. Always brightens me up.'

Linda gorged herself on cream cakes – she didn't care how much she ate, especially at present – and departed after ensuring that the children said thank-you to Uncle Keith and Auntie Tamsin. Keith cleared away the tea things and poured drinks.

'You thought about having a kid, Tam?'

'Obviously you have,' Tamsin replied. It was easy to see that the afternoon with Linda had been devised to lead to this apparently casual question.

'Well, it's something I wouldn't like to miss out on, not altogether.'

'I see.'

'It's nice for kids to have young parents. I'm thirty – maybe that's what made me think about it.'

'And I'm thirty.'

'Hard to believe, love-girl, but you are.'

Tamsin said reflectively: 'I can't say that I feel what Linda does.'

'You could get round to it.'

'I probably could.'

'You don't exactly have anything against it, sweetie?'

'No. It would make a difference to the way we're living – you've got to take that into account. For me more than for you. There's my job.'

'If you left that job for a spell I'm sure they'd have you back. Or you could work part-time. We'd have an au pair, of course – somebody who's good with kids, not just a maid. It would work out, one way and another.'

'You really have been thinking about it, haven't you?'

'Well, will you?'

'Think about it? Yes.'

No more was said that evening or during the next week. Presumably Keith didn't want to put pressure on her, especially about giving up her job. He was careful not to appear as a male chauvinist or an example of machismo (these phrases were just coming into fashion). But doubtless he was confident, as he had been confident that she would love him and marry him. And this was equally important to him; she was certain about at. For him, having children was the necessary complement to his er triumphs. Perhaps it hadn't been necessary, or had scarcely been saged, in the first place: but it was now.

could see that Keith would be an excellent father. He was a great ite with his nephews and nieces. He amused them and played vith them, but he also took them seriously as individuals and listened to what they said. Just this Sunday, Tamsin had noticed that more than before. Whether of set purpose or not, he was learning about children. Bringing up children would be his new skill and he would count on making a success of it, like everything else.

Tamsin couldn't entirely believe in herself as a mother – a real mother like Linda. She was daunted by the demands that would be made on her: guiding, advising, conferring a shape on another human being. However, that was looking a long way ahead and Keith would take most of the responsibility. Probably it was true that men thought about children while women thought about having babies. Making an effort, she did begin to feel something of Linda's readiness to embark on the steadily ascending process of nurturing new life in her body. Secretly, in the bathroom, she ran her hands over her thin waist and hips and imagined them richly swelling, month after patient and deliberate month. Yes, the feeling was there – attended by detachment and scepticism, like all her feelings, yet authentic enough.

It would be something positive to fix her mind on, at all events. She had got bored with parties and with the foolish glitter of the pop scene, as she'd expected. She was glad to have found the job with the housing trust, but wasn't involved in it at any significant level. Having a baby might, as Linda put it, brighten her up – avert the menace of indifference. It was a negative motive and it was also commonplace (it was often the reason why women wanted babies, she supposed) but if it was valid it shouldn't be rejected.

Above all, if having a child was the completion of Keith's love for her, then it must likewise be the completion of her love for him. Love was what bound them together; she couldn't risk being divided from him in anything so vital. For her own sake as well as his, she couldn't deny him what he wanted so much.

She preferred not to make a dramatic announcement. One night, when they were lying peacefully in bed after making love, she said: 'By the way, I've stopped taking the pill.'

Of course, Keith responded with delight. 'That's great! Fantastic! Oh, my sweetie-honey-bunny! I knew you would!' She had to laugh. After all, she had merely stopped doing what the immense majority of wives throughout history had never done in the first place.

But for Keith, she saw, the reality was one with the promise. He' always been like that. When Tamsin went to bed with him, she loved hi When she was his girl, she was necessarily his wife. When she stop taking the pill, she was already pregnant.

He began talking about the child. Tamsin wasn't surprised t that he wanted a daughter, and therefore was sure of having a da

He racked his mind for names, as though this were an urgent problem. Some of the names he liked best had already been used in his family, and naturally his daughter couldn't be the namesake of a cousin. Best, he decided, to choose an unusual name, one that would make the child practically unique. Tamsin, entering into the right spirit, suggested Persephone... Iseult... Clotilde. As her names became more far-fetched (Saxophona, she proposed with only the flicker of a smile) he complained that she wasn't taking it seriously. She wasn't. For one thing, she wasn't pregnant yet. For another, she had a private intention of demanding to call the child Jane, or John if it was a boy.

Provisionally, Keith referred to the daughter as Tamsinette. He wanted a Tamsin who would be his from the beginning: a Tamsin without secrets, without a life in any way withheld from him.

Meanwhile, Tamsin still wasn't pregnant. She had always been perfectly regular with her periods, and so she continued to be. The first time she didn't miss – the first time after the mental conception of Tamsinette – Keith asked in a perplexed tone: 'Are you sure?' The second time, he said: 'Well, bloody hell, nobody can say we aren't trying.' But he went on talking about Tamsinette with the same enthusiasm and confidence.

As the months passed, the periods became a wry joke like a run of bad luck in gambling. Keith wasn't so disappointed as she would have imagined. For him, the process of conceiving a child had begun, was irrevocably launched, was merely taking longer than he had reckoned.

Ever since they'd been married, Keith had been talking intermittently about moving from the flat to a house. Tamsin didn't care. She had never attached much importance to what kind of home she had. If anything, she liked the flat – the freedom from neighbours, the fine view of London, and the amusing improbability of a flat at the top of an office building. But Keith connected houses with stability, with being properly married.

Tamsin had been assuming that nothing would happen, at least for a considerable time. Keith aimed at a big house, although she found the flat quite big enough. He also aimed at a modern house; his brother had acquired a rambling Victorian house in Lee Green, but this didn't fit Keith's conception of a setting for himself and Tamsin. Big modern houses in London were difficult to find, and Tamsin refused to live in the ʳuburbs or the country. But now he stepped up the search, for to his ʳnd a family demanded a house even more emphatically than a marriage. ʳas great for a kid to be able to run out to a garden, he said. So getting a ʳe was urgent – leaving aside, once again, the fact that Tamsin wasn't ʳly pregnant.

ʳe way that things happened for Keith, the ideal house suddenly became available. It belonged to a pop singer who decided to live abroad for tax reasons. Being a friend of Keith's – and indebted to Keith, like most pop stars – he was willing to let it go at less than its market value.

The house had been built in the 1930s, and to historians of architecture it was a period piece; indeed, it already had a preservation order. But since domestic architecture in England had yet to advance again with such dramatic boldness, it made an impression of being ultra-modern. When Tamsin saw it, she considered it utterly ridiculous. It was not only big, but designed to seem bigger than it was, to present vistas and perspectives instead of points of rest, to replace the usual idea of a house by the geometrical concept of area. There were lots of rooms, and yet because of the open-plan principle there were really no rooms. One was impelled to be perpetually on the move and perpetually on display. One couldn't hide, except in a bathroom. She was sure that Ann and Linda would marvel at it, and then thank God that they didn't have to live in it.

Still, she reminded herself that she didn't care what kind of place she lived in, and Keith was very keen on this house. It did suit him – suited what she admired and loved in him; one had to be impressed by a man who had the confidence to take it on. Also, it was in Hampstead and she wouldn't have to live in the country. She kissed him and said: 'All right, let's.'

What she hadn't foreseen was that the house made the child necessary. For, whereas the flat had been on the right scale for a couple (a wealthy couple, of course), the house certainly wasn't. Indeed, only a child – say, a particularly boisterous three-year-old, always rushing about and throwing things and making echoing noises – could find this house a natural environment. So Tamsinette was missed just as though she existed, had grown up here, and had been lost or kidnapped. Wandering about, Keith seemed to be looking for her.

One night – about three in the morning – he came home from a party in a state of what Tamsin called to herself aborted drunkenness: that is, he had drunk enough to be plastered, but wasn't. She recognized this state because he lost his usual breezy cheerfulness; a stranger would have thought him more sober than early in the evening. She hadn't gone with him. Nowadays, although it disappointed him, she seldom went to parties. However, she wasn't in bed. Since coming to live in th' house without rooms, she had got into the habit of taking naps on couch or in a chair wherever she happened to be.

'Hello,' she said. 'How was the party?'

'OK.'

He stood staring at her across a desert of parquet floor.

'I was thinking about you,' he said.

'Yes.' She understood how that could be true at a party, in the crowded loneliness.

He walked steadily, but for him rather stiffly, to a table on which there was a tray of drinks and poured himself a vodka. Tamsin watched him swallow it, Russian fashion. It couldn't make any difference to him.

He said abruptly: 'I can't understand why you're not having a baby.'

She didn't answer.

'It's a whole year now.'

'Is it?'

'Yes, it bloody well is. Didn't you realize that?'

'I'm not so impatient as you are, Keith.'

'What does that mean? Don't you want to, after all?'

'Yes, I want to. I mean impatient as a person. You are – you know you are.'

'I'm impatient about this. D'you blame me?'

'No, only it doesn't do any good. Look, Keith, a year isn't very extraordinary. Take my parents, for instance. Four years between when they got married and Sheila, then three years between Sheila and me. And I'm sure that wasn't planning.'

'I'm talking about us,' he said (of course) impatiently.

She saw what he meant. Her parents were thin-blooded people. For Keith and Tamsin, it ought to be different.

'Cheer up, darling,' she said. 'You shouldn't drink so much, you know.'

'I'm not drunk.'

'No, but it isn't a good idea all the same. Alcohol is a depressant. Especially for you, it seems. Come on, let's go to bed. It's frightfully late.'

As soon as they started to undress, he did cheer up.

'Hey, sweetie, tonight might be it, mightn't it?'

'No reason why not.'

But the wretched period came round again. Tamsin's periods had become the dominating events of Keith's life – his life, rather than hers. They were no longer mere delays, but defeats, like unsuccessful auditions for an actor or rejection slips for a writer.

'I think you ought to see a doctor,' he said.

'That's ridiculous. A year's nothing extraordinary, you've got to believe it.'

'You're not afraid of finding something out, are you, honey?'

'No. I just don't see the point. What would you do, anyway? Trade in for a model that gives better results?'

'Now you're being ridiculous. I don't know what I'd want to do. Adopt a kid, that's one possibility.'

'You don't want to adopt a kid. You want to make one.'

'Right, I do. So I want to know what's holding things up. I should have thought you'd want to know, too.'

'You're the one who thinks there's a problem, not me. Anyway, I don't like being mauled about by doctors.'

'There's no mauling to it. They carry out tests.'

'I'm perfectly all right, Keith.'

'How do you know?'

'Want to bet?'

Keith was insistent. She went to see the doctor.

'How often do you have intercourse?'

'Every five minutes,' she said.

The doctor smiled and said: 'Congratulations.'

'Well, that's what it feels like. It's our main activity.'

'Too often, perhaps?'

'Oh no, I didn't mean that. I love it.'

'You see, if you have problems about sexual harmony, or about your marriage in general, they could be relevant. I'm not a psychiatrist. But it's a possibility.'

'We're very happily married,' Tamsin said emphatically. She certainly didn't want to see a psychiatrist.

The tests showed that there was no reason why she shouldn't have a child. But among fertile women, the doctor said, some were more fertile than others. A year wasn't long; he had known cases of couples waiting for ten years, and not in vain.

Keith heard her report with an air of resignation. 'Well, we'll just have to keep hoping,' he said.

'Stop worrying about it so much, darling. Think about the other things in life. Things are fine, really, aren't they?'

'Oh, sure. Things are fine. But . . .'

'But what?'

'It's just because things are fine, in every other way, that this is so incredible.'

To him, it was incredible. The one explanation that never occurred to him was that he couldn't fertilize her. Logically, the fact that he didn't even consider it was extraordinary. It didn't require any imagination; it could be arrived at by a simple process of elimination. But that it never did occur to him, Tamsin was quite certain.

And if in one sense it was extraordinary, she thought, in another sen it was natural. He had this invincible confidence; he had his male pri Pride in the gallons of sperm that he had generated in his life (if sp was the right word) – load after load of the stuff, readily and re gushing, distributed among goodness knows how many girls, carefully trapped in condoms and caps, then poured freely and with ardent purpose into Tamsin. It must be unthinkable for him that it could lack the vital ingredient.

She didn't suggest the wounding idea. It would merely be to pin the blame on him, to confront him with his failure. She recoiled from such an act of enmity and revenge. Anyway, what was to be gained? If they couldn't have a child, then they couldn't have one. Tamsin certainly didn't intend to adopt one. Her desire, so far as it existed, was not for the child but for the growth within her body.

'We've got each other, darling,' she said.

'Oh yes, love . . . I know.'

They still made love often, although she had stopped thinking about ever having a child and it was once again for the sake of making love. She still loved Keith – she clung to that. Certainly she needed him. She had no one else, after all. She was keenly conscious, at this time, of having scarcely the thinnest kind of intimacy with any other human being. Her friends – the people she knew, rather – were so utterly concealed by their public masks that it was impossible to know them as real people.

Real people . . . it was a catch-phrase in smart circles, at the same time patronizing and self-deceptive. Occasionally, Tamsin was asked about her job and had to describe the housing trust tenants. She was told: 'I do envy you, getting to know people like that.'

'You mean poor people?' she replied bluntly.

'Oh' – this always caused embarrassment – 'real people. They sound so genuine.'

She wasn't sure about that. They were genuine in the sense of being, defencelessly and unavoidably, what they were: poor and without fame. They did, out of their loneliness, entrust confidences to her. But they also presented themselves as they wished to appear to her. Their reality was their own. Perhaps that was why she didn't care profoundly about them, or about the job.

The one she liked best was the old sailor, Frank. This, she recognized, was because he was a man: a man on his own, and anxious to present himself as a man who had been successful with women. It had occurred to Tamsin recently that she didn't know a great deal about men. Brain and Keith, so dissimilar and each in his own way so unusual, were not a representative sample. Frank, by his own account, was what most men – she supposed – were like. He had loved a number of women, without being impelled to devote his life to any of them. He always used the word 'love' in this old-fashioned sense – 'I loved her all that summer.' It implied both affection, sincere if not overwhelming and sexual possession. He never admitted to having taken a woman simply out of physical need, like Keith. But then, he had never been in love with a woman whom, he wasn't actively 'loving'. 'Out of sight, out of mind,' he said candidly. (Candidly, or as he presented himself.)

'Why didn't you ever get married?' Tamsin asked.

'Ah.' Frank clearly had a prepared answer to this question. 'I did think of it. But it's hard to give up the thought of the next woman, see, beyond the one you're loving at the time. It's being a sailor, I reckon. There's always the next journey. Later on, I came to wish I had. But maybe it's all for the best. I wouldn't want to watch a woman grow old, a woman I'd loved.'

'Still, you might have had children.'

'Ah.' Frank gave her a sly smile.

'I bet you did. With all those women.'

'Only once that I know of,' Frank said. 'Girl in Liverpool. Very sweet girl, never tried to make me marry her or any of that carry-on. I told her I'd pay so much a week – take an interest in the kid, you know. I would have, too. But she got it adopted.'

'Did you go on loving her after that?'

'Oh no. I was quite annoyed, see, about her having it adopted. I didn't see why she had any cause to do that.' Frank frowned, but soon cheered up. 'Still, I was glad I'd done it. You like to know that. A man does, I mean.'

When Tamsin came home she used to roam about the big house, sometimes sitting down for a while to read or watch television, but driven sooner or later to move on again. She felt that she was looking for something, and often that was literally true. Since the house was nothing but an open space, there was no allotted place to keep this or that object and she had no idea where she'd left things or where the maid might have put them. But what she was really looking for she didn't know. For herself, perhaps? Her reflection confronted her wherever she went, since the last owners of the house – the pop singer and his girl-friend – had covered or rather obliterated the walls with mirrors. Yet she never stopped to stare into these mirrors. They showed only their cold and polished surface, and a figure painted on glass.

In the course of the next year, the idea that she and Keith were hoping to have a child gradually receded. He still spoke of it, but wistfully or with a brave attempt at a cheerfully casual tone, as though it were a standing joke. His confidence had dwindled, not indeed to an admission of failure, but to uncertainty. He didn't take well to uncertainty – it was unnatural for him – but he made the best of it.

She noticed a presumption, on the part of Keith's family and her own parents, that she and Keith had chosen to be childless. Linda's visits were rarer, either because she had a toddler to cart about or because Keith didn't invite her. When she did come, with her brood of four, she said to Tamsin: 'They are a bloody trial, I've got to admit that.' It wasn't what she believed, but it was a gesture of tolerance toward Tamsin. Probably she thought that Tamsin was a selfish bitch and was afraid of losing her slender figure. Tamsin didn't care.

So far as she was concerned, the episode was over. The feeling of willingness to become pregnant had left her. She could almost believe that she had simulated it like a frigid woman simulating sexual eagerness, or at least persuaded herself into it. Anyway, the time had passed. She still didn't know for sure whether Keith was sterile or whether they might ultimately have a child. But the idea of having one when she had outlived the desire – accidentally, so to speak – was unwelcome to her. Without saying anything to Keith, she began to take the pill again.

4

One morning, Tamsin received a letter from Dorothy, Brian's mother. As she read it, she realized that for some time she had been expecting that she would see Brian again. Expecting this to happen, not intending to see him; but she wasn't altogether sure that the distinction was valid. It had been by chance that she'd seen Keith again after years apart from him, and yet perhaps not what people called sheer chance. She could have bought cheap soup plates at any street market instead of going to Portobello Road, where (she remembered later) Keith had taken her when she was his girl-friend.

The letter – or note – was brief, and merely said that Dorothy wished to discuss something if Tamsin could spare the time. It contained no expressions of affection, but they had never been in Dorothy's line. Relations between mother-in-law and daughter-in-law had been honest and frank but not warm. Dorothy had approved of Tamsin, considerably more than she had approved of Brian. When the marriage broke up she had sent a similarly brief note extending her good wishes, and implicitly absolving Tamsin from blame.

Tamsin rang up and suggested lunch. 'Come to my club,' Dorothy said. It was the first time Tamsin had been to a club of this kind, though she'd been with Keith to plenty of the other kind. She half expected to see elderly and distinguished men discussing Gladstone's Home Rule policy, as in period films and television serials, and indeed a number of such men – or extras, she thought irreverently – were scattered about the spacious, high-ceilinged rooms. However, this club admitted women. Perhaps it had been forced to by pressure from women like Dorothy.

Dorothy was waiting, reading *The Economist*. They shook hands –

kissing wasn't in Dorothy's line either – and went in to lunch. The food was uninteresting; as it was just like Dorothy's cooking, she ate her way through it contentedly. They had half a bottle of wine, just over a glass each.

Dorothy mentioned that she was on a Royal Commission considering benefits for the disabled. This struck Tamsin as not quite appropriate; she would have expected Dorothy to feel, though not explicitly, that disabled people ought to make greater efforts to help themselves. Anyway, she was enjoying the task. There were a great many details to master, she said with satisfaction. No one had ever looked at the services for the disabled comprehensively and systematically.

'I don't know how you fit it in,' Tamsin said.

'I'm jolly glad I've been given it. I didn't know what I'd do with myself after retirement.'

It hadn't occurred to Tamsin that Dorothy would have retired, or could ever retire. But she did look older. She seemed to have shrunk, and didn't look taller than Tamsin, or not so much taller as before. Her tweed suit – she bought tweed suits to last for years, like a man – was loose over her shoulders and arms. She had lost weight as she lost power, apparently.

'Has Robert retired too?' Tamsin asked.

'Robert is dead. He's been dead for three years.'

'I'm so sorry. I had no idea.'

'I should have thought you'd have seen the obituaries,' Dorothy said rather sharply.

'I'm afraid I don't read the papers properly.'

Dorothy wasn't much put out, however, nor was she affected by a remembering of grief. She described her husband's death in a matter-of-fact way. He had recognized – making his own diagnosis and merely asking a colleague to confirm it – cancer of the stomach. He had decided to take an expensive holiday and flown to Ceylon in the middle of the winter; he had declined Dorothy's offer to go with him. And he had died there, in his hotel room. Presumably he had taken an overdose. Dorothy said that, on looking at the bank statement, she had found that he'd bought a one-way ticket. Tamsin was impressed. A dignified, unsentimental ending to an unsentimental life.

'You've kept on the house,' Tamsin remarked.

'Yes, one doesn't want to move after thirty years. It's too big for one person, of course, but it was too big for two people. And although I'm not attached to possessions I shouldn't enjoy going through everything, deciding what to keep and what to get rid of.'

'No.'

'I see that you're living in that Bauhaus place, Tamsin. That's pretty big for two people, isn't it? Or have you got children?'

'No, we haven't got children.'

'I hope you're happy, Tamsin.'

'Reasonably,' Tamsin said. Considering their former relationship, she wouldn't have wished to give Dorothy the impression that her second marriage was ecstatically happy. Not that Dorothy would have minded much.

Ordering the trifle to follow the roast lamb, Dorothy came to the business of the meeting.

'Have you kept any of Brian's poems?'

Yes, Tamsin said. She had them all, in a cardboard box – not only his published poems, but copies of poems which hadn't been accepted, or which he had chosen not to submit for publication, or which he had abandoned as failures in the midst of revising them. Sometimes she had rescued them from his pockets when taking his clothes to be cleaned; sometimes she had picked up crumpled balls of paper from the floor and smoothed them out when she was alone. She wasn't at all guilty about keeping them after the divorce. It was for her, more than for Brian, that they still lived.

For years, she hadn't looked at the poems. Keith certainly wasn't aware that she had them. But she had been looking at them lately; this made her feel that the approach from Dorothy was no coincidence, or at least that coincidences came when they were due. She didn't so much read the peoms as stare at them – at Brian's almost illegible writing, at the tangle of deletions and alterations. They seemed, as she retraced her steps through time, to be mysteriously reasserting their original significance.

Dorothy explained that she was planning to have the poems published as a book if there were enough of them. It might revive Brian's reputation. That was a long shot, admittedly; but at least it would tell him that he was still valued.

'You're going to pay for it?' Tamsin asked.

'Yes. But Brian won't know that.'

'Oh, he will. He knows how these things work.'

'No, it won't be a vanity press production. That's the phrase, isn't it? It'll be a genuine publisher.' Dorothy named the firm. 'You see, I know a man there. In fact, he's my cousin. He's seen Brian's poems – the few that I have – and he thinks highly of them. He would publish the book without a subsidy if it were an economic proposition. So the deception is legitimate, I think.'

'I wasn't criticizing. I'd like to see this happen. But I don't think Brian will care. He never did care much about being published.'

'He'll care about the advance,' Dorothy said tersely.

'Oh, there's to be an advance?'

'Since it's a question of a real publisher there will naturally be a contract, and therefore an advance.'

'I see.'

'You'll scarcely be surprised to hear that Brian is perpetually in need of money.'

'Without me to support him?'

'As you know, Tamsin, I'm well aware that you did more than anyone had a right to ask of you. In fact, when you . . . separated, I thought it might be good for him not to have you to depend on any more. Unfortunately it hasn't worked out like that.'

'Do you often see him?'

'When I can induce him to come and see me, and thus give him a square meal. It's intermittent. I last saw him about a month ago.' Dorothy finished her trifle and lit a cigarette. 'He says he has various jobs. Casual work, evidently. It can't amount to much. Honestly, I don't know what he lives on.'

'Poor Brian,' Tamsin said softly. Dorothy didn't hear.

'So a publisher's advance – say, a hundred pounds – would come in very useful for him. There might even be royalties if the book sells.'

'Poetry doesn't sell.'

'I suppose you're right. Still, as I say, the advance will be welcome.'

'It's a rather complicated way to give somebody a hundred quid, isn't it?'

'I doubt if he would accept it from me directly. I should be perfectly willing, of course. Goodness knows I can spare it, with my pension and what Robert left. But . . .' For once, Dorothy looked embarrassed. 'He's a grown man,' she said.

Tamsin didn't believe that Brian was likely to turn down a cheque, or for that matter a pound note, from his mother. She saw the point, however. Dorothy would have considered Brian demeaned by that kind of largesse. It would have been an admission of his helplessness, an admission that she didn't want to make and didn't think that he should make. Whereas he had earned the hundred pounds, by writing the poems in the first place.

There was a short silence. Tamsin found herself thinking of the poems, few but precious, that Brian had written about her – 'Paleface', she remembered, and 'At six o'clock she comes home'. Poems that were an ineradicable, a still potent part of her life.

'Does he ever talk about me?' she asked.

Dorothy replied diplomatically: 'He doesn't talk much about anything.'

Tamsin gazed across the dining-room; most of the tables were by now deserted and littered. She hadn't expected a yes, but it was saddening not to get one.

Unexpectedly, Dorothy said: 'I'm sure he would like to see you again.'

'D'you really think he would?'

Tamsin tried to accompany this question with a neutral smile, but her voice was unsteady. She felt herself blushing, as a young girl would have blushed at being told that a man was interested in her.

'Oh, I believe so,' Dorothy said. 'When I allude to something that happened during the time when you were together, it clearly means a great deal to him. After all, that was the best time of his life, although he didn't know how to value it or preserve it. I've no doubt he often thinks of you.'

'I often think of him.'

Yet Tamsin didn't exactly mean this. She didn't, even when she looked at the poems, think consciously of Brian. She felt the other dimension of her life; she moved along the other track through time.

Dorothy looked at her keenly and said: 'Perhaps I shouldn't have said what I did just now. You're a very loyal person, Tamsin, as I've always appreciated. You shouldn't feel the slightest obligation to see him again. I can understand that it would be painful for you.'

'It wouldn't be painful,' Tamsin said. 'It would be . . . oh, I don't know.' And she didn't, at this moment, know what it would be like: simply that it had become a necessity.

'Disturbing, then. You have your life, as you've fortunately been able to remake it.'

'I'm another man's wife, you mean?' Tamsin said, smiling.

'Well . . . When I said that I hope you're happy, I meant that you deserve to be. Believe me, I got in touch with you solely to ask about the poems.'

'Oh, quite so. But one thing leads to another, doesn't it?'

'So it seems. Perhaps my action was mistaken from the outset – inconsiderate. If so, I'm sorry. It's all rather outside my experience. Robert was the only man in my life.'

'You shouldn't apologize. If I can't look after myself now I'll never be able to, shall I? Where does Brian live?'

'I could invite you next time he comes to see me.'

'I'd rather choose the occasion. It's a question of mood, to a certain extent. You just give me the address, that would be best.'

'He lives in a ghastly little room,' Dorothy said, with an attempt to make this amusing. 'It's really slummy.'

'We mostly lived in slummy places, if you remember.'

'Not like this. However, since that's your decision you'll see for yourself.'

Tamsin went about a week later, at the failing end of a cold grey afternoon; she was scrupulous about not using her working time for a private errand. The address was near the cheap end of Portobello Road, where Keith had kissed her under the bleak struts of the motorway. The slummy house didn't surprise her. She felt at home, through imagination as much as through experience, in this part of the social landscape: the territory of the great scene-painters of classless poverty and urban solitude, of Balzac and Dickens and Dostoyevsky.

There was no way of telling where Brian's room was, and no one about to ask. He would be either in the basement or at the top, she decided. The basement seemed to house a family, for she could hear the chatter of a television set and the wailing of a child, either punished or ignored. So she went up to the top. The last flight of stairs had no light. She climbed them cautiously, holding on to a banister which wobbled as though it might come loose with a tug. When she reached the landing she tossed up mentally between the two doors and knocked on the one to the left.

There was not a sound from inside the room, but she was sure that Brian was there, in his zone of silence. She had never needed to see him nor hear his voice to know that she was close to him. She opened the door, went in, and closed it behind her.

He was standing – waiting for her, of course, since he'd heard the creak of the banister. He raised his right hand slowly, touched her face, and made a gentle movement along the slope of her cheek.

'I'm real,' she said.

She wondered if he was going to kiss her, but he didn't. There was no need, she thought. They hadn't generally kissed when she came in at six o'clock.

'What were you doing?' she asked.

'Nothing.'

'Just nothing?'

'I do a lot of that.' He gave her his quick, deflecting smile, the smile that he had developed to go with such admissions.

'Did Dorothy send you?' he asked.

'She told me where to find you.'

'I'm not hiding.'

'You still wear that sweater,' she said.

'Why not? But you look quite magnificent.'

She was wearing a new coat, bright red with large golden buttons. It didn't fit her idea of herself – or the idea of her that Brian would recognise – but Keith had chosen it and as usual she had accepted it. She thought of taking it off, but it seemed best to content herself with being here. Besides, the room was cold.

'When did you see Dorothy, then?'

'Last week. She wrote, and then we had lunch.'

'A working lunch to discuss this business of getting my poems published, am I right?'

Brian was supposed to get a letter from the publisher; he wasn't meant to guess that a scheme had been hatched. Still, Tamsin wasn't surprised.

'Right,' she said.

'And are you paying for it, or is Dorothy?'

'Dorothy is.'

'I couldn't make up my mind whether it would be her idea or yours.'

'If it had been mine I'd have asked you first, don't you think?'

'Yes, I did think that.'

'Dorothy got in touch with me because I've got the poems. I've kept them, Brian, all of them.'

'I see. I never did believe that you would have let them go.'

'No, indeed.'

'It's interesting, Dorothy's becoming quite sentimental in her old age.'

'If you don't want this done, you should say so, Brian.'

'I don't mind. I'm not hiding myself, so why should I want to hide the poems?'

'You should be proud of them. Anyway, I am.'

'That's the stuff, Tam,' he said ironically. But not altogether ironically. She saw that he hadn't quite ceased to be proud of the poems. Or, seeing her again, he remembered to be proud of the life they had shared when he wrote them, and of her belief in him.

Was he glad to remember – glad to see her again? The phrase was too temperate, too much of a sensible Dorothy conception. It was impossible, it would always be impossible, for them to meet as other divorced couples meet, on easy and friendly terms, calmly and a little wistfully recalling the completed episode of their marriage. Time for them was not divided into past, present and future, but eternally enclosed them. While she was in this room, they were together.

And they had never dealt in words like 'glad' and 'happy'; what they gave each other was immensely more. She had a sense of shouldering once more, after a restful lull, the full weight of life. What she would have wished to say was what she had said when she first came to him in a room like this: 'Brian, I can't live without you.'

It could not be said. She had confessed in misery and defeat that she could not live with him, not all the time. An hour with him – she stayed for about an hour – was all that she could bear now of the close and silent intensity.

She didn't go straight home, but steered the car right and left at random, then parked and walked – aimlessly, seeing nothing – through the cold streets. When she was tired of that, she went into a pub and had a cheap, acrid-tasting whisky. It had more effect on her than three or four drinks in the usual way, so she went in somewhere else and had a cup of coffee. She had forgotten where the car was parked and had to try several side-streets before she found it. Then she looked at her watch, regained the ordinary scale of time, and drove fast to Hampstead.

'Hello there, sweetie,' Keith said. 'Wherever have you been?'

'I got tied up. I'm sorry.'

'It's OK. The incarnation's making dinner.' They had a Spanish maid this year, Encarnacion. 'She says she likes cooking, so it's a lucky break for her.'

'Good.'

He kissed her, and continued to hold her firmly while he went on talking. She felt that he was reasserting his possession of her, insistently or even anxiously. But no, she must be imagining that.

'I had one of those bloody awful days too. Everything took twice as long as it ought to've done. It's nice to get home in this stinking weather. We'll have a lovely homey evening, listen to some music, how about that?'

'Sure.'

Brian had said nothing about wanting to see her again. But she knew that she would go again; it was inevitable, just as going to Keith's flat had been inevitable after the first time.

She went when she was in the mood, as she put it to herself – in fact, when she was captured by the necessity. She never made any advance arrangements; she didn't want to, since the sudden and irresistible compulsion was what gave her a wild delight. Anyway, Brian couldn't be reached by phone. Sometimes she went on two or three successive days, but sometimes not at all for a month or so. It didn't seem to make any difference to him. Once they were together, the intervening time was unreal.

As a rule, she went in the late afternoon. But after a while she became less scrupulous about her working hours; she always got through the work easily enough and the tenants didn't expect her at any particular time. So she went to Brian at any hour of the day. Occassionally, if Keith was at a party, she went at night. Once she got out of bed after sleeping for a couple of hours, put a sweater and trousers over her naked body, and got the Mini out of the garage. She drove home through empty streets, hitting sixty miles an hour and shooting red lights, and got into bed again. Keith came in five minutes later. Although she wouldn't have made any deliberate plans to keep him in the dark, his ignorance of this escapade gave her a certain gleeful amusement.

Brian was almost always there. Only once, when she pushed the door open in the afternoon, she found the room empty. He must have gone out for a short time, she thought; later, he told her that he never locked his door because he had nothing worth stealing. She waited for three hours, longer than she normally spent with him. When she realized that she would have to go without seeing him – that night, at Keith's special request, she had agreed to go to a party – she collapsed into bitter, painful sobbing. When had she last cried? Not since she had left Brian.

At the party, she behaved without any effort as though this had never happened. She smiled, laughed, yelled, flirted and danced, all just as usual – or rather not as usual, but as enthusiastically as in the first year of her marriage with Keith. She simply never gave a thought to the small cold room, the agonizing disappointment, her helpless tears. On the way home Keith said 'I knew you'd have fun, darling. It's just great to see you like this.' She pressed close to him in the big car, rubbing her leg on his, kissing him at all the traffic lights. As soon as they reached the house they threw some cushions on the floor and made love riotously.

There was no connection – none at all. I'm leading a double life, Tamsin thought sardonically. But she felt each part of this life to be authentic and sincere. She didn't have to make pretences, either when she shared the magical tranquillity of Brian's room or when she laughed and chattered with Keith. She was doing what, at the given moment, she had to do. When she lay still and calm on Brian's bed, she felt that she was experiencing the only reality. But when she returned to her life with Keith, she recognized that this life too – despite its absurdities, despite the detachment with which she could observe it – was entirely real to her. She was unhappy only when she was alone, either in the big house or, that one daunting time, in the small room. Then she was left to pursue the endless and baffling search for her ultimate self.

In a sense, she had been through all this before, during the time when she was Brian's wife and Keith's mistress. But only in a sense. Then, there had been the awareness – and the obligation, as she saw it – of choice. It had been a period of change, a process with a determined ending which she first admitted as a possibility and by degrees consented to. Now there was no choice and no foreseeable resolution. She couldn't return to living with Brian. She no longer had the courage, and there was no sign that he wished it; when she was with him, he had what he needed of her. Nor did she want to leave Keith. She understood fully what she had tormentingly glimpsed all along – that she was bound inexorably to both these men.

Keith was sure to find out that she was seeing Brian. He wasn't perceptive, but he couldn't be blind for ever to the powerful force that was acting on her. Besides, although he didn't often get home before her, it happened now and again. She told him small lies without much compunction, but she found it distasteful – and really, too much trouble – to build up a system of deception. She didn't want to hurt Keith, and yet she was somehow untouched by the prospect of his knowing, for at bottom she felt that she had a right to her hours with Brian.

Several times she made up her mind to tell Keith, if only to forestall being detected and put in the wrong, and also out of impatience at his lack of insight. But perhaps he knew, and couldn't face talking about it. Or perhaps he imagined that she was having a casual affair with someone or other, which would blow over if he was patient. Or he might be having an affair himself – she didn't enquire where he'd been when he came in late, sometimes very late – and they were drifting peacefully into 'that kind of marriage'. This wasn't very likely, as he was delighted with her company whenever he could get it, and made love to her as vigorously as ever . . . but then, Keith's capacity for affection and his virility were both well above average. Anyway, she let things slide.

One evening, she came back from Brian's room after eight o'clock. She had fallen asleep. Lying on the narrow bed, she did sometimes doze off; it was only a further stage of the peace she found there.

Keith was standing in the middle of the emptiest space in the house, puffing at a cigarette. He wasn't a heavy smoker; he had a habit of lighting a cigarette when he was annoyed or impatient and stubbing it out half-finished.

'You're late, honey-dove,' he said.

'Sorry. Did you get Encarnacion to start dinner?'

'We're going to Paul and Julie's. Don't tell me you'd forgotten.'

She had. It was the first obligation that she'd forgotten in all her time as Keith's girl-friend, fiancée, mistress and wife. At once she felt accused, vulnerable.

'We ought to be there now.'

'I'm sorry, I'm sorry.'

'Where have you been, anyway?'

'I went to see Brian.'

'You what?' Plainly this was a revelation to him.

'I went to see Brian,' she repeated. Her voice, in her own ears, sounded unnaturally loud.

Keith stubbed out his cigarette, which required a walk of several yards. Then he asked: 'Not for the first time, I take it?'

'No.'

He was about to say more, but checked himself.

'We've got to dash. Wear your gold kaftan.'

'I'll go in this dress. It's all right.'

'It's crumpled,' Keith said sharply.

Tamsin felt herself blushing, and hurried off to change.

In the car, they didn't speak. The dinner-party seemed to go very well, but once Tamsin saw Paul and Julie exchange an amused glance. It struck her that she and Keith were behaving with excessive brightness, as couples do when they have had a row before leaving home or when their marriage is getting rocky.

In the car going home, they sank again into silence.

She undressed quickly and got into bed. Keith undressed too, but stood staring out of the window. She didn't know what to expect from him, and this disturbed her, for she had become used to calculating his reactions.

Suddenly he pulled the sheet away, threw himself on her, and forced her legs apart. She was relieved. He was playing rape, one of their range of games. She started dutifully shouting: 'Help! Save me! Rape!' and waited for him to close his hand over her mouth. But when she looked at his face, she saw that he wasn't playing.

When he released her, she put on a bath-robe and walked straight out of the room (or rather the bed area). She went to a bathroom at the far end of the house, mainly because there was a door to close. She lay in the bath a long time, feeling her body soothed and softened. Keith had been really violent; she had a large bruise on one thigh.

Later, she roamed about the house, started to read, gave up, and turned on the radio. It was very late now, but after some fiddling among the foreign stations she eventually caught a voice speaking solemnly in Russian. She didn't understand a word, but the music of the language pleased her.

She saw Keith coming a long way off, as one always did in this house. He was naked. The mirrors reflected him as he advanced. She looked at her own reflection; she had let her robe fall open. It was like a scene from a portentously decadent film.

'Didn't you sleep?' she asked.

'I did, yes. Then I woke up and wondered where you were.'

'Oh, I haven't gone anywhere. I just wasn't sleepy.'

'What the hell are you listening to?'

'It's a declaration of war. The Russians are landing in Essex. But it won't affect us.' She switched the radio off.

'I thought we told each other everything, Tam. I assumed that, until now.'

'I did tell you. I could have said I'd gone to the movies, or anything.'

'I mean, all along. I thought we had a really good thing going.'

Tamsin was half irritated and half charmed – as she often had been – by the modish, earnestly youthful phrases in which he tried to express what in fact was deeply serious for him.

She said: 'So we have. Only, it's impossible for me to stop caring about Brian. He's . . . he was important in my life.'

'He wasn't good for you. You know that.'

'That isn't the point.'

'I thought it was the point between men and women. I try to be good for you.'

'You are. Look, Keith, if you feel threatened you couldn't be more absolutely wrong. My seeing Brian is . . . something entirely different.'

'It's nothing to do with me, is that it?'

She didn't answer.

'I love you so much, sweetie.'

He knelt in front of her, seizing her round the waist, and caught sight of the bruise.

'Christ, darling, did I do that?'

'It's all right. I enjoy being hurt. We decided that a long time ago, didn't we?'

'Nobody could love you the way I do, Tam.'

'I know. I do know.'

'Let me kiss it better.'

They found their way, inevitably and to Tamsin's relief, to their familiar domain of sensuality. It was better than talking, she thought – better than thinking. She welcomed, as an addict welcomes the effect of a drug, the unfailing responses and the timely excitement.

In the mirror, she saw a woman sprawled in a deep chair with a man's head between her legs. Herself? At all events, Keith's Tamsin.

5

Brian's poems got three reviews, two of them favourable though not enthusiastic. One critic wrote: 'Here is a new and interesting talent, of which we may hear more in the future.' Brian found this funny.

Tamsin was still seeing him when she was in the mood. Sometimes she said to Keith defiantly: 'I saw Brian today.' Sometimes she didn't, not for concealment which had become pointless, but because the experience of seeing Brian was closed and she didn't wish to mingle it with the resumed experience of living with Keith. But Keith always knew, showing a sensitivity with which she hadn't credited him –or she believed that he knew, and that came to the same thing.

The double life was all that she could cope with. She gave up her job – abruptly, from one day to the next, indifferently leaving the housing trust short-handed, and without even saying goodbye to old Frank and the other tenants. She had never been guided by a social conscience; it couldn't be helped. And if her own life was so disordered she couldn't claim to help other people with theirs.

Keith wasn't pleased. 'I thought that job meant something to you,' he said. It was a change from his conception of her, from the Tamsin whom he wanted to admire as well as to love. He also thought that she was making herself free to see Brian more conveniently.

Altogether, he was hard hit by being faced with a situation beyond his resources. It was worse for him than it had been during the years when he was completely deprived of her. Then he had found some pride in his lonely devotion, and of course he had been sustained by hope. But now he had less hope – she hadn't after all escaped from her obsession, and he couldn't see where it was to end. He was maddened by having to go through the loss of her again, not for a settled period to which he could compose himself, but repeatedly on unpredictable afternoons. He couldn't accept that his possession of her was incomplete, limited to a part of her.

Tamsin was distressed to see how badly she was hurting him; but she didn't know how to help it, since ceasing to see Brian was impossible for her. It was Brian who had once said: 'I don't want to share you.' He was willing to share her now, to have the part of her that needed him. But Keith wasn't.

The fact that, strictly speaking, she wasn't unfaithful to Keith appealed to Tamsin's sense of irony; but she knew that it was irrelevant. She would have made love with Brian, naturally, any time he wanted. He didn't want to, and she took this as a sign that they were giving each other what was essential. He didn't say, but evidently thought, that making love would bring them back to what they had failed at: living together, a complex of effort and activity, marriage. He reserved for Tamsin, and she reserved for him, the rarer achievement of peace.

Meanwhile (back at the ranch) she not only made love with Keith whenever he wanted, but also took the initiative more often than before. This had begun, for an unexpected reason, to cost her something. She was having trouble with her spine. It ached when she lay beneath Keith's weight, and caused acute spasms of pain in acrobatic games. The osteopath said that there was no cure, only a degree of relief. She was so thin – she seemed to be thinner than ever – that nothing cushioned her; she felt as though her bones rasped on her skin. But she didn't tell Keith (though she told Brian, as she told Brian everything) about this trouble. She found a stern pleasure in offering him what he had always desired. It was important because it was the language in which they communicated. With Brian she used the language of words – sometimes not many words, but each one charged with subtleties of meaning – and the yet more eloquent language of silence, of their tender stillness. With Keith she had the insistent and forceful language of love. Of love or of sex; she didn't make the distinction.

It took her some while to realize that Keith was no longer so keen on making love. She was so used to his displays of virility, his sexual pride, his assumption that this was the way to assert his possession of her, that she was incredulous. He had made love to her demandingly in every phase of their life together, and it had been his first reaction when he found out about Brian. But apparently, as she continued to see Brian, he came to feel that she was fobbing him off with this recompense for the part of her life that wasn't his. Sadly, she recognized that this was more or less true.

Well, it showed what a hopeless tangle she was in. If she made love eagerly with Keith, she was rewarding him for his tolerance. If she didn't, she was indicating that she belonged to Brian. She couldn't win.

Absurdly, just at this time they couldn't get away from sex. About a year ago they had got to know Nick and Gina, who had bought a house directly across the street. These young people had a good deal of money; Nick worked, though not very hard, in his father's stockbroking firm, while Gina was a model in considerable demand. They were enthusiastic about pop music – though no longer teenagers, they were avid readers of Keith's magazines – and still more enthusiastic about sex. Coming to live so near Keith and Tamsin, they declared, was the best thing that had ever happened to them.

They invited Keith and Tamsin over with embarrassing eagerness and frequency, and unavoidably they had to be invited back. But they also came without being invited – they crossed the street when the whim seized them, assuring themselves of a welcome by bringing a bottle, a supply of Moroccan hash, or a new porn book. One evening, when they were rashly admitted by Encarnacion, Keith and Tamsin were wearing bath-robes and had obviously just been making love. This convinced Nick and Gina, not that they might sometimes be intruding, but that their company was the one thing needed to enhance Keith and Tamsin's already delectable sex life. 'We're four of a kind – let's face it, we're all sex maniacs,' Gina used to say. Her new friends were evidently expected to live up to having a house with so few doors and so many mirrors. Wife-swapping and games *à quatre* were doubtless what Nick and Gina had in mind, but they were happy with sexual chit-chat.

Then there was the new maid, Encarnacion's successor. As a maid, Daphne – she came from Cyprus – was the best of the sequence. She polished the parquet floors until they shone, she cleaned the mirrors incessantly, she scrubbed the baths every time they were used, and if Keith and Tamsin came home in the small hours she appeared to ask whether they needed anything. She dressed, of her own choice, like a traditional maid in a black dress and white apron. But since she was beautiful – genuinely beautiful, not merely pretty or attractive – she didn't look like a maid so much as like a famous actress playing a maid. So it was disturbing to have her about. In plays, the beautiful maid is irresistible to the husband and the famous actress thus takes command of the stage.

Daphne, in fact, was in love with Keith. In love . . . what that meant to her, one couldn't be quite sure. Devoted, one could certainly say. Her favourite task was looking after Keith's clothes, doing all the things that Tamsin seldom remembered to do. He was scarcely aware of a loose button before Daphne had sewn it tight, or of a stain before she had sponged it. She received his thanks with solemn, grateful happiness. However, her modest demeanour covered a recognizable sexual alertness. A true peasant girl, she was at the same time simple and shrewd. Beyond any doubt, she had caught the gist of the talks with Nick and Gina; she had sensed Keith's virility; she had seen that things weren't right between him and Tamsin. She waited, humble but watchful, to accept his summons with the same solemn, grateful happiness.

Daphne hardly ever left the house. Other maids had claimed set periods of free time to see boy-friends or attend English classes, but she simply worked. Also, whereas other maids had been taken on for a year, Daphne had made her home in England (an uncle was vaguely responsible for her). Keith and Tamsin hadn't quite grasped this at the outset, but she was with them unless they sacked her, which they could scarcely do since she was such a good maid. She was a permanence, like Nick and Gina.

Tamsin couldn't help finding all this comical, and by degrees she grew weary of feeling sorry for Keith. In various ways, he wasn't having such a bad time. He had his work – or game of skill, or whatever it was – at which he was more successful than ever. He went constantly to pop concerts and clubs and parties, maintaining his eternal youthfulness and always welcomed for it. Although he groaned when he saw Nick and Gina coming, he got some fun out of the sessions with them. He was flattered by Daphne's devotion, too. He could take pleasure at the same time in her willing availability and in the virtue of declining it (so far as Tamsin knew, though she didn't much care). She could have done with an equivalent boost to her own self-esteem.

Yet he was unhappy, she knew that. And she felt that it was unfair of him. She gave as much of herself as she ever had; it wasn't her fault if he imagined that he possessed her entirely. Besides, to be unhappy was out of character for Keith, as it wasn't for herself and for Brian. She had put her trust in him because of his strength, his confidence and resilience. If that strength did not sustain him, it was she who was betrayed.

Sometimes – and this was the worst betrayal – he was unhappy when ͏e made love to her. More exactly, he made love to assuage his unhappi-ss. He turned to her with a new kind of desperation in the early ͏nings, as though to reassure himself that he could regain her after the ͏nging solitude of sleep. The reassurance didn't always succeed. ͏at wasn't her fault either, she thought.

͏l you're not with me, sweetheart,' he said.

He was sitting on the edge of the bed, no longer touching her. It was a grey dawn, with rain falling like gravel on the concrete patio.

'I'm not?'

'Not like you used to be.'

'You're imagining things. It's always been good with us and it still is. I always come. What else can I do?'

'It used to be more . . . I don't know . . .' He made a vague, clumsy gesture.

'It's going a bit stale, maybe. I don't feel it, but you might. Why don't you fuck Daphne for a change? You know she'd love it.'

He stared at her and said: 'I honestly think you wouldn't mind.'

'I shouldn't take it tragically. It's just a suggestion.'

'You couldn't have made that kind of suggestion before . . .'

'Oh, it's a joke, for Christ's sake.'

'It didn't sound like one.'

'I'm not at my best, I'm afraid. I'm going back to sleep.'

Another time, he said suddenly: 'You think about somebody else.'

This was on a night when they hadn't made love, but gone to bed yawning like any other married couple. Tamsin was reading. She had thought that Keith was asleep.

She asked: 'D'you mean . . . ?'

'Yes, when we're making love. That's what it is. You always come, and all that, but you're thinking of somebody else.'

'No,' she said. 'Really not.'

In fact, it was not true. To think of Brian, she had to be either with him or alone. But, now that she considered it, she didn't think of Keith when they made love. She must have ceased to do that when it was no longer a language in which they communicated. She thought about her own pleasure, or about her spine when it hurt.

'I often thought of you when I was with other girls,' he said.

'Oh, did you? That is nice to know.'

'You're the only woman who's ever mattered to me.'

'You should be glad that life's been so simple for you.'

He didn't answer, and she returned to her book. But after a few minutes he said: 'Well, there it is – Brian was your first man.'

'Oh, is that what's worrying you?'

'I know it could all have been different.'

'No, it couldn't. But both of you were my first man, that's how seems to me. Anyway, I never think of Brian when I'm with you. when we're making love, not at any time.'

'And you never think of me when you're with Brian.'

'If I went there to think of you I shouldn't go at all, should I?'

'You go to get away from me – is that what you're saying?'

'No, it's not. I never want to get away from you, Keith. Maybe I want to get away from myself. Can't you allow me this? It's a small corner of my life.' As she said this, Tamsin fixed her eyes on the book she was holding; it was the worst lie she had told Keith yet.

She never knew when he was going to say something about her visits to Brian. Clearly, the role of jealous husband embarrassed him and ran counter to his notion of the modern sophisticated marriage, proof against all strain because it rested on tolerance and flexibility. He couldn't admit that in reality their marriage wasn't like that at all. So, for days or even weeks at a time, he was his usual self: affectionate, cheerful, chatty and slightly drunk when he came home after work. But the bitterness was there, merely contained. It burst out unexpectedly, sometimes when she hadn't in fact seen Brian recently. She learned to avoid being silent and pensive; he wouldn't believe that she wasn't thinking of Brian. They lived in an atmosphere of enforced, almost desperate vivacity.

This was more easily maintained, of course, when they were not alone. Sometimes it was a relief to see Nick and Gina trotting across the street. Gina, especially, could be quite entertaining. In her youth, she'd had an exuberant career as a groupie and had succeeded in getting fucked by several pop stars whom Keith knew. She also recounted stories of breathlessly spontaneous intimacies with men whom she'd met at parties or in pubs or, if one were to believe her, in the street. She didn't specify whether a given incident had happened before she married Nick or since. He let her prattle on, however, as though her enthusiasm for instant sex without emotional attachment constituted her charm, or ought to in Keith and Tamsin's eyes. Prattle it was, Tamsin thought: the innocent prattle of a child, still unable to relate experience to value.

'Did I ever tell you' – Gina's stories always began with this phrase – 'about what happened to me on the beach at Carry-le-Rouet? There was this tiny little beach, see, in between the cliffs, where I used to go and sunbathe. So there I was, absolutely starkers, with my face down on my towel, and I suddenly felt this hand grab hold of me and turn me over. It was one of the local boys – must have been fishing, they do a lot of fishing there. He was ever so young – when I touched his face I knew he'd never shaved. Ever so brown and beautiful, though. D'you know, neither of us said a word. I don't suppose he knew English and I couldn't think in French. Would have spoilt it, too. Mind you, he was up to all the tricks. It wasn't just in and out. We were rolling about, all covered in sweat and sand, for Christ knows how long. It was fabulous. I was out of world, I was flying, I blew my mind, I just flipped.' Gina waved her about, trying to stretch her miniscule vocabulary. 'We both went off like bombs. Then, d'you know, I shut my eyes, and when I opened them there was nobody there. Just the sea and the sky. Like, really far out.'

'This was at Carry-le-Rouet?' Nick asked.

'Sure.'

'You must have been crazy. Him, too. Could have been arrested. The main road goes right along the beach.'

'No, it doesn't. There's the cliffs.'

'Which beach was this, then?'

'A tiny little beach. I discovered it.'

'Which way d'you go from the town? Say you're at the post office, there's two roads, which way d'you turn there?'

'Oh, shit, honey, how do I know?'

'There's just the two beaches. They're always full of people.'

'OK, OK,' Gina said, pouting. 'I made it up.'

Tamsin started to laugh. She laughed because it didn't matter. It was much the same whether Gina lay on beaches day-dreaming of beautiful boys or whether they materialized. Her whole life was a fantasy, including what happened to her.

But Keith, to everyone's surprise, was annoyed.

'What d'you mean, you made it up? This is ridiculous. There's no point in telling us something like that if it isn't true.'

'Well, I have done it on the beach,' Gina said. 'If it wasn't at Carry it must have been somewhere else.'

'But this actual thing was just made up. You said so.'

'Gina's got a lot of imagination,' Nick said indulgently, 'Should have been a writer. Shouldn't you, pusscat?'

'We can all make things up . . .' Keith persisted.

Tamsin caught Gina's eye and they both giggled helplessly. It was Keith who was being ridiculous. Yet in his protest there was also a certain dignity. He had a great respect for the truth, Tamsin reflected. The trouble was that he couldn't stand very much of it.

In spells of detached analysis, Tamsin considered the state of her marriage. Clearly, it wasn't what it had been at the time when Keith had confidently taken all his illusions for realities, and when she too had enjoyed illusions of being safe and contented. Yet the marriage wasn't rocky. They didn't fight; they were careful not to hurt each other in small ways. There was no danger – or, looking at it another way, no hope – that the marriage would ever break up. It would go on as it was maimed and distorted but tenacious. For, in defiance of logic, what had weakened was the ruthless power of love: his love for her, and no l her love for him. It held them locked together, or not so much loc as for ever colliding, straining and groping, dashing themselves against each other. Though she no longer thought of being happy with him, she couldn't imagine not being in love with him.

It wasn't sufficient for her, this love. It never gave her peace, as she found peace with Brian. It wasn't a purpose of her life, but a force driving through her life. Yet it wasn't open to her to abandon it, for it wouldn't abandon her.

Keith was busy with an enormous pop festival to be held on the August bank holiday weekend. He had found an excellent place for it – the park of a stately home. There wasn't a Duke, Keith admitted with a grin, but there was an Earl and he had promised to declare the festival open. Apparently this Earl and his Countess were fairly young and had proved sympathetic as soon as the idea was put up. The estate manager, with whom Keith had actually negotiated, had been concerned about possible damage, but his fears had been allayed. Keith had recruited a corps of two hundred responsible young people to stop any of the fans getting near the house or the ornamental gardens. In return, the Earl had used his influence with the Chief Constable and no police would enter the grounds.

Tamsin agreed to go, for Keith insisted that he wouldn't enjoy it without her. If he really meant that he couldn't leave her for a long weekend in London, free to be with Brian, he didn't say so.

They arrived on Friday afternoon. The weather was very hot and, with Keith's usual luck, the forecast was good. Fans were thick on the road, driving old cars decorated with slogans or flower patterns, packed into vans and Dormobiles, riding motor-bikes and mopeds and simply bikes, hitch-hiking. Keith gave a lift to four of them in the Jaguar.

In the home park, tents and sleeping-bags were all over the place. They left the car in a reserved enclosure behind the great house and walked in the direction of the main stand, where the more famous groups were to perform. Tamsin didn't see anyone she knew. The pop enthusiasts whom she met at parties, despite their fervent straining after youthfulness, didn't go to festivals like this. This scene belonged to the kids, the genuine kids, who lived on hamburgers and coke and slept on the ground. Some of them looked at her with surprise. No doubt she looked old to them, or else they guessed somehow that she had never belonged with them. But it was different for Keith. Many of them recognized him; they called him Keith and chatted to him easily. She let him
e into the crowd and strolled about by herself.

he found herself following two people who were strolling at the same
rely pace. One was a woman wearing a very smart long dress,
le for Ascot rather than for a pop festival, and a hat with a wide

brim. Tamsin herself wore a shirt and slacks; they were expensive, like all her clothes, but more or less in tune with the occasion. With the smartly dressed woman was a young man in the standard teenage uniform of T-shirt and jeans. Tamsin guessed that he'd hooked an older woman, probably wealthy, and was introducing her to his scene.

They turned. The woman at once gave a beaming smile and exclaimed: 'Tamsin, how marvellous to see you!' It was Amabel.

Tamsin smiled too, but speech was suddenly rendered impossible by the deafening sound of an electric guitar – they were near one of the stands. Both women started to laugh and clapped their hands over their ears.

'Let's go where we can talk,' Amabel shouted.

'Yes, let's.'

The young man said: 'I want to listen.'

'Yes, you do what you like, darling,' Amabel replied. Tamsin saw that he wasn't exactly a young man, though he was taller than Amabel, but a boy of about thirteen. He was extremely good-looking, indeed beautiful, like a fantasy of Gina's.

'That's my eldest,' Amabel said as they walked away. 'He's pop crazy, of course. He plays one of those things himself, when he's allowed to. I say, it is the same Keith – your Keith – who's running this show?'

'Yes. My Keith.'

'You did marry him, then? It's funny, I had an idea you didn't. I must have been told wrong.'

'I did eventually. I was married to Brian first. You remember Brian?'

'Oh . . . yes.' Amabel gave Tamsin a curious look. 'You married Brian and then you married Keith, is that right?'

'That's right.'

'You do seem to have stuck to the old Alma Mater. I lost touch with all that bunch, I'm afraid. You'll have to fill me in. I was quite surprised when I heard it was Keith doing this; that's why I thought it might be another chap with the same name. He wasn't in the jazz club so far as I can recall.'

'He isn't so much keen on jazz – pop – as he's keen on running things.'

'Well, he's obviously very good at it. This is going to be tremendous. They're still pouring in.'

'Did you come with your son, Amabel?'

'Did I . . .? No, you see, I live here.'

'You're the Countess?'

'Yes, if you marry an Earl you've got to be a Countess. You ɪ meet Charles. Not that I know where he is, it's chaos today. Anˑ

come in and have some tea, or a drink, whichever. It's sweltering out here, isn't it?'

They had tea, with cucumber sandwiches and currant cake, served by a matronly figure whom Amabel addressed as Mrs Thoresby. The room – drawing-room, Tamsin supposed – was comfortable and not very large; except for the leaded windows and the stone fireplace, it could have been in any ordinary house. Amabel explained that the family didn't use the main rooms, which were on show to the public.

'It's no big deal being an Earl, Tam. You're half a museum curator and half a farmer. Charles prefers being a farmer.'

However, over the fireplace there was a full-length oil painting of Amabel, dressed in riding kit and leaning gracefully against a five-barred gate.

'Wish I looked like that now,' she said, following Tamsin's eyes.

She had changed, certainly. She was thick round the waist and hips – she'd never been exactly slim – and her complexion was florid. She had reached the stage at which a woman is described as 'still very attractive', with a faint emphasis on 'still'. But the change wasn't principally in her appearance. It was in what – as she glanced good-humouredly at the portrait and took another slice of cake – she evidently accepted of herself.

The portrait seemed, perhaps through the artist's insight and perhaps because of what Tamsin knew about Amabel, to have caught her at the point of change. She gazed into the distance, across the home park no doubt, with a relaxed smile; but this smile was also a little mischievous, a little mocking, a smile that remembered student high jinks. It was the portrait of an Amabel with no uncertainties about being the Countess, yet not altogether used to it. But she was used to it now, clearly. She was entirely contented, entirely safe, and able to enjoy the pleasures of nostalgia.

'D'you ever think about that crazy trip we had, Tam?'

'Sometimes.'

'D'you remember getting your bottom pinched on the Acropolis? Christ, you were furious.'

'I expect I was. It hurt. I had quite a bruise.'

'And that ship we went on? I'm afraid I got you into that. That bloody first mate, the one who fancied you. Wasn't he repulsive? You did have a raw deal – the captain was gorgeous. Still, I stuck with you when you decided to get off at Tangier.'

'I've always been grateful.'

'Oh, I didn't care that much about him.'

'I mean, for the way you stayed with me when I was ill.'

'Oh yes, you were ill, weren't you? I'd forgotten about that.'

Mrs Thoresby cleared away the tea. Amabel lit a cigarette and said: 'I met Charles soon after we got back. I never would have dreamed I was going to get married, but all of a sudden it looked right. Sort of a reaction, I suppose.'

'It has been right, obviously.'

'Oh, sure. Some men are good for a whirl, some are husbands. Charles could only be the husband. Anyhow, that's why I lost touch.'

'I got married soon after we got back, too.'

'To Brian? It's funny, I thought you were really stuck on Keith.'

'It's been my misfortune to be stuck on two men.'

'Oh, come on, if you've married them both that isn't such a misfortune. More of a rich life.'

Tamsin smiled, but said nothing.

'So this is what Keith does – putting on these festivals?'

'Yes, and owning clubs, and promoting groups, and running fan magazines. The pop scene, generally.'

'It must be thrilling.' But instead of pursuing the subject, Amabel asked: 'What did Brian do after he graduated?'

'He's a poet,' Tamsin said firmly.

'Still?'

'How d'you mean, still?'

'I don't know . . . lots of students write poetry, don't they?'

'Brian was very talented.'

'Oh yes, he was.'

'I didn't imagine you read poetry, Amabel.'

'I read Brian's.'

Tamsin stared. Amabel said: 'I mean . . . Well, you see what I mean, evidently. But didn't you know?'

'No, I didn't.' Tamsin sat quite still for a minute, while the distant sound of pop music filtered into the room. Then she attempted a laugh and said: 'I'd have guessed you and Keith, more likely.'

'Actually, no. I did miss a few. Pity. Too late now.'

'It wouldn't occur to me that Brian was your type.'

'Are you upset, Tam?' Amabel asked gently.

'I believe I am. Isn't it silly? It's just . . . I can't explain.'

'I wish I hadn't come out with it like that. Still, it is a long time ago.'

'I know.'

'I hope we're friends.'

'Oh, we are. I'm so glad I met you again.'

'That's fine, then. Are you staying all the weekend?'

'Yes.'

'Not in a tent?'

'No, Keith's booked into a hotel, I don't know where.'

'Oh, nonsense, you must stay with us. You simply must. You should have let me know you were coming.'

'But I didn't know you were the Countess, did I?'

'Nor you did. I'm absolutely bonkers today. Must be the heat.'

It was an odd weekend, divided between the fervour of the pop festival – more like the self-intoxicating ritual of an extreme religious sect, Tamsin thought, than a musical event of any kind – and the ordered comfort of the house. The noise began about midday and went on all night, amateurs taking over when the big-name groups left off. From indoors, one had the feeling of being besieged by an army of fanatics, dervishes or something of the sort, celebrating the coming triumph of their faith. But these fanatic-fans were in no way hostile. Now and again they peered in at the windows, as though to see whether the Earl and the Countess were getting on all right, and obeyed cheerfully when moved on by Keith's volunteers. The TV news reported that it was the best-behaved festival crowd on record. In point of fact two boys were stabbed and three girls collapsed from bad trips, but publicity was avoided.

Keith rushed about incessantly, very much in his element, and slept only for a few hours before breakfast. Tamsin spent a certain amount of time sitting on the grass in the midst of the crowd, usually with Amabel's children – the beautiful boy and two beautiful little girls. It was strange, but it was also pleasant, to be surrounded by so much . . . not exactly happiness, but so much belief, so much unquestioning acceptance, so much simplicity. Late at night, she didn't want to move. The boy had to remind her that the girls ought to be in bed.

In the house there was simplicity too, and also real happiness. Charles was an enormously tall man with slightly bandy legs, no doubt an affectation although he was in fact devoted to riding. He put on a consistent performance as a horsey aristocrat. This involved making frequent unfunny jokes, loudly professing his ignorance of politics, the arts, the sciences and simple arithmetic, and generally claiming to be stupid, though it was clear that he was intelligent. He also claimed to be under Amabel's thumb: 'You're quite right, dear . . . I'll do that, dear.' When they were alone, presumably they abandoned the role-playing and had rational discussions. But no doubt they were intuitively in agreement most of the time. They understood each other perfectly. They were securely and deeply in love.

The children were fascinated to hear that Tamsin had gone hitch-ing with their mother before she was married. Where did they go? they have adventures? 'Well, your mother kept changing the plans,'

Tamsin said. They couldn't imagine this Amabel – frivolous, impulsive, unsettled. But it was the unsettled quality in Tamsin that attracted them.

Who would have thought it, when Tamsin was a serious girl while Amabel was the college scatterbrain and the college sexpot? For it was Amabel, Tamsin recognized, who had grown and matured, found a fitting shape for her life, and was now advancing without complications or uncertainties. One could see Amabel (eating currant cake, putting on more weight) enjoying her son's progress as a student, guiding her daughters through their affairs, mildly teasing her husband about growing older.

While Tamsin...

On Tuesday the festival was over. Keith, in a satisfied and expansive mood, insisted on being given a chance to repay Charles and Amabel for their hospitality. They would make an effort, they said, but they hardly ever went to London. They stood and waved, together with their children, as the Jaguar moved away down the drive.

The heat wave hadn't ended. Nick and Gina came over for a swim in the pool – the four of them naked, which supplied something of the atmosphere that Nick and Gina sought if not all the activities. Tamsin paced again the cage of her life.

PART FOUR

I

Mr Paterson was much distressed when Tamsin told him that she was giving up her job. As she knew quite well, he would have liked her to be his mistress. She had forestalled any approach by mentioning, the first time he took her out for a drink, that she was not only married but happily married and, as she put it, absolutely wrapped up in Brian. They had, nevertheless, a wistful and delicate kind of relationship, maintained by occasional drinks in the lounge bar of an old-fashioned Bloomsbury hotel, which somewhat relieved the emptiness and futility of his life. It was only for Mr Paterson that she broke her rule of being home at six o'clock.

'I've never contemplated the possibility of losing you,' he said. 'You've been here . . .'

'Three and a half years.'

'So it is. We've come to depend on you. And I've had the impression that you like the work, as well as doing it to perfection. If I was mistaken, I much regret it.'

'No, no, I've enjoyed being here. That's not it at all. Brian and I are going to live in the country.'

'Oh dear. So I shall lose sight of you altogether.'

'I'm afraid so.'

'Where are you going?'

'To the Scottish Highlands. We've found a cottage – you know, a croft. It's a marvellous place. Very remote, very beautiful. We've decided that Brian needs surroundings like that to do his best work.'

'And you? Won't you be bored? You're such an active person.'

'Oh, there'll be lots to do. We're going to grow our own food.

It'll be a completely new life.'

'You're very courageous, my dear.'

'I'm looking forward to it.'

It wasn't true that Tamsin had enjoyed being at Paterson's, doing tedious work under the command of the detestable Miss Fowler. She had twice tried to change her job, without success. True, she wouldn't have thrown up the job without getting a new and better one if she'd been a single girl. But of course, it was Brian who mattered. He wasn't progressing as he should – as he deserved to. He still had only a few poems printed every year and a few broadcast. That in itself wasn't important, or she kept reminding herself that it wasn't, although she longed for him to receive greater recognition. What was serious was that there was no advance in the quality of his poems.

It was Brian himself who said this. Tamsin had, until lately, refused to agree. As she saw it, he criticized himself too scrupulously and allowed his confidence to waver, so he needed her to encourage and fortify him. But each new poem really did give her a thrill of admiring excitement.

'It's great, Brian. I don't see how it could be better.'

'No. But it could.'

'How? You just explain to me in what way it could be better.'

'Ah, if I knew that it would be.'

'That's just a logical double-bind.'

'There's something . . . There's another poem like this, the poem I haven't written. It's floating about, out of my reach.' He made a gesture with both hands, like a man trying to catch a butterfly.

Was she at fault? She wanted every poem to be a triumph, obviously. Because he ruthlessly scrapped all his weaker efforts and wouldn't let her see his drafts while he was trying to perfect them, she assumed that if he announced a poem as completed it must be entirely successful. She felt a surge of joy – and simply relief – when he said : 'I think I've done it'; that is, she felt this before she read the poem. So she began to wonder whether she was really doing him the best service by her unquestioning enthusiasm, and whether this enthusiasm didn't arise partly from her own needs.

She made a deliberate effort to read the poems as though she had seen nothing of the labour of composition : as though they were by a stranger, not by the man whose strivings and achievements were the centre of her own life. One Sunday she sent him out for a walk, saying that she wanted to give the flat a thorough cleaning, and read through all his poems. The early ones were just as exciting as she'd thought at the time. The recent ones, she had to admit, didn't show any advance – any greater depth or power. The early poems weren't actually better, but they were bolder and fresher. It seemed that his doubts and his toil had clouded this freshness without bringing any compensating gain. To put it simply, he was going a bit stale.

Also, he wasn't writing much. Tamsin felt that this ought not to worry her; with poetry, surely, quality was everything and quantity was irrelevant. Yet she reflected that almost all the poets she admired had written rather a lot. Most of them had written a fair amount by the time they were Brian's age. She had been hoping that by this time he would have a book published. But he wasn't ready for that; when she spoke of it, he said: 'I'm not going to churn out poems just to make a book.'

There might, after all, be some connection between the quality and quantity – between the fact that Brian wasn't conquering new poetic domains and the simple fact that he didn't write much. Writing poetry was difficult, but perhaps it didn't need to be so difficult as this. The trouble might be that Brian didn't have the best conditions for his work.

She was much concerned about his being interrupted, especially by the phone. They inherited the phone with the flat and Tamsin suggested having it disconnected, incidentally saving a bit of money. Brian said that one could always just not answer it. However, she suspected that he did answer it. Letting a phone ring demands unusual strength of mind.

He had several friends whose jobs, mostly in journalism or the BBC, allowed them to take long lunch hours and who evidently thought that it was a kindness to ask him to lunch. The process, including Brian's journey from Muswell Hill to Soho and back, took three or four hours out of his day. Indeed, it killed his whole day. He never did his best work in the morning; and in the afternoon, stuffed with heavy food and wine, he was likely to fall asleep.

'You don't have to go,' she pointed out to him.

'No, of course not.' But he did go. He found pleasure, not exactly in the lunch, but in being asked and then asked again.

Tamsin was inclined to disapprove of these lunches, which seemed to be a male prerogative, since all the women she knew had jobs that permitted exactly sixty minutes for lunch, or else were kept at home by children. They were also an excuse for wasting time. Brian didn't scheme to waste time, of course, but his friend Norman did. Norman had written a successful novel (secretly, Tamsin considered it shallow and meretricious) which was made into a film. Having banked the cheque, Norman no longer did any work. He had to recharge his batteries, he said. So he was in the habit of ringing up Brian to suggest a lunch – even worse, an afternoon watching cricket or a search for second-hand books.

Brian nearly always went, and they nearly always ended up in a pub. If Tamsin found the flat empty when she came home, she could reckon that Brian was with Norman.

She didn't grudge Brian his relaxations. Writing poetry was not like office work, or even like writing a novel. The intensity was what counted, not the continuity – not the hours. If a poem wouldn't come out right, it was more sensible for him to take a break than to stare at the words and torment himself. What she doubted was whether he had the right sort of relaxation: whether he was aided and restored or merely diverted. When he had been with Norman, she noticed, he came home tired.

Norman liked crowded places. He was happy in pubs and restaurants where you had to shout to be heard and struggle to be served; he was happy in Petticoat Lane, Hampstead Heath on a bank holiday, and Oxford Street just before Christmas. All this, he said, was Life with a big L; in fact, he drew on it greedily for his novels. But Brian's need was for quiet places, for space and peace and beauty. He and Tamsin had discovered certain quiet places – a part of Epping Forest that was well away from the road, and the far side of Virginia Water – which now belonged to them by the right of affection. They used to go by bus, taking a picnic lunch, on Sundays. When Tamsin could get a day off they went on a weekday, which was better. But if you knew where to go, you never met many people; and the people you did meet passed with an apologetic smile, since they also wanted to be alone or at least recognized that it was a place for being alone.

They were all places with tall, stately, venerable trees, and for such trees both Brian and Tamsin had a deep fondness. He had written beautifully about trees – about the patient cycle of their life and their dignified resignation to death. Among the trees, at all seasons, he was truly happy. The days when she could go with him and see him like this were precious to her, but she was glad too if he went to their special places without her. She knew that he would come back refreshed and strengthened.

It would be good, she thought, if he could live with this restoring peace – this true relaxation – constantly available, at the door, without the long and tedious bus journey. So she got the idea of living in the country.

There would be loss as well as gain, inevitably. They both enjoyed seeing friends, dropping in at the pub round the corner, going to an occasional party, walking the London streets late at night. They enjoyed seeing the sort of films that didn't get on the circuits and the sort of plays that ran briefly at little theatres. In fact, they were Londoners. Tamsin especially – she was drawn to the core of the city, like most people who have grown up in the suburbs, and would have lived a stone's throw from Piccadilly Circus had it been possible. She liked spending a few days in the country, but on her own account she would never have chosen to live there. Still, it was Brian who mattered . . . or, since her life and his were one, her fulfilment through Brian. It didn't occur to her that she was being unselfish. Unless Brian reached his full stature as a poet, she herself was diminished.

When she made the suggestion to Brian, he said at once: 'Tam, that's a great idea.'

She threw her arms round him and kissed him, as a different woman might have if her man had agreed to satisfy some wish of her own.

'Oh, I'm so glad! It'll make all the difference, won't it?'

'Yes, that's right – it'll make all the difference.'

She hadn't heard this note of certainty and of unclouded hope in his voice for what seemed like a long time.

'We'll have to go somewhere really terrific,' he said. 'I don't know where it is, but I can see it. Wild mountains, huge forests, everything ten times the size. Not another house in sight. Is there anywhere like that, Tam? Wales, d'you think . . . Scotland? You know, I've never been anywhere. I don't know my own country. I've been abroad with Robert and Dorothy, that's all. But we won't go abroad. That would feel like a holiday. You come back from a holiday.'

Tamsin had thought of somewhere like Devon. They would be living in the country, but there would be a town within reach and she would get a job. However, she saw at once that Brian was right. She didn't really want to have anything to do with a dull, bland small town. If she was bored by her work at Paterson's, she'd be driven round the bend by any job she would find in Devon. And surely she had enough resources to occupy herself.

She had been to Wales, and remembered wild country and mountains. But perhaps it wasn't remote enough, for she also remembered traffic jams on what should have been lonely roads, and recently she had heard about English people buying Welsh cottages as second homes and sending the prices up. Scotland might be more what they were looking for. She had never been there, but she imagined it – the Highlands, any-way – as beautiful and empty. When she looked at a map, there did seem to be a lot of space. Besides, she could encourage herself with a notion of finding her ancestral roots, for she had been called Tamsin after a Scottish grandmother. She asked her father: 'What part of Scotland did your mother come from?' Characteristically, he didn't know.

When her summer holiday came round, they used it to explore Scot-land. To save money which they were bound to need in the future, they hitch-hiked. Progress northward was slow, because the university term had just ended and the motorway junctions were thick with hitch-hikers. They could feel the precious fortnight draining away. But once they were in the Highlands everything looked hopeful. The landscape was magnificent. Right and left from the main road, narrow roads on which there was practically no traffic climbed to deserted moors. It didn't rain, either, although they had been warned of rain in the Highlands. A pale blue sky – more beautiful, they agreed, than the intense blue of the Mediterranean – spread from horizon to horizon.

A Scot who was driving a removal lorry told them that if they were planning to settle in the Highlands they ought to go still farther north. Anywhere up to Inverness the cottages were being bought as second homes, just as in Wales. Sutherland was the place – it was too far for the the city-dwellers. And it was grand country.

In Sutherland, sure enough, Brian and Tamsin found their dreams coming true. The countryside had an air of being unknown and yet welcoming, of waiting for someone to be bold and understanding enough to discover it. The air was pure, the water in the streams was delicious, nothing was in any way soiled or tarnished. Towns whose names became familiar by appearing on signposts thirty miles away turned out to be tiny settlements – a small grey church with a small grey school beside it, a couple of shops, a post office. When they bought food, the shop-keepers asked where they came from and implied that meeting a stranger was an event. Cars belonging to tourists hurried along, apparently intent on reaching the north coast, soon to vanish and leave the solitude undisturbed once more. Chances of getting a lift were poor, but Brian and Tamsin no longer bothered about that – they walked. It would be absurd to be carried past the spot they were seeking.

They found it by chance – no, by intuition. They came to a road-fork and decided to take the turning to the left, because that road hadn't been repaired for years and grass grew down the middle of it. It had a destination, according to the signpost, but it was hard to believe that it went so far. They passed a croft. A man carrying two buckets across the yard stared at them as though to memorize details in case of questions about their disappearance. The road climbed steeply, crossed a saddle between two mountains, and then ran straight across a broad plateau. The contour map showed it as a bowl, and there were mountains all round shutting out the travelled world. But the open moor seemed to be as high as the mountains, so they had the feeling of being on the roof of the world, lifted above all plains and villages and towns and enclosed places of whatever description. In this immensity there was exactly one house, built of square-cut grey stone like all the other traditional houses in Sutherland.

When they reached it they knocked on the door, intending to ask the owner if he knew of any houses to rent in this part of the country. There was no answer, so Brian lifted the latch – houses in the north of Scotland were never locked – and they went in. The rooms were furnished; at least, they contained two sagging but capacious armchairs, two upright chairs, a sturdy kitchen table, a dresser which would have been marketed by Ted Goldman as a valuable antique, and two beds upstairs. But there were no sheets on the beds, no cups or plates, no personal possessions anywhere, no carpets or curtains.

Brian and Tamsin walked back to the croft below the saddle. The man who had stared at them was now tinkering with the engine of a rather battered car.

'Did ye take the wrong road?' he asked.

'We're having a look round,' Brian said. 'That house up the road – is it empty?'

The man removed a plug, looked at it critically, returned his attention to Brian, and said: 'Aye.'

'You see, we're looking for somewhere to live.'

'Ye are?' The man considered this gravely. 'Well, it's empty,' he said.

'What happened to the last people who lived there?'

'He died. She's away to her son in Glasgow.'

'Did they own the house?'

'No, it belongs to the estate. All the crofts belong to the estate. Ye'd have to see Mr Millan, the factor, in Tongue. I've to go there. I'll take ye when I've cleaned these plugs.'

It was a long drive. Tamsin sat in front with the crofter; he wasn't talkative, but she liked his way of saying plainly and clearly as much as was needed.

'What do people do round here, mostly?' she asked.

'Sheep. There's not much but sheep.'

'Oh, I don't think we could keep sheep.'

'There's little paid work for a young man.'

'We're just looking for a place to live. My husband's a writer.' Tamsin sometimes preferred not to say that Brian was a poet; people tended to have a caricatured notion of poets. The crofter didn't ask what Brian wrote, but merely said 'Aye', implying that he didn't concern himself with how other people arranged their lives.

The factor was clearly surprised at being presented with a tenant for the house. It had been empty for three years, he said.

'There's no services, mind. Neither electricity nor drainage nor water.'

'What did they do for water?' Tamsin asked.

'There's a burn inbye the croft. Boil the water for drinking maybe. But it ought to be pure.'

The rent was one pound a month. They didn't hesitate. The place was manifestly ideal; besides, they had been away from London for eight days out of Tamsin's fortnight and they had no more time for searching. The agreement was to run from the first of September, allowing Tamsin to give a month's notice of leaving her job.

The factor said: 'I hope it suits you. Anything you want to know about the locality, you can ask Mr Macbeth.'

'Who?'

'The man who drove you in. Your next neighbour.'

'Is he really called Macbeth?'

'It's his name,' the factor said without a smile.

When the time for the move came, Brian hitch-hiked to Scotland again. Tamsin was to go by train with their belongings – suitcases, a box of household things, another box of books, and a rolled bundle of sheets and blankets. She was alone for five days and missed Brian desperately, achingly. Everything about London seemed unbearable: the flat, the tube, the office where she was working her last week. She couldn't imagine how she'd put up with it.

The train on the Friday night was packed; she had to sit on her bundle in the corridor. She cheered herself up by gazing at Scotland in the light of dawn. With the heather in flower, it was more beautiful than ever.

She took a bus (also packed) to the fork in the road. Brian was supposed to meet her, and to have made some arrangement for getting the luggage up to the house. When she didn't see him, she started to worry. He couldn't still be stuck trying to hitch-hike, could he? Here at the foot of the impassive mountains, she suddenly felt very alone and almost daunted. But soon she saw Macbeth's car lurching down the road, and Brian was in it.

They kissed passionately, making a pledge and a resolution, as they had kissed in the basement room when she came to say that she could not live without him. Meanwhile, Macbeth loaded up the luggage. She wondered whether he would charge some kind of taxi rate, or take them up to the house for nothing in neighbourly fashion. In fact, when she took out her purse he asked for exactly the cost of his petrol.

After the car had gone, Tamsin felt the solitude again. But now that she was with Brian, she rejoiced in it.

'Isn't it splendid?' she said, holding his hand and gazing round their domain.

'It's perfect. Thank you for it, Tam.'

The house was warm and cosy. Brian had bought a sack of anthracite for the old cooking range and found out how to get it working. They wouldn't need a fire yet, he said, and when they did they could forage for logs. He had bought an oil-lamp, candles, a stock of food and a bottle of whisky.

'You must have spent quite a bit, Brian.'

'Oh, it's just to start us off.'

So they began their new life, a life of freedom and self-reliance. The only tie to the outside world, Tamsin supposed, would be the need for shopping. The one shop, which sold everything, was miles away; she decided to ask Lady Macbeth – they must call her that, obviously – on which days she went and arrange to share expenses. But Lady Macbeth explained that no one in Sutherland went shopping for food. She and her husband never left home except for rare trips to Tongue. Mobile shops came round, even along Tamsin's road which passed a string of remote crofts. The butcher came on Tuesday, the fishmonger on Wednesday. The baker, who also sold groceries, came on Monday and Thursday. This was good news for Tamsin, for she had never enjoyed shopping – the hurry and bustle, the queue at the check-out counter, the fatuous conversations with women she generally failed to recognize. All that was part of the rejected London life. The vans came as Lady Macbeth had said; the drivers were polite but not chatty, so she swiftly picked out what she wanted and paid.

She was glad that she had no need to descend from her plateau. When she stood at the door of the house, she had an enriching sense of the beauty and grandeur all around. She was never satiated with it and never got bored. The weather wasn't always fine, of course. Sometimes dark clouds gathered, darker than she remembered seeing anywhere else, and rain fell in torrents. She stood at the window and stared at it, like a child. In Scotland the weather seemed to be peculiarly localized, or else it was simply that one could see for miles; anyway, it was seldom raining everywhere at the same time. There were islands of clear sky, patches of sunlight on the flank of one mountain or another, and magical shafts of light streaming through the clouds. The scene changed from hour to hour, almost from minute to minute, providing a continual drama. Sooner or later all the clouds rolled away and the serene blue sky was restored, fresher and cleaner than ever.

They went for walks – short walks, giving merely a taste of what was at their disposal, and also long walks. They didn't cross the saddle and go down toward the Macbeths' house, but in the other direction they walked for hours. The wild open moorland stretched on and on, still deserted except for crofts almost as lonely as theirs, of which some were inhabited and some were empty, indeed ruined. They discovered more mountains, rushing streams, and small limpid lakes. The character of the country was always the same, always generous and spacious, but every fresh view was a revelation.

One day, soon after the beginning of their new life, Brian shouted: 'Hey, Tamsin, come and have a look at this.' She hurried into the kitchen. He always worked there, at the table, while she stayed in the other downstairs room.

He had written a poem that came directly out of living on the roof of the world, a poem of vision and celebration. She saw at once that it had just the qualities that had been eluding him: the freshness and the vibrant enthusiasm, the true blaze of creative power. He had been for a long walk the day before, alone. Just as she had hoped, the beauty that surrounded them was transmuted into the beauty of words.

'It's your very best,' she said.

'It's pretty damn good, isn't it?' He paced round the room, taking long energetic strides, as he did when they started out on a walk. 'I'll have to work on it a bit, I suppose. I've done it in a rush. But I couldn't help showing it to you.'

'Brian,' she said, 'why don't you send it off right now?'

'I've only just written it. I never do that.'

'This time you ought to. You won't gain anything by fiddling with it. You'll lose something, more likely.'

They set off right away, going down past the Macbeths' house for once and covering the six miles to the post-box – which was at the fork in the road – at a marching pace to catch the collection. Tamsin had persuaded him to submit the poem to a paper with real prestige.

'Of course it's good enough for them. They're lucky to get it. Besides, they pay properly. You're not going to let this poem go for peanuts – not this one.'

The poem was accepted. The literary editor wrote: 'I hope you'll send us more in this vein. Your flight to the wilderness seems to have served you well.'

2

Brian and Tamsin began their new life with a small amount of capital: or rather Tamsin did, since he never bothered about money. She had started a savings account with the cheques that Robert gave her to buy pretty dresses. Since deciding to leave London, she had been saving from her salary. Finally, there was a farewell cheque from Mr Paterson – out of his own pocket, she guessed, not from the firm. So they would manage, she reckoned. They would be living cheaply, and Brian would get a lot of poems accepted.

She soon discovered that food cost more in Scotland than in London, instead of less as she had expected. She was shocked by the price of standard items like butter or frozen peas. Presumably she was paying for the petrol used by the mobile shops, and of course they had no competition.

Growing food turned out to be a romantic illusion. She had imagined that one could always grow food if one had a bit of land, and she'd bought a book called *A Practical Guide for Smallholders*. But the plateau had no soil; it was stony on the mountain slopes and swampy near the house. Lady Macbeth said that nobody in Sutherland grew vegetables, except potatoes. Tamsin didn't see the sense of trying to reclaim swampy land to grow potatoes, which she didn't much like. Anyway, it was harvesting time, not planting time.

The free wood for the fire was another miscalculation. There were great forests somewhere in Scotland, perhaps, but not here. The only trees were birches, growing in small clumps along the streams. They looked pretty when the sun was shining, but she missed the huge, sheltering, comforting trees of England, the oaks and beeches and elms.

Those trees gave shade while they lived and warmth when they died, but the birches were useless as fuel. The puny logs, sucked into damp earth, were soaked to the core and had to be dried for hours on the cooking-range. When they got dry (and some of them never did) they flared delusively and were quickly consumed. It wasn't worth carrying them home.

So, in addition to the anthracite for the stove, they had to buy firewood for the chilly evenings. Both could be delivered. But they weren't on a regular route for the anthracite merchant or the wood merchant, as they were for the mobile shops, and the cost was appalling. They were paying for living the simple life, now a rarity. Other people cooked on calor-gas – well, they hadn't got a modern stove. Again, other people had electricity for light and heating, and the tariffs were cheap in Scotland, but there was an impossible connection charge.

Tamsin disliked having to bother so much about being comfortable indoors, for the point of leaving London had been to live an outdoor life. The walks were splendid . . . for the first few weeks. But unfortunately there was only one walk, along the road. The moor turned out to be a morass of swampy ground and dark little pools, from which tufts rose like steep-sided islands. One could progress only by jumping from tuft to tuft, which really couldn't be called walking. It took all one's concentration, it was very tiring, and one didn't always land safely. Several times she got her feet soaked, and once a shoe came off and sank beyond recovery – a good new shoe whose loss she could ill afford. For all she knew, the swamps might be bottomless. One might be sucked down to a miserable death; she had heard of such a thing. She wondered how anyone had kept sheep here. Perhaps they'd grazed high on the mountains, where the ground was firm and a tough, dwarfish kind of grass grew among the rocks. Once, Brian and Tamsin got through to this firm ground after two hours of tuft-jumping and climbed one of the mountains. The expedition took all day and they returned, dangerously, after dark. They didn't try again, so they were limited to walking on the road.

In October, Tamsin began to admit to herself that she sometimes felt lonely. She was dismayed and guilty – what had they come here for, after all? But she hadn't fully envisaged the effect of the monotony, the sameness of day after day. She found herself standing at the door and waiting eagerly for the mobile shops. When they came, she tried to keep the men chatting, but they didn't respond. The brevity of this kind of shopping, which she'd welcomed at first, brought a sense of disappointment. 'Well, that's that for today,' she said to herself as the van moved on. And the time from Thursday to Monday, with no vans, seemed very long.

Apart from the shops, there was only the post van. She got into the habit of waiting for it too and wondering whether it would stop. It seldom did. Now and again it brought a letter from a poetry magazine. Acceptances were good, rejections were bad, but in either case these letters didn't take long to read and the event soon belonged to the past. They had very few other letters. People in the twentieth century, especially big-city people, communicate by meeting or by phone; Tamsin hadn't reflected on this before, though she had behaved like anyone else. She felt ignored – forgotten. She wrote a long letter to Norman. He replied with a chatty, entertaining letter, full of news about various friends and sharp, witty comments; she cherished it and read it several times, with a worrying feeling of nostalgia. She wrote again, but Norman didn't. She wrote to some other friends – they didn't have many, now that she thought of it. Either they didn't answer, or they answered after a long delay, or they sent hurried notes: 'So glad you're keeping well – must be a great life, we do envy you – sorry I'm a bit rushed just now.' Eventually, Tamsin even wrote to her parents. She was at a low ebb, she couldn't help feeling, if she looked forward to hearing from them.

Day after day, she talked with no one but Brian. She had expected to find contentment in that. They did have long intimate talks, enriched by their seclusion and by the endlessness of time. Tamsin fought against the treacherous notion that this wasn't enough for her. It was the truth that she cared supremely for Brian and, on this level of feeling, didn't care a rap about anyone else. But apparently she missed – she actually needed – just the sort of conversations that she had rejoiced at escaping from: casual, superficial conversations with people to whom she was indifferent.

It might have been better after all, she thought, if they'd gone to live in a village. She began to find excuses to leave the plateau. She went to see Lady Macbeth for one reason or another, though Lady Macbeth talked sparingly, like her husband, and always seemed to be busy. She trudged to the shop, convincing herself that she'd forgotten something essential when the van called. Sometimes she bought newspapers (which they needed to light the fire, anyway) to relieve the dullness of listening to the news on their transistor radio. Occasionally she went to Tongue, either getting a lift from Macbeth or taking the bus despite the expense. It was a real treat, she thought sardonically. She was thrilled by crowded pavements, by going round a small supermarket, by queuing in a fish and chip shop.

She tried for some time to conceal her loneliness from Brian, but the integrity of their life together depended on having no secrets. And he soon guessed; his insight into her feelings could not fail.

'Well, I'm at a loose end sometimes, that's natural. I'm not writing poetry, after all.'

'Solitude isn't much in your line, is it, Tam?'

'Oh, I wouldn't say that. I have to make the adjustment. I'll be all right, don't worry. I'm all right anyway when I'm with you. But I can't be with you all the time or you wouldn't do any writing, would you?'

'We're living at a high pitch. The low pitch is appointments and lunches and so forth. It's not so easy being continually face to face with oneself.'

'Yes, that's just it.'

Some time – a couple of weeks – after making this admission, she realized that Brian was feeling the strain too. One morning, when she was setting out for Tongue, he suddenly said: 'I'll come with you.' The day turned into a spree. He went recklessly through the shops buying things that were 'bound to come in useful' – an elaborate sort of penknife, a powerful torch, a woollen cap for each of them. It suddenly started to pour with rain, so they dashed into a pub and drank three whiskies, the first they had touched for weeks. After this they had lunch in the hotel, which Tamsin certainly hadn't intended. Finally, Brian insisted on buying a bottle of whisky. In the evening, still in a state of excitement, they broke it open. It should have lasted for weeks, but they were so appalled by their extravagance that they went wild and finished it. Brian staggered to the door and was violently sick – he was never a good drinker.

The money had to be made up somehow. At Christmas they would want a turkey and another bottle of whisky, or anyway a bottle of wine if such a thing could be found in Sutherland. Tamsin began to buy mincemeat instead of joints, margarine instead of butter. Meanwhile she put out of her mind all thoughts of going to Tongue again, or even to the local shop lest she might buy something they didn't strictly need.

So there she was, confined to the house and the habitual walk. Confined . . . she hadn't felt that before. But space and time, the infinities in which she had exulted were now contracting.

The days became shorter. Of course one knew that the days were shorter in winter than in summer, and considerably more so in the north of Scotland. But to know it was one thing and to experience it as a dominating factor in life was another thing. At their shortest, the days were only five hours long. They got up late because it was so miserable to get up in the dark, and had a combined breakfast and lunch. Hardly any time seemed to have passed before, with a sinking of the heart, they saw that it was getting dark again. Besides, unless the sun shone it never became properly light at all. Daylight, so-called, was a grey miserly twilight. In the old house with its small windows, it was scarcely possible to read.

She had counted on beautiful clear nights unobscured by city murk. There were nights like that, when the moon shone with icy brilliance or the stars glittered. But mostly a thick layer of cloud made the grey day sink into a black night, unrelieved, crushing, suffocating. Even out of doors, it was like being shut in a dark cupboard. The darkness was a nullity, a blank in creation. So it continued, for eighteen or nineteen hours.

The oil lamp gave a yellowish glow, gentle and restful as a change from electric light, but so weak that after a time they found it depressing. And oil cost money, so they lit the lamp only when Brian was working or when Tamsin (rather guiltily) wanted to read. Often, through the long evenings, they talked or listened to the radio by the light of a single candle.

Rain fell almost every day in October, and usually went on falling for hours. It was a fierce, stinging rain; if you walked toward it, it struck your face like darts. Going for a walk, picking your way among the deep puddles on the road, was no longer a pleasure but an act of desperation when sitting indoors became intolerable. And as the year waned, it became colder. On the first of November, snow fell for the first time.

By now, it was always cold in the house. Tamsin bought a roll of felt, and spent a whole day tracking down draughts and sealing them off. Then she bought a paraffin stove; it was ugly and smelly, but it saved firewood and it could be carried up to the bedroom. And yet, even when they used up wood recklessly and had a blazing fire, it was still cold.

'We'll just have to wear a lot of clothes all the time,' Tamsin said. They had come with what served in London for winter clothes, but clearly they were not equipped for Scotland. They also needed more blankets, although they now spent the night in their sleeping-bags and even made love, not very comfortably, in Brian's sleeping-bag. So she made another trip to Tongue.

She bought the blankets, and bought long underclothes of the kind that raised laughs in old productions of Ben Travers farces, but that was all. The shops were full of thick, beautiful, enticing Fair Isle sweaters; however, it seemed that these were meant for tourists and the prices were impossible. An idea came to her as she stood irresolutely in the street – why not knit sweaters? And thick socks, which they needed badly, and gloves, which they never wore in London. She hadn't knitted for years (as a child she's been taught to knit and sew by her mother and had hated it) but she could recall the simple skill, she supposed. So she bought a quantity of good strong wool, which was quite expensive for a start.

Knitting was trickier than she had imagined. She had forgotten the code in which the patterns were written, and had to figure them out like puzzles. She soon abandoned the attractive decoration and made the sweaters plain. Even so, she made mistakes and was forced to unpick and begin again. But it was getting colder every day, so there was real urgency. She knitted hour after hour, long after her fingers were stiff and swollen. Now and then she couldn't help thinking: 'I used to have a job in publishing.'

When they put on the sweaters they stared at each other and collapsed in helpless laughter. Tamsin didn't know why she'd gone wrong, but she certainly had. Shapeless, ambisexual, they looked like survivors of an earthquake clothed from relief stocks. And that was how they continued to look, all day and ever day. After a time, it was no longer funny.

When the knitting was finished, Tamsin had nothing to do. The housework didn't take much time. Washing clothes by hand was the most laborious chore, but she did it only once a week. Her cooking was necessarily simple. She had read all the books they'd brought and started again on *The Brothers Karamazov,* but the light wasn't good enough for sustained reading. There was always the radio, but she didn't like to disturb Brian with the noise, and anyway she couldn't pick up Radio 3 and was limited to the boring Scottish service.

It was all worth while, she told herself stubbornly, if it helped Brian to write. But, as the fine autumn days and the long walks had spurred him, the cold and the darkness paralysed him. If she went into the kitchen she found him gazing vacantly at the wall, his notebook open on the table but the page blank. When he came into the other room at the end of his stint, she dreaded seeing him slump into an armchair and hearing him say: 'Sorry, no good today.'

In London, of course, Tamsin had realized that he didn't write all the time. But being so close to him, being aware that he wasn't writing, was different. Was he pursuing an idea that might become a poem, or wasn't he? It was exasperating not to know.

'Brian,' she said at last, 'what's the trouble?'

He gave her his thin smile, the smile of a boy caught out in an evasion, and said: 'You mean, no poems?'

'No poems, it seems.'

'I can't write to order. You know that.'

'Who's ordering you? You want to write, surely.'

'I don't know.'

Tamsin felt the touch of fear.

'What d'you mean, you don't know?'

'I don't think I ever *want* to write. There are times when I must write – I'm driven to it. It happens, or it doesn't happen.'

'Yes, I see that. But I did think that living here would cause it to happen more often – more naturally.'

'I thought so too,' Brian said in a flat voice.

'It must be the winter. This bloody darkness.'

'You think it's that.'

'What else could it be?'

'It could be that the darkness is in me.'

'Oh no – no!'

She knelt by his chair and seized his hands.

'I believe in you, Brian. You're a poet. It has to be true. Otherwise everything's false, everything's meaningless.'

After this flash of drama their life continued undramatically, without triumph or disaster. Brian produced a poem. He worked steadily for several days, covering pages of his notebook, more like a prose writer than a poet. The poem was, unusually for him, a long one. Secretly, Tamsin didn't think it was very good. (Secretly – she hated to hide her thoughts from him.) She suspected that it had been written for her sake and not out of his own need; it wasn't real, in the same sense as his other poems. But it was accepted and brought in a welcome cheque.

By now, to save fuel, they were spending twelve hours or more in their sleeping-bags. Nothing broke the silence except the noise of the wind. There was a fierce wind almost every day and every night – sometimes carrying rain, sometimes snow, sometimes the one mobile element in a clear sky, but always persisting with an inexhaustible cosmic energy. Living in the lonely house was like being a ship, not so much voyaging as seeking to survive in a vast dark ocean.

One night, the usual noise was varied by a sudden clattering.

'Christ!' Brian said. 'What's that?'

'Tiles coming off the roof, could it be?'

In the morning they found the tiles, six of them, on the ground behind the house. It was impossible to put them back; they didn't know how, they couldn't climb up the sheer wall of the house, and they had no ladder. Anyway, three of the tiles were broken. It began to rain – the pitiless Scottish rain, as cold as snow. Almost at once, it seeped through the ceiling. They hadn't even a bucket to catch it, and had to use saucepans which soon filled up. By evening it was still raining. They abandoned the bedroom and carted the beds downstairs.

Tamsin went to see the factor – another trip to Tongue.

'I'm sorry, but the estate has no obligation. It's a repairing lease.'

'How do you mean?'

'You're responsible for repairs. After all, you're only paying a pound a month. But somebody will do it for you. There's plenty of handymen all round these parts.'

She took the bus back and consulted Macbeth. There were no handymen, he said. The last tiler had gone off to Aberdeen, to work for steady wages, five years ago.

'Your man will have to look to his repairs. It's what we all do.'

His advice was to use tiles made of rubberoid. You could nail them to the roof-frame – it didn't require any skill, he implied. 'I suppose ye've no ladder?'

She admitted this. With an air of pitying resignation. Macbeth agreed to lend his ladder. She didn't dare to confess that they had no hammer or nails, so she bought them at the shop along with the rubberoid tiles. These were shoddy-looking things, made of some sort of plastic composition and a bilious green in colour. Tamsin remembered having seen them on garden sheds in the London suburbs and felt that they were an insult to the old house.

As soon as Brian clambered on to the roof, several more tiles clattered down. Nailing on the rubberoid, with freezing hands and in lashing rain, took him a long time. The stuff cracked and split; the roof-frame, made of oak apparently, was very hard; he dropped the nails and Tamsin had to hunt for them. It got dark before he'd finished and he had to return to the job next day. In the end the house looked merely patched, provisionally rescued from its sad inevitable decline.

Christmas came. Turkeys cost more in Scotland than in London, like everything else, so Tamsin bought a chicken. There was no bottle of wine because the weather was rougher than ever, and she convinced Brian that it would be stupid to walk to the shop. Christmas was only a formality, they'd always said; for the last three years they had spent it with Robert and Dorothy and considered it a bore. Yet they felt the emptiness of this Christmas. They couldn't even listen to carols because the radio had run down.

Then the real winter set in. What they'd had so far, they realized, had been merely a warning. The winds raged and howled, battering at the house, which seemed to suffer mutely like a living thing – like a tree, or like some big clumsy animal far from shelter. One couldn't even tell the direction of the winds; they were a riot, an elemental chaos. Snow fell incessantly, all day and all night. The flakes whirled about in the gusts and eddies, carried upward as much as down. But each flake did in the end escape from the tumult and sink to the ground.

Brian and Tamsin wore their ungainly sweaters, their gloves and two pairs of socks all the time, and didn't undress to go to bed. In the house they were like people trapped by street-fighting, preferring to be imprisoned than to risk venturing out. The moment the door was opened, the wind burst in with a boom of triumph and swept snow into the room. More tiles were torn off the roof, including new rubberoid tiles, and couldn't be found. It was out of the question to make repairs while the blizzard kept on. The firewood stacked behind the house was invisible under a load of snow. They cleared it and carried it indoors. The stream was frozen, and when Brian attacked the ice with the hammer he found it solid to the bottom. For water, they had to use melted snow.

On the fourth day, the winds abruptly ceased. The silence was strange, almost disturbing, like the silence when a familiar piece of machinery is switched off. And everything looked different, for the snow had hidden all that had made the moor look rough and uneven – the tufts of earth, the cleft of the stream, the scattered rocks. The whole plateau was smooth and level in its unbelievable whiteness, beautiful certainly, but as feature-less as a desert. It seemed to have been raised and remade. The house, with snow to the ground-floor windows, looked as though it had been sunk into a pit when it was first built.

The road was hidden, too. Tamsin stood in the doorway – Brian was still in bed – and tried to trace it, mostly by memory. It was a Monday morning; the post van was due in another hour. She supposed that it was someone's job to clear the road, now that the blizzard was over. But she and Brian were responsible for the track, about fifty yards long, between the road and the house. She fetched a spade, one of the few tools left behind by the previous tenant, and set to work, glad to have a positive task after the days of blank waiting and mere survival.

The day passed in the same uncanny silence. The post van, of course, didn't come; nor was there any sign of the road being cleared.

The next day, again, nothing happened. It was the butcher's day, and already the baker was a day overdue.

'Brian, I'm getting worried,' she said.

'About what?'

'We don't actually know if they clear this road, do we?'

'Oh, they must.'

'Well, it's not a very important road.'

'How much food have we got?'

'A few tins. The bread's going stale.'

By Thursday, there was no coffee for breakfast and they were eating their last slices of bread, stiff as rusks.

'I'll walk down to the shop,' Brian said. 'I've got to, haven't I? It's not a bad day – it might snow again tomorrow.'

'All right. I'll come.'

'You stay here, Tam. It's going to be quite tough.'

'I don't want to stay here by myself.'

'Let's make a start, then. We don't want to be coming back in the dark.'

They took the spade. In some places it was possible to walk, or rather take single laborious steps, sinking each foot into the snow and heaving it out again. In other places they had to dig out a path. The snow had frozen hard; it was like attacking blocks of ice. Once, they lost the road and found themselves walking on the moor. By the time they were over the saddle and in sight of Macbeth's house, half the short day had gone.

Tamsin said: 'We'll never make it to the shop and back again in time. Let's see if the Macbeths can help us out.'

Macbeth was smoking a pipe after finishing an excellent lunch, of which the remnants were on the table and the smell lingered in the room. He was in shirtsleeves and a waistcoat; Lady Macbeth wore a thin house-coat over her dress. It was astonishing to see people taking warmth for granted – a coal fire glowed tranquilly – and dressed for indoor comfort.

'Food?' Macbeth said, eyeing Brian like a bank manager considering an overdraft. 'Did ye no have a stock of food?'

'I'm afraid not.'

'Ye'll be needing a stock of food in winter.'

'We thought the road would be cleared.'

'Did ye now? It's only yesterday they cleared the road to Tongue.'

Macbeth slowly folded a piece of paper, touched it to the fire, and relit his pipe.

'Ah well, wife, what can we do for these poor folk?'

To be despised by Macbeth – it was hard to take. Tamsin saw Brian give his quick vulnerable smile. But, from Macbeth's point of view, it was mere childishness to come to Sutherland and invite cold and hunger. The wild north wasn't his dream; it was the situation dealt to him by life. He accepted it on terms – the terms being electricity and television, his well-maintained and insulated house, his car, his coal fire. Without these he would have gone away, as other crofters had gone away.

A few days later, the snow melted and the vans came again. So did the post, for which they were waiting restlessly; Brian had sent off two poems before Christmas. When the post van came in sight, Tamsin rushed to meet it. It brought a delayed Christmas card and two rejection slips.

The winter went on. She had imagined that it would be beautiful here, with high clear skies, crisp healthy air, and the constant vision of the snowy landscape. There were days like that, but only rare days, intervals amid every kind of bad weather: harsh stormy winds, rain, more heavy snowfalls, and sometimes dense fog. The only certainty was that it was always cold. 'Another bloody awful day' – neither Brian nor Tamsin tried to hide a dull, dragging gloom. So much was ahead of them, too. Spring came late in the north; they would be cold until April, probably May.

Brian was writing less than in London – almost nothing. A few poems came from him laboriously, without any feeling of joy or triumph, nor even confidence. Sometimes he scrapped them and sometimes he sent them off, but he knew and Tamsin knew that none of them was really good.

It was harder for him to write here, after all, not easier. Brooding in isolation didn't lead him to an intense and concentrated use of his powers, but merely to a tormented desperation. In London he sat at his work-table as long as the writing went well, and when the difficulties were too great he had lines of escape. Here, hemmed in by the cruel weather, he was denied relief when he was void of ideas, when his efforts had crumbled into failure, when he could only think of why he had failed and wonder how long it would be before hope returned. He was unremittingly face to face with himself in the sad grey light or in the darkness. She hadn't sufficiently imagined what that must mean for someone who depended on the unpredictable, the never-assured moment of creation.

So she had been wrong, she had simply been wrong. The failure wasn't caused by the unexpected problems and hardships, but by the falsity of the whole idea. And the idea had been hers, so the blame was hers.

They must go back to London, she decided, and the sooner the better. If she had injured Brian, she could at least make some recompense. She didn't know where they would live (the flat must have gone) or how they would live. But they would manage, for naturally she would work.

She was determined not to let Brian think that they had to leave Scotland because he hadn't written much. No – she must convince him that she was the one who couldn't stand the cold, lonely house any longer. But in any case there was a solid and indisputable reason why they had to go: they were running out of money. She hoped that Brian would see this as a matter of high expenses, not of low earnings. The fact was, she saw when she looked at her account, that they hadn't enough for the train fares to London. They couldn't very well hitch-hike in winter. Much as she disliked the idea, she supposed that they would have to borrow for the journey from Brian's parents.

Now that she had made the decision, she found herself strangely reluctant to speak of it to Brian. It might be a relief to him – but then, it might be a blow. It was possible that he had reconciled himself to the lonely life more tranquilly than she knew, and that he looked forward to a burst of achievement in the summer. She wasn't sure what he thought in the silent hours. She hadn't in reality come closer to him, she reflected sadly – perhaps the contrary.

In the darkness of the evening, kneeling in front of the fireplace, she suddenly began to cry. The immediate reason was that she had failed to get the fire to burn, she had no more newspapers, and they would have to face the cold with the smelly cheerless paraffin stove. But that had happened before. She was weeping for the death of her hopes.

He knelt beside her and put his arm round her.

'Come on, Tam. Look at me.'

She obeyed, wiping her eyes with the rough wool of her sweater.

'We've got to give up. Is that it?'

She said nothing.

'That's what you want to say, isn't it?'

'Oh, my God, Brian, I feel so bad about it. I can't carry on, I just can't. I thought it wouldn't matter – the cold and all that – so long as I was with you. But I can't take it, after all.'

'Don't cry, Tam, please.'

'I'm crying because I've failed you.'

He held her firmly and let her rest on him with her face pressed against his shoulder. He was the strong one, betrayed by her weakness but forgiving her. That wasn't true ... she knew it wasn't, and when he was face to face with himself he would know. But she hoped that he would believe it while they carried through their retreat.

Perversely, painfully, their last days in Scotland were lovely: the skies clear, the air sharp and pure, the sunlight brilliant on the snow-tipped mountains. The road, waterlogged since the last thaw, dried out in hard frosts. They went for long walks every day. But they went for walks because Brian didn't try to write, so they could persuade themselves that they were having a holiday. They had made no mark here; the Macbeths would soon cease to think of them.

When they crossed the saddle for the last time and left the plateau as undisturbed as they had first seen it, they didn't dare to look back.

3

Sometimes she doesn't come for weeks, but when she does come we are exactly where we were before. We lie on the bed together and escape from time. Any words (but we are beyond words) that submit us to the measure of time are equally true or equally untrue. We have no future . . . we are already living in our future . . . we are still living in our past. We cannot grow old . . . we are already old. We can neither lose nor increase what can with equal truth be called our resignation or our contentment or our despair: at all events, our understanding.

The bed is cheap and hard, like all the beds we ever had. The room is small, like all our rooms. I touch her pale cheeks in silence, in grey light or in darkness. Our clothed bodies lie side by side in calm endurance, as they did in the house in Scotland.

In that house, I began to understand. By bringing me there Tamsin made me her supreme gift, although she couldn't know what it was, and indeed it was the opposite of what she intended. I discovered my true nature and set the course of my life. I had imagined, and Tamsin had believed with perfect faith, that my vocation was to write poetry. I learned, that winter, that it was to fail to write poetry.

At the time, it was a terrible discovery. I could do nothing for weeks but sit at the table – my work-table, as it should have been – numbed by the cold and frightened by the wolf-howl of the wind, shuddering with misery and shame, feeling the blood seep from the wound. I had lost everything, I thought; I was reduced to zero, to non-existence. The memory, even now, is like the memory of a death – my own death.

But then I looked back, as the grown man looks back to childhood, at the man who had travelled hopefully to Scotland – the poet. What I thought I was losing, I had never really possessed. I had been able to write poems, and some of them were good. But I had always written reluctantly, with a crushing effort, with persistent doubts, driven and subdued by the task. I understood that the doubts were the truth; the effort was a violence against my real self.

So I dedicated myself to my vocation: the vocation of failure. A hollow and sterile negation, I thought at first. But once I accepted it, I saw what was positive in this vocation of stillness, of silence, of endless persistence without triumph and loyalty without reward. It was given to me to do, clear-eyed, what other men merely stumble into doing, or vainly struggle against because they cannot bear the knowledge. And I began, in those cold and lonely days in Scotland, to be a success at being a failure.

When we came back to London, I was tempted to renounce my vocation. Not to resume the illusion of writing – that was finished – but to be drawn into some other career: to become a teacher or a doctor or an architect, or whatever. I could have studied again and qualified myself. There are grants; Robert would have backed me with considerable relief; Tamsin likes working, or she did then. Or I could simply have got a job. Jobs can be found by presentable inoffensive young men with arts degrees, and at the time I had friends. The BBC is full of ex-poets.

That was the easy way out. I'm proud that I rejected it. I was faithful to myself.

I could say nothing of this to Tamsin. She couldn't have accepted it then; she had believed in me as a poet so much more firmly than I had believed in myself. She imagined that she was there to help me, to encourage me as I wrote, to wield the lash of hope. She had all the qualities for doing that – for the poet whom she had married, she was the perfect wife. And now, as I renounced the achievement that she longed to share with me, she was my judge. She could never be my enemy but she was my opponent: the opponent of my failure.

Yet I was sure that what bound us together, for the whole of life, was something truer than hope. In the end she would understand what I understood; we should cease to be opponents and be the guardians of our strange, secret knowledge. She would have to arrive at the understanding of her own accord – to be told was useless. I didn't know then that she would first have to leave me, but if I had foreseen that I should have accepted it, as I did accept it when it happened. It hasn't divided us. We are together still, in the timeless silence of our small room; nothing can divide us.

4

When they returned to London on the overnight train from Inverness, they stayed with Robert and Dorothy for the first few days. They had the house pretty much to themselves; it was comfortable and impersonal, like a good hotel out of season. It was fun to laze in a hot bath, sleep between clean white sheets, toss their dirty clothes into the washing-machine, and adjust the central heating.

Robert and Dorothy asked a few questions about life in the northern winter, but made no comment. For them it was an episode in Brian's protracted development: rather silly, in fact a waste of time, but of course to be tolerated. They delivered no lectures – that wasn't their style – and refrained from asking what he meant to do now. Robert also refrained from offering any more money, or else didn't think of it.

Of course, Brian wanted to see Norman. At his flat – the first floor of an ample Victorian house – the atmosphere of cheerful disorder was more congenial. 'Why don't you camp out here till you've sorted yourselves out?' he said. They accepted, drawn by the promise of lively talk and the renewal of friendship. Beer-bottles were stacked on the floor; new books (review copies) waited for anyone to dip into them; people were always dropping in and staying for hours. One couldn't disturb Norman, Tamsin assumed, because he did practically no work. But she discovered that it was his choice to give this impression. Actually he got up at seven and bashed the typewriter for three hours before getting into his 'lazy' personality. He was working simultaneously on a novel, a film script, and a serial version of *Roderick Random* for TV. His system was to demand huge advances for 'research' and 'trying out ideas' and refuse to commit himself to delivery dates, while quietly getting on with the work so that

157

it could easily be knocked into final shape when necessary.

Louise, an elegant woman several years older than Norman, slept with him intermittently but never prevented him from being up at seven. It appeared that she was dividing her time between Norman and Mark, another successful writer. Neither made any exclusive claim; they were good friends, and in any case Louise's marriage still had a background existence. Her husband, a property developer, kept her in funds and hoped for her return, a possibility that she didn't altogether rule out. Did she prefer Mark or Norman? She hadn't decided and was in no hurry to decide. She and Norman discussed the question enjoyably and without intensity, often in front of Brian and Tamsin or anyone else who was in the flat, and also with Mark who dropped in now and again, to depart at a late hour either with or without Louise. She was the kind of woman that Tamsin most disliked – dependent on men but basically indifferent to them.

'What does Brian write?' Louise asked.

Tamsin replied: 'He's a poet.'

'Oh, is he? Tough on you.'

'He doesn't write TV serials, if that's what you mean.'

'Yes, that is what I mean.'

Tamsin said nothing. Louise stretched her arms – a favourite movement, revealing her well-shaped and sedulously shaved armpits – and asked: 'What do you do, then?'

'I'm in publishing,' Tamsin said. 'I'm looking for a job at the moment.'

Yes, she was looking for a job. These days of getting up late, sitting about the flat, drinking coffee and beer and Scotch and coffee again, chatting and gossiping – she'd soon had enough. Besides, Brian wasn't likely to write any poems here. By the time he was out of bed, the social round was beginning. But until Tamsin earned something, they couldn't get a place of their own.

She rang up Paterson's and talked to Penny. Mr Paterson had been ill and had been forced to go to the West Indies for the whole winter with his awful wife. He was virtually out of the firm and Miss Fowler was in complete command. Penny didn't think that she would have Tamsin back even if there was a vacancy, which there wasn't.

So Tamsin read the ads and applied for four jobs – none of them definable as interesting (two in non-literary publishing firms, one with an encyclopedia, and one as research assistant to a trade union) but that couldn't be helped. All sent her forms to fill in, and indicated that the interviews wouldn't be for a month or more.

'Let's go to the theatre,' Brian said. 'There's quite a few good plays on.'

'We haven't got any money.'

'Oh, that's all right.' She recognized his guilty smile. 'Norman's staked me a bit.'

'Brian, I don't like borrowing from Norman.'

'We're eating off Norman, aren't we? What's the difference? Anyway, he's loaded.'

'We owe your parents already.'

'What, for the train fare? They wouldn't think of asking for that back.'

They went to the theatre – Tamsin couldn't resist it. But she felt the urgency of getting some kind of job, and read the ads in the local paper. There was a job in a bookshop.

She was given the job readily, but it turned out to be part-time. The shop had a number of assistants, mostly wives with children at school who liked working in the mornings. Tamsin could work three weekday afternoons and all day Saturday. The pay was bad.

However, she went off straight away to find a flat. Rents in their old neighbourhood had gone up sharply; she had to settle for a very small flat with no view. Even so, the rent would take most of her earnings and there wouldn't be enough left over, on the most rigorous calculation, for food and essential spending. She took the flat, all the same. They could meet the deficit with the money Brian had borrowed from Norman – he had evaded telling her how much it was, but it wasn't exhausted and she guiltily dismissed the idea of early repayment. Of course, she would soon get a decent full-time job. And of course Brian would write more poems. One couldn't go through life without some hopeful assumptions.

She was interviewed for the four jobs, and didn't get any of them. This was depressing, not only for financial reasons but because by this time she hated the bookshop. It was a silly, pretentious place, trading in fashions that she despised – mysticism, occultism, trendy radicalism, pseudo-liberated sex books. There were few real customers; young men and girls used the shop as a meeting-place, lounged about and chatted – but not to Tamsin. She didn't fit in, somehow. Young men and girls . . . at twenty-five, she was already detached from them. She wore jeans, but she didn't wear jeans with ragged holes or strings of beads, which had conquered London without her noticing. She didn't talk by grunting and mumbling, nor could she attempt the strange new accent, with confused elements of the consciously working-class, of American and of Australian. The customers (for want of a better word) leafed through the books with dirty hands, read while they waited for their friends, and left without buying anything. They stole books, she was sure, but so cunningly that she never caught them in the act. She watched one man read a book – Sylvia Plath's poems – from cover to cover and then replace it on the shelf. When she tried saying 'Can I help you?' or

'D'you find that interesting?', she was rebuffed and her employer was annoyed. 'Don't chivvy people, I'm not running that kind of shop,' he said. It would be ironical, Tamsin thought, if she got the sack from this absurd place. Ironical, but not funny.

Anyway, she had to earn more money. She didn't know how to live, like the people she listened to in the shop, by borrowing, stealing ('ripping off', they said) and devising tales for the Social Security. It wasn't exactly that she disapproved; she didn't believe that she had the knack.

She tried again to get a job in publishing, and failed again. It was a bad time, friends said, though they didn't explain why. Presumably she would have to take any job she could get – 'general office work' was the phrase. She considered learning to type. Wherever she went she saw ads for secretaries, often at good wages. But she had been warned years ago that once you typed, you were doomed to type for ever. Anyway, she couldn't pay for the course. Or would it be right to use Norman's money? She had almost resigned herself to this when she read an ad that attracted her: 'Writer urgently needs bright young woman to help with projected book.'

She phoned. The writer said: 'Come round and let's meet.'

'What sort of book is it?' she asked.

'Oh, that's right, I didn't put my name. I'm Farrell Branston.'

'Ah, I see.'

Tamsin had never heard the name, so she went to the library and consulted *Who's Who*. Farrell Branston was a science-fiction writer, with numerous books to his credit. Tamsin was ignorant of science and never read science fiction, but she couldn't afford to be scrupulous. She took out one of his books and read it in the course of the evening.

When she rang the bell of Mr Branston's large detached house, a voice shouted: 'Come on in. It's the room on your right.'

The writer, recognizable from the book-jacket, was lying on a couch with his right leg encased in plaster.

'Excuse me not getting up. Obvious reasons. I'm going to call it skiing, but it was a car crash. Then I was breathalysed. So I can't drive for a year even when I throw my crutches away.'

'I can see why you need help.'

'Damn right. I'm in shit up to the neck. I'm getting divorced, too. My wife's a number-one bitch but I'd have postponed the bust-up if I'd known this was going to happen. Well, look, there's all this stuff to sort out.'

The room was littered with books, magazines, scientific journals, and innumerable loose sheets of paper covered with scribbled notes.

'That's the raw material. Normally I just roam about and pounce on what I need. You're going to roam and pounce for me.'

'Entomology,' Tamsin said, picking up a journal. 'I'd better be frank – I don't know the first thing about it. I took an English degree.'

'Not to worry. I can see you're bright. You've got some idea how these books get written, I expect.'

'Well, I've just been reading *The Rose-Pink Death*. I sat up half the night with it.'

'Great. Have a drink. It's over there. I'll have brandy and soda. OK, this time it's radio-guided scorpions. This bunch of revolutionaries, they programme the scorpions to bite their way through the ruling class. OK, you've guessed it, the scorpions get to communicate with each other and take over. So there's a fair amount of detail – scorpions, and radio, and politics. No problems, though. Just slog.'

'It sounds absolutely fascinating,' Tamsin said bravely.

'We're going to be friends. Cheers. Is your name Stella?'

'No, it's Tamsin.'

'That's a fine name. Stella would have been a coincidence, though. You remind me of Stella, my first wife. She too had a perfect arse. You do know you've got a perfect arse, Tamsin?'

'I must tell my husband.'

'If he hasn't told you he bloody well should have. When can you start?'

'I've got a job to get rid of. Monday, I should think. May I ask what you're going to pay me?'

'Ah, that's the bad news, I'm afraid. My overdraft is killing me. I'm paying for two wives and four kids, I've got doctors' bills, they've trebled my car insurance, and the tax man's got me by the balls. I can't actually afford to pay you at all, but it's the only way to get the bloody book done.'

So Tamsin was to be paid less than a typist. More, however, than at the bookshop. She accepted Branston's offer without trying to bargain and went home in high spirits. The job was going to be fun, she was sure. The nonsense about the scorpions amused her, and she liked Branston already.

'He says I've got a perfect arse,' she informed Brian.

'Does he? What does the job consist of, did you say?'

'Oh, I reckon it's all talk. Anyway, he's immobilized.'

The day before Tamsin was due to start her new job, she realized that she was pregnant.

Soon after they were married, she and Brian had discussed whether they should have children and decided to wait. It wasn't, as Tamsin remembered it, much of a discussion. Their sense of perfect unity and sufficiency kept them from desiring what would alter the shape of their life.

She douched and used a cap. She disliked this business – disliked the intrusion into her body of manufactured products. But she managed to take it for granted and to suspend thought while she prepared herself. It was the mundane aspect of being a woman, like having periods. It had nothing to do with herself as Tamsin, as a unique individual.

Brian, she saw, disliked the business more than she did. It interrupted what shaped itself for him as a single process, from the compact made by their eyes to the final harmony. Often she had to free herself from his arms and remind him: 'Just a minute, darling.' And sometimes they had made love 'without anything'.

It was her fault – she accepted that, since remembering the cap was her responsibility. It had happened for obvious reasons: in Scotland because she hated wriggling out of the sleeping-bag and going through the business in the cold; in London, both before they lived in Scotland and (on one occasion) since, because she was a bit drunk or not fully awake. Still, she admitted when she thought about it, there was more to it than that. Perhaps she wanted the elemental satisfaction of making love untramelled, naked to Brian within as well as without. Perhaps some deeper impulse, running counter to her conscious wishes, urged her to conceive a child.

At all events, these rare happenings – a dozen or so in over four years – left her with a memory of extraordinary joy and sweetness. In the morning, she reproached herself: she had been silly and reckless; really, it must be the last time. Yet she cherished the memory as one might cherish the traces of an elusive dream. It seemed to be unreal, in that the cap and the douche were proofs of reality. Recalling it during the day, she half-believed that she had actually dreamed it. The sense of unreality was reinforced by the fact that she didn't become pregnant. True, she hadn't been reckless often, and the commonsense conclusion was that she'd been lucky. But she began to feel that she wouldn't get pregnant unless she deliberately tried to. She knew better, of course, and yet she couldn't quite accept the notion of such a real consequence stemming from an act clouded in unreality.

Well, here she was. They were living from hand to mouth, they were in debt, Brian hadn't got back into his writing stride, she was about to start a necessary and congenial new job . . . and she was pregnant.

She was quite sure about it, since her periods had always been regular, but she went to a pregnancy advice centre for a test. Positive, as she'd expected. Mrs Dean (brisk but kindly, as suited the role) asked her what part of London she lived in.

'I'll put you in touch with an ante-natal clinic. They're pretty good in north London.'

Tamsin said with an effort: 'I'm not sure if I want to have the baby.'

'Ah.' Mrs Dean settled back in her chair, prepared to deal with this situation. 'You aren't married, dear?'

'Yes, I am, but my husband doesn't earn much and we've got a tiny flat. This wasn't planned.'

'What kind of contraception d'you use?'

'A cap. I must have skipped it once. In fact, I know I did.'

'Once is enough, isn't it? You'd be safer with the pill.'

'I thought there were health risks.'

'Oh no, those stories have been disproved. I'd definitely advise you to use the pill in future. However, that's not the problem right now, is it?'

'No.'

'Well, if you decide on a termination it's quite possible now, as I expect you know.' Abortion had just become legal – one of the few instances of fortunate timing in her life, Tamsin thought. 'But do remember, millions of women have been grateful for children that weren't planned. You needn't make your mind up just yet. You'll be discussing it with your husband, of course. Don't rush into anything, dear. You've got to be sure of your feelings. Think it over carefully, then come and see me again.'

Tamsin didn't rush into anything, but she wasn't able to think it over carefully. It was her first week of working for Farrell. The job absorbed her: not so much the job as the satisfaction of working closely with this quick-witted, energetic man. She remembered about the pregnancy only at odd times, on the bus for instance. It was still unreal. Or it was like an embarrassing secret, a problem that was irrelevant to her real life and would go away if she hoped for the best. If she had idiotically stolen something from a shop and was wondering whether she'd be prosecuted or not, she would have felt much the same, and avoided the thought in just this way.

She worked hard at the science-fiction research – darting about the room, hunting down references, filling notebooks and amassing index cards. Farrell was delighted with her; he had never tackled a project so systematically or made such quick progress, he said. She helped him to limp to his desk and he was able to type the first few pages. But they worked only in bursts, about two hours in the morning and rather less in the afternoon. Farrell really wanted company and moral support. He obviously missed his wife, though he delivered tirades against her. There was a daily help, but Tamsin found herself more or less running the house; she cooked lunch, went out to buy cigarettes and liquor, reminded him to answer letters, struggled with his chaotic accounts and told him how close he was to his overdraft limit. The rest of the time they talked, and also drank a fair amount. Farrell had never written anything but science fiction and with disarming honesty didn't consider himself 'a real writer', but he read appreciatively and his enthusiasms tallied with hers. He was gregarious in his profession and a figure in the Society of Authors, so he had stories to tell about writers whom Tamsin would have liked to know. ('We'll have a party when I get off my crutches,' he promised.) He had travelled widely, too. So he was constantly entertaining; but he treated Tamsin as a person with a life of her own – she would tell him as much or as little about it as she chose, he implied – and not merely as an audience. They were friends, in short. After only a week, she realized with grateful surprise that Farrell was the best friend she'd ever had.

She let the week go by without telling Brian that she was pregnant. He was so pleased because she had an interesting job that she was reluctant to spoil the new stability with her unfortunate problem. And the truth was that she was scared. Scared because he would say flatly that she ought to have an abortion, or scared because he might want her to have the child? She didn't know. She had no idea whether he would want her to have the child or not. They had 'waited', she supposed. The sense of being apart from him, of having to guess at his feelings, was strange and disturbing for her.

Then, in the second week after the test, the pregnancy became real. At night, when she woke out of inchoate dreams, she felt it taking hold of her. It wasn't a problem she could think about; it was an experience through which she had to pass – already an experience, even if it was to be curtailed. She could compare it only to the terrible illness at Tangier. It was as intense as that, rendering her alone and helpless, piercing to the heart of her existence. But if it was comparable to the illness in its mysterious power, it was also the direct opposite. Instead of knowing what it was to die, she knew now what it was to feel alive to the point of exaltation, to be possessed by the creation of life.

She stirred Brian to make love to her while she was in this state – in the middle of the night, in the sweet dreamy way, without her cap (this didn't seem to tell him anything). It was wonderful, more wonderful than ever before. If she went on with the pregnancy she would have months of this, she thought. She felt a great continuance between making love like this and what was growing within her body. In the morning she told herself: if I'm going to put a stop to this I'd better do it while I still can.

One evening, Brian said: 'What's going on, Tam?'

Absurdly, she blushed. She had been miles away, not really thinking but floating into her secret experience.

'I can see there's something,' he said. 'Some great new plan?'

'Certainly not a plan. There is something, though. I'm pregnant.'

He was simply amazed.

'D'you know, that just never occurred to me.'

They discussed it; that was clearly what they had to do. Indeed, they
discussed it for hours. But the discussion, she felt, was somehow beside
the point. Either having the child was a fulfilment of desire and need,
joining them beyond all possibility of doubt like their first need to live
together – and this they would have known in a moment – or it was
not.

She said: 'Frankly, you've never seen yourself as a father, have you?'

'Have you ever seen me as one?'

'No.'

'I don't look beyond the togetherness of you and me – changeless, an
eternal present tense. When we make love, it's to renew and preserve
that. It's not to leave in you any perpetuation of myself. I don't have
that kind of pride.'

'I see.'

'I've answered your question, Tam. I haven't tried to tell you what to
do.'

'Oh, sure.'

There was a short silence. Then she said: 'Well, from the practical
point of view...'

From this point of view, the position was clear enough. It was to be
hoped that Tamsin could go on working for Farrell, maybe for years –
she had kept the far less enjoyable job at Paterson's for three years,
after all – provided that he wanted her when he was off his crutches.
If he didn't, they would still need money and she would have to find
another job. Brian couldn't very well write poetry in the little flat
unless they paid somebody to look after the child. And they couldn't
afford to, on her likely earnings and his irregular cheques.

The next day, Tamsin phoned Mrs Dean to say that she wanted an
abortion. She was directed to a hospital to have her blood-pressure
tested, and this and that. While she waited, it came to her mind that she
had told Brian nothing about the experience of being pregnant, the
peculiar sense of intensity and enrichment. He hadn't asked, had he? He
hadn't said that if she wanted to have the child he would match his
determination to hers . . . he would get a job, they would manage
somehow...

But it was too late to think about that now.

'Would you come this way, please?'

Tested, booked in and committed, she decided to be sensible. Could she have really chosen, for the sake of an emotional experiment, to stop Brian writing poetry, give up working for Farrell, and reduce her life to a commonplace pattern, like her sister's? Of course not. Ridiculous.

She was obliged to spend three days in the hospital. With legalized abortion a novelty, they weren't risking possible ill-effects and press publicity. Brian phoned Farrell to say that she had 'flu. The doctor was jovial, the elderly ward-sister was elaborately polite, and the nurses were off-hand, impressing on her that she wasn't really ill. A woman in the next bed grumbled aggressively: 'Suppose we're going to get the hospitals crowded out with these abortions. Nobody thought about that, did they? Been waiting a year to get my hernia done, I have.' There was one other abortion case: a muddled, frightened schoolgirl who sobbed incessantly. Tamsin consoled her. Ironically amused by her unaccustomed role as pioneer of women's rights, she had no time to examine what she felt about her own abortion . . . or managed not to.

'I missed you,' Brian said.

'It's stupid, having to stay in all that time. Well, thank God it's over. I'll be going on the pill now, by the way.'

Farrell also said: 'I missed you.'

'I'm sorry. It was such a nuisance. There's a lot of 'flu about.'

She sat down at the desk and began to go through her notes. Farrell lit a cigarette and watched her. After a few minutes, he said: 'You've been having an abortion, right?'

She closed a notebook slowly, stared at him, and asked: 'How the hell did you know that, Farrell?'

'I've paid for a few in my time.'

'But is it that easy to see that a woman's had an abortion?'

'It is if one's really interested in women, I suppose.'

'How?'

'I should say by her air of disappointment.'

Tamsin started to laugh. But to her surprise, she found that she was crying.

5

After she stopped working for Farrell, she had her hair cut short and started to wear a dress instead of jeans. The idea of the dress, in the first place, was that she was looking for a new job without much confidence and thought it might help at interviews. When she got the job it didn't matter what she wore, since she worked in a small office by herself and her employer wasn't interested in her appearance, nor in anything else about her except her efficiency. But she had no wish to go back to jeans. They represented what she had relinquished: youth, freedom, and hope.

The job was with a press-cuttings agency. Every morning, Tamsin was confronted by a stack of newspapers of whose existence she hadn't dreamed, such as the *Northern Echo* and the *West Lancashire Gazette*. Her task was to search for mentions of people who subscribed to the agency. The item had to be clipped, pasted to a slip giving the newspaper and the date, and sent to the subsciber.

She had a card-index of subscribers, but she was soon able to remember dozens of them and anticipate their names in the appropriate columns. There were politicians, sportsmen, actors and actresses, and also writers. It was curious for her to be so well-informed, considering that she and Brian had never been more than occasional newspaper readers. She looked forward to Thursdays, when *The Times*, the *Guardian* and the *Daily Telegraph* had book reviews. When one of her favourite writers had a new book out, she knew at once and went along to the library. She wasn't above being interested, too, when one of these writers was cited for divorce or found guilty of drunken driving. In an odd way, she had a kind of acquaintanceship with the people about whom Norman and

Farrell had told intimate stories. She would never meet them now, but she kept up with them.

Now and then, there was an item about a poet who had been a friend. He was giving readings, or he'd won a prize, or he'd made a challenging speech at a conference. She and Brian seldom saw any of these former friends. The winter in Scotland had made a break which proved to be final. She had the addresses because of her work, and when she saw the names in press stories she thought of getting in touch, but she didn't. What would have been the use? Of course, she never mentioned to Brian that So-and-so had won a prize.

After two years at the agency, she never thought about looking for a different job. She didn't mind the routine so much as she had minded the routine at Paterson's. That had been her first job, and she had regarded it as a stage on the way to something better. But now she had no such illusions. It wouldn't be much use applying for a job at a good publishing house and presenting credentials from a cuttings agency. Actually, she had landed this job only at the end of several weeks of unemployment and financial strain. So it made sense to resign herself to staying.

Farrell Branston was not among her subscribers, but she came across his name quite often as she scanned the papers. She knew that she would never see him again. It was strange that she had counted on being his assistant and his friend for a long time.

He had kept her on, as she'd hoped, when his leg was mended: for one reason, because he was banned from driving and needed her to drive him about. It was summer, he was keen to get into the open air after being cooped up, and so they used to go off for a day in the country, happily tramping about and discussing new twists in the scorpion plot. She enjoyed these days; she enjoyed, even more, the days she spent in his house, days pleasantly divided between work and talk. The house had become a second home for her. She understood later that she fitted only too well into it and into his life, and this was just why what she took to be their friendship couldn't last.

'You know I'm in love with you, don't you?' he said all of a sudden.

He chose a moment that must have seemed to him not only favourable but natural. She was pretty well defenceless, for they were both sitting on the couch which he'd used as a day-bed while his leg was in plaster. They had finished work, she could have gone home but hadn't, and they'd had a couple of drinks. Yet she was taken completely by surprise. No doubt, her surprise – her naïveté – would have seemed to most people more remarkable than his attack.

An attack it was, sure enough. He was all over her in a matter of seconds, pressing her down on the couch, planting kisses on her, ripping her blouse open. She at once recognized this kind of determination and confidence in sweeping aside any resistance, though she didn't reflect until afterwards that she recognized it because of Keith.

She fought – she really fought. She felt it to be outrageous that Farrell didn't even propose to talk her into bed, but to strip her and fuck her right there on the couch. After punching him hard on the mouth, she managed to get free and dash to the door.

Farrell took a swig of her drink – his had been knocked over – and said: 'Right, we've had the scrap. Now you listen to me, Tamsin. You've got a man in love with you. You're not a kid, you know what love is. It's the genuine bloody article, I assure you. It's all yours. So don't pass it up, my angel.'

'You're making a big mistake, Farrell.'

'Oh no, I'm not. I've made my mistakes, but this is the one that can't go wrong. You're for me and I'm for you.'

'You're imagining it. It's out of the question. It's impossible.'

'Nothing's impossible. That's what love's all about. Don't raise problems, Tamsin, they're irrelevant. You just get yourself headed in the right direction and everything else'll sort itself out.'

'Oh, stop it,' she said. 'I'm going.'

'Not yet you aren't. We've just started this.'

He moved toward her. She grabbed her handbag and raced out to the street.

On the way home, she decided that she had been silly to take the job with Farrell, or anyway to stay after he got off his crutches. She had been misled by the ease of their friendship, but that was just what ought to have told her that she would suit him nicely as a mistress. And clearly he wasn't a man to be content with a wistful might-have-been, like Mr Paterson. She was angry when she thought of the casual, jovial crudity of his assault – a caricature of the boss grabbing his secretary. Yet she didn't rule out, or didn't want to rule out, the possibility that Farrell was really in love with her. She would never know. It would be like him to claim to be in love, and indeed to convince himself of it, when he wanted a woman as much as he'd undoubtedly wanted her. She wasn't sure what he meant by love . . . or what anyone meant.

Anyway, Farrell would have required her to be in love with him. He would have demanded the central place in her life. Which was impossible, because of Brian. Or more exactly, perhaps, because of Farrell's dismissal of Brian as a minor irrelevance. 'Everything else'll sort itself out' – by that he'd meant, presumably, that she could either leave Brian, or stay married to Brian and be Farrell's mistress, whichever arrangement she preferred. That was when she had felt a spasm of disgust, felt the whole situation to be no longer menacing but simply demeaning. Until that moment, she had been hoping to restore their friendship – they would have another drink, they would laugh about his pardonable try-on. But when he said that, she had to get out.

As soon as she got home, she wrote a letter giving up her job. She told Brian that Farrell had suddenly decided to go abroad. She was fairly sure that Brian guessed what had happened, but he didn't say anything. To her relief and amusement, soon afterwards she read in a newspaper that Farrell had gone abroad.

Two years later, in the deadened peace of her little office at the cuttings agency, she still missed her last interesting job, missed her last friendship – missed Farrell. She would have liked Brian to thank her because she'd turned down the chance to be Farrell Branston's mistress for the sake of her marriage. Her marriage to Brian . . . she had begun to wonder, as she could never have wondered before, just what it was. It was sad, certainly, that she could think of 'marriage to Brian' and no longer of total and unquestioning identity.

Brian had stopped writing altogether. For Tamsin this was a disaster, since the reality of Brian as Brian, and therefore the merging of her life with his, had been of a single piece with his writing. But there was a disaster beyond the disaster and a sundering beyond the sundering. She didn't understand why he had ceased to write – didn't begin to understand how such a thing could be possible. Nothing that he said explained it, or helped her to accept it.

He said: 'It's pointless to write unless you write the very best. When you think of it, out of all the millions of poems that have ever been written only a few really matter. I mean, the poems that enrich the world. You know the difference. Those poems aren't a few degrees better than other poems, they're of another nature. And the others, ultimately, aren't worth having. Do you want me to write poems to add to the heap? I can do it any time, but it's of no value to me or to anyone else.'

'But surely,' Tamsin said, 'poets don't know whether what they're writing will enrich the world or not. They simply write.'

'Either they reconcile themselves to the valueless, which I won't. Or they feel the power of true achievement. I don't feel that now.'

'You have to write, Brian. That's how the power comes.'

'Try and try again, like the spider?'

'You used to.'

He stared at her for a moment, and then said: 'It could be that my achievement won't be poetry at all.'

'What else, then?'

'Silence.'

This frightened her. She could see nothing in it but a blank resignation or a consoling delusion. And it was meaningless, really. If silence was what had to be overcome, how could it be an achievement?

'You'll get over this,' she said. 'Don't think about how your poems rank – think about being a poet. You can't lose that, Brian. It's in you. It's got to come out again.'

But, although she went on saying this, the truth was that she was saying it to herself.

So there was a dull vacancy in their life, which had been so complete and ardent. Tamsin seldom thought of Brian while she was at work. Why should she be drawn to think of him, when he wasn't writing? She didn't exactly know what he did all day, and avoided asking him. He spent a good deal of the time with Norman and Louise and their crowd, she suspected. In the evenings and weekends, they didn't talk as they had before. He seemed to be cultivating his silence. Sitting in the same small room with him, and lying in bed with him, she was nevertheless apart from him, condemned to her bleak disappointment and her lonely incomprehension.

They didn't make love so often. This she took to be another expression of his silence, if that meant all abstention from giving himself. She was hurt and depressed, but she knew that it would do more harm than good to make sexual passion the rescuing bond. Like that, the essential intimacy could be lost for ever. The too frequent surging of her physical demands was a nuisance to her. If she'd allowed it to rule her life, she thought, she would have married Keith, or been Farrell's mistress.

If it had to be like this, she told herself, it had to be. She still had her marriage to Brian, whatever it had become; without it, she would have nothing. She hadn't married him on the condition of his success, nor on the condition of knowing what they must endure together. She hadn't married him for happiness. She hadn't married him from choice at all.

Once a month or so, they spent Sunday with Brian's parents. Robert was averse to intervening in the lives of adult people, and didn't feel responsible for his son, but as usual he was concerned for Tamsin.

'You're still doing that stupid job?' he asked her. They were sitting in the garden after a solid lunch. Brian had volunteered to wash up; he was always ready to do that kind of chore, perhaps as a defence against the charge of idleness (and idleness, Tamsin certainly granted, was too simple a label). Dorothy, summoned by pressure on the pound, was at the Treasury.

'Oh yes,' she answered, 'I don't mind it.'

'It's a rotten life for you. Why can't Brian have a job?'

'Brian?' Tamsin had never considered this.

'Well, we don't hear of a lot of poetry being written.'

'No. He's in a bad patch.'

'One's got to do something. I can't understand a man doing nothing.'

'Ah, but you're doing a job you enjoy. What sort of job d'you think Brian ought to do?'

'I don't know. There are jobs. He could try a press-cuttings agency. Fair's fair. You could write poetry.'

Tamsin started to laugh.

'No, seriously, d'you mean you've never put it to him?'

'I never have. You can if you like.'

'All right, I will.'

Tamsin distrusted the idea. She was afraid that it might be the end of Brian's writing. They might drift into a colourless, 'respectable and responsible' middle age, in which even the memory of their hopes would be blandly effaced.

On the other hand, most poets had jobs. Eliot had worked in a bank. Brian would write again if the will and the power returned to him – it depended on that, not on time. 'I'd write poetry on Sundays if I wanted to,' Robert had remarked, unanswerably. Perhaps the job would not be the end of his writing, but on the contrary the end of his passivity. Anyway, he wasn't writing now. Scotland had done no good; Tamsin's self-sacrifice (as Robert and doubtless other people considered it, though she didn't) had done no good either. So it might be right to try anything.

Brain said: 'I'll do it if you want me to, Tam.'

'I don't know what I want. It wasn't my idea. You could try it . . . see what happens.'

'All right, then. I'll get a job.'

'It isn't so easy getting a job, mind.'

But Brian soon found one, behind the counter of a travel agency. She had expected him to try for something more intellectual – perhaps to rustle up his old contacts at the BBC and in the world of literary magazines. She was shocked by his setting his sights so low and contenting himself with the kind of job that she herself now accepted with resignation. But to Brian, no doubt, any job was the same as any other.

She didn't give up her own job, as Robert had presumably wished. They would have been where they were before, or very slightly better off. As it was, they could enjoy small luxuries – theatre seats, dinners in Soho – and go to the pub without thinking twice about it. Tamsin controlled both pay-packets, and scrupulously saved three pounds a week.

When they came in from work, they asked each other dutifully: 'What sort of a day did you have?' This wasn't a success, for Tamsin's day was always the same and Brian wanted to forget his. He got on all right with the boss and the rest of the staff, he said, but the customers were a trial. They asked endless questions, but expected him to arrange everything in five minutes; they demanded the perfect holiday, and then complained about the prices as though he'd personally fixed them. Tamsin saw that he found the job taxing, even exhausting. He didn't have her knack of working methodically, of combining indifference with efficiency.

However, he got up at the same time every morning, he shaved and brushed his hair, and he got used to wearing a tie and the Marks and Spencer suit which had been the necessary investment in the job. There were days when she had an impulse to weep at the completeness of his submission. She was losing the real Brian, her Brian. But then, she had been losing him inexorably for years. Sometimes she hoped that pegging away at the job would give him a kind of pride. That was what she got from pegging away at her job, after all. But sometimes she wanted him to rebel.

'D'you hate the job, honestly?' she asked.

'No, I don't hate it. I can't say I love it, of course. You don't love your job, Tam.'

'If you want to chuck it, I shan't complain.'

'No, no. I'm not going to do that.'

Then she came home one afternoon and found that he was already in the flat. He was wearing his old sweater. Time had run back; she didn't know whether she was glad or sorry.

He gave her his guilty-schoolboy smile and said: 'I've got the sack.'

'Why?'

'Oh, I made a muddle. This chap had booked tickets and I never got them for him. I must have written it down on a bit of paper and lost it. I don't remember. Well, he came in for the tickets and I hadn't a clue. He's supposed to fly to Ibiza on Saturday, but the flights are all full.'

'So they've sacked you?'

'Yes, on the spot.'

'Well, fuck them. You can get another job. Let's go to the pub.'

She was determined to treat this setback as a minor incident, indeed as a joke. Nobody was suffering, not even the customer – he would be sent somewhere else, and for such customers one beach was like another. Brian had been given his week's wages, so they got rather drunk in the pub. Yet she wished that he'd quit the job. She couldn't help remembering that she had never got the sack.

'Listen,' she said a few days later, 'you don't have to get another of those boring jobs. Look around a bit more. We've got some money saved.'

But in the weeks that followed she half-regretted saying this. He applied for 'interesting' jobs – in publishing, and as a lecturer at a polytechnic – went to interviews, and was rejected. Trying to become a lecturer was obviously hopeless, she could see, since he had a pass degree and no teaching experience. He amused himself in the evenings by reading the ads and picking out the most extraordinary jobs . . . Professor of Statistics at the University of Fiji, Appeals Organizer for the British Leprosy Association, Curator of the Agricultural Implements Museum. The search was becoming a fantasy. The savings, of course, dwindled.

All of a sudden, he got a job – and, marvellously, a very good job. Like most good jobs, it landed in his lap by luck, thanks to a chance meeting in an afternoon drinking club (she hadn't realized that he went to afternoon drinking clubs, but never mind) with a man called Bill Fairbairn who had been at university with them. Fairbairn had gone into public relations and now had his own firm. One of his 'ideas men', he told Brian, had just been stolen by a rival. It was infuriating; you thought you could trust somebody, you regarded him as a friend, and he left you flat.

'Hey, you wouldn't like to give it a whirl, Brian, would you?'

'I don't know anything about public relations.'

'That's great. I need somebody who doesn't know anything about PR. A critical eye, questioning the fundamentals. A totally fresh vision.'

What most impressed Bill, so Tamsin gathered, was that Brian had done nothing but write poetry since they'd been students. Brian didn't mention that he was looking for a job, still less that he'd been sacked from a travel agency. As Bill – a man of impulses, and at this point by no means sober – saw it, Brian would be doing him a favour by condescending to work for him.

'You married Tamsin? Sure I remember Tamsin. Fantastic girl. I say, how's she going to react to you getting into PR? Very high-minded girl, I always thought.'

'I'll have to talk to her about it,' Brian said gravely.

The job, once Brian started it, was certainly quite different from the travel agency. There were no fixed hours; he seldom got up until Tamsin had left the flat. He went to the office in his old sweater. Discussions, among the staff or with clients, took place over long lunches or drinking sessions. If Tamsin phoned the office during the day, Brian generally wasn't there.

The salary wasn't very high by PR standards, apparently, but to Brian and Tamsin it was startling, and it was likely to be increased 'assuming everything pans out', as Bill put it. Although Tamsin wasn't preoccupied with social justice, she reflected that Brian was being paid far more than a hard-working hospital doctor. What Brian actually did to earn the money she didn't know – couldn't have explained, at all events, to the hospital doctor.

'What sort of ideas do you put up?' she asked.

'Oh . . . this "ideas man" thing, it's all part of the jargon really. Mostly I knock down other people's ideas. That seems to be my function.'

They moved to a better flat. It wasn't much bigger – what did they want with a big flat? – but it was central. In fact, Tamsin could walk to work. The flat was in a solid, old-fashioned block not far from Tottenham Court Road. It was the first time they hadn't lived in a converted house, and the quietness seemed strange.

Once again, she didn't give up her job. Her drab little office and her routine gave her a sense of continuity. There might be crazy ups and downs, but this remained.

It occurred to her that, from the financial angle, they could have a child now. But she didn't much want to. Perhaps what appealed to her was an unplanned pregnancy – the mysterious outcome of a dream-impulse – and not a planned one. Perhaps the brief, intense experience had been enough, and what Farrell called the disappointment had at some deep level seemed to her fitting, or deserved. In any case, Brian hadn't wanted a child before and presumably still didn't.

This time she didn't handle the money that Brian earned, nor indeed see much of it. He was paid monthly by cheque and the rent of the flat was paid quarterly in advance, also by cheque. She did the day-to-day shopping out of her wages, as before, and managed it easily since the rent was taken care of. There was nothing else she wanted. She bought no new clothes, and although she replaced a few worn or broken household possessions she hadn't any urge to make a more attractive home. The furniture that went with the flat was undistinguished but sufficient. She didn't try to save; she assumed that there was something left over out of Brian's ridiculous salary, but didn't know or care how much. The new luxury was not having to think about money.

They could once again afford to have dinner out and go to the theatre, but they seldom did. Brian usually came in late, and he usually came in drunk: slightly drunk, or decidedly drunk, or now and again very drunk. When he was really drunk he complained of feeling ill, said that he didn't want anything to eat, and fell asleep slumped in a chair. Once, when Tamsin had bought theatre tickets, he came in drunk at eight o'clock and had obviously forgotten all about it. She said nothing, and settled down to read. She spent many of her evenings reading.

She was irritated and sometimes disgusted by his drinking, but she didn't worry a great deal about it. Clearly, it was an aspect of being in PR. She reckoned that Brian didn't actually drink so very much, bearing in mind that he'd always had a weak head and could be knocked off balance by an amount of alcohol that would have made no visible impression on – for instance – Farrell. Emphatically, she didn't propose to nag.

But was she to be, after all, the unseen wife of an overpaid, cynical PR man with a bit of a drinking problem? No, she couldn't believe it. Rather, it seemed to her that Brian was working his way through a succession of assumed personalities: the striving poet (she had been certain that this was the real Brian, but she might have been wrong), the devotee of silence, the dutiful clerk, and now the PR man. And she had to look on; she could do nothing else.

As for the drinking, she decided that the best way to endure it was to drink too. Brian had started to buy bottles and set up a bar in the flat, on the grounds that Bill Fairbairn or someone else might drop in – though this didn't happen. They drank steadily through the weekends, giggling at silly jokes and conducting long-winded arguments, in which neither he nor she ever conceded a point but they were too lazy to get angry. It passed the time.

One evening, when he was fairly drunk, Brian tried to find an office memo which he had brought home and mislaid, and which Bill now needed. He opened drawers at random, flinging the contents on to the floor, and came to the drawer where he kept – or rather, where Tamsin kept – his poems.

'Look at all this stuff, Tam. I thought we'd got rid of it ages ago.'

'Brian, those are your poems.'

'I don't need them. What the hell use are they now? It's waste paper, just waste paper.'

He was skimming the poems across the room, like a wilful child.

Tamsin controlled herself and said: 'OK, don't make such a mess of the flat. We'll get rid of them if you like. The dustman's coming to-morrow.'

Soon afterwards, he fell asleep. She collected the poems and packed them in a cardboard box. Next day she took it to her office, and after finishing work she took the tube to Barnet, to her parents' home. She hadn't spent a single night in her old room since she'd been married. but as her parents never had guests it was still as she had left it – 'Tamsin's room' – and it still contained some art books and other bulky possessions for which she had never found space in the succession of small flats. The poems would be safe there.

But, although she hadn't looked at them for a long time, she found that being without them made a difference. The flat, already impersonal, confronted her every day with its emptiness, which was the emptiness of her life and Brian's. Nothing in it had any value or any meaning.

Their well-paid, absurd life continued. She didn't imagine that it would last for ever, but she didn't care one way or the other. In fact, it lasted for three months. Then Brian came home, earlier than usual and only slightly drunk, and said: 'Well, that's it. I shan't be working for Bill any more.'

'Won't you?'

It hadn't been clear to her – perhaps not altogether clear to him – that he was on three months' trial. Bill had chosen not to make the appointment permanent.

'What did he say?'

'He just said it hasn't panned out.'

Tamsin asked no more questions. Presumably it hadn't been sufficient for Brian to knock down other people's ideas without contributing any of his own. Or he had got drunk too obviously and too early in the day. Or he had made some ludicrous muddle – possibly, had again forgotten what he'd written on a bit of paper.

This time, he said nothing about finding a new job. Nor did she. It was understood, without words, that the experiment was over. He had proved that his most durable role was as the resigned failure, the man of silence. This she would have to accept as the real Brian. It was, after all, his achievement; he had made the final discovery of himself. It would be wrong, by trying to comfort him, to deprive him of that.

The immediate effect was that he drank more than ever. She continued to keep pace with him. At weekends she drank enough to get crazily drunk herself – why should he be the only one to escape from thinking? They would end up staggering about the flat, trying to dance to music on the radio, stumbling into the chairs, knocking things over, smashing glasses or the plates from the last skimpy meal. Sometimes Brian threw up – usually in the lavatory but once on the carpet. Then he passed out, or simply fell asleep, and she went to bed.

One Saturday, at about six o'clock – they were middling high by that time – he said: 'Sod it, that's the end of the bottle. I'll go out and get some more.'

'All right.'

He looked at his wallet. 'Can you let me have some money, Tam?'

'No, I can't. I've just got enough for the week's food.'

'Oh well, let's have some coffee.'

And that was the end of the drinking spell. Tamsin had never believed that he was likely to become an alcoholic. Not that he could have resisted it; he simply happened not to have the disposition. Besides, it wasn't necessary for him. He could be a failure without it. Cold sober, he was already withdrawn from the outer world into which he had briefly ventured.

She called at the bank and found that their account was almost down to zero. This was a relief rather than a shock; she was in charge of the finances once more. To her further relief, there was no one for Brian to borrow from. Norman had at last given up his on-off affair with Louise and had gone to live in the Bahamas to avoid paying tax.

'We'll have to move out of this flat when the quarter's up,' she said.

'OK.' Obviously, it didn't matter where they lived.

She set off on another search. Muswell Hill had become too expensive. After trying various parts of London, she found a flat they could afford (that is, she could afford) west of Shepherd's Bush. It was a shabby district, but lively, with a mixed lot of people – some who seemed to be middle-class and down on their luck, some working-class, some black. But she didn't make friends in the neighbourhood. She never had. She must have always felt that they wouldn't be staying.

In the mornings, while she dressed and made coffee before Brian was up, she looked at the flat – the shoddy furniture, the faded wallpaper, the stains on the ceiling – and wondered vaguely if she might do something to improve it. A coat of paint, or at least a couple of bright posters? But the time for that kind of effort . . . that kind of pretence . . . had gone. And the flat, if one could attribute feelings to something so lifeless as this flat, didn't seem to want any attention. The house was due to be demolished sooner or later in a road-building scheme, which struck her as fitting.

Like the flat, she wanted nothing much. Her hopes had been so far eroded that they were better abandoned than remembered. She had never cared much about pleasure or comfort or money, and if it was depressing to have so little of these, that was because doing without them no longer had any purpose. But she had begun to long for some measure of safety.

6

'Something happened today,' Tamsin said.

Brian looked at her – focusing his attention slowly, as he often did nowadays – and said: 'You've quit your job.'

'What? Why d'you say that?'

'You look pleased with yourself.'

To her annoyance, Tamsin blushed. She said: 'No, I'm not pleased with myself. And I haven't quit my job. I couldn't, not today anyway. It's Saturday.'

'Oh, is it? Well, what's happened?'

'I met Keith.'

Brian said nothing. She looked intently at him, but couldn't discern any reaction.

'I went to his flat.'

Brian still said nothing. She said, forcing the fact on him: 'We went to bed.'

I hope I don't sound pleased with myself as well as look it, she thought. Pleased . . . not at all the right word, of course; but she had been stimulated, shaken up, in a sense brought back to life. One could feel that, she supposed, at the same time as feeling confused and unhappy.

'Why are you telling me?' Brian asked.

'Why am I telling you? Where would we be if I didn't tell you a thing like this? I can't imagine it. I can't have another life outside our life. Secrets . . . lies . . . all that stuff.' Tamsin made a grimace.

'But you must have a reason for telling me. Or is simply to demonstrate your honesty?'

'That's not what I'm concerned with.'

'Then is it meant to hurt me?'

'Please, Brian...'

'Perhaps it's meant to do me good, is it?'

'No, no ...'

They argued about this until they reached a point of weary exasperation. Then Tamsin cooked a meal, which they ate in silence. She felt drained, exhausted; she went to bed long before Brian.

But all they'd talked about, she thought as she tried to get to sleep, was that she'd told him – never about what she'd told him. That was fantastic, absurd. Yet it was true.

Although she had felt tired, she found after a time that she was wakeful and tense. She was waiting for Brian – waiting to be close to him again; and actually waiting, the familiar signals of her body told her, for him to make love to her. Was she a woman who could make love with two men, casually moving from adventure to reassurance, marking the interval by a shower and a bus journey? It didn't seem possible. She was appalled by what it could reveal of herself. 'Why are you doing this?' Brian would ask.

When he got into bed, she pretended to be fast asleep.

The next day, Sunday, she said that she wanted to go for a country walk. They took the bus to Virginia Water, deliberately seeking memories of better times. Brian was almost his old self: alert and talkative, grateful for her good idea, affectionate to her. She wondered if, without intending it, she had carried out the most banal of marital exercises – letting her husband know that he mustn't take her for granted. They clung to each other and kissed under the shelter of the great trees, and as soon as they got home they made love. This was like old times, too. She felt herself enriched by the generous and healing tenderness that they had always been able to give each other when it was most needed.

What had happened the day before now seemed to her entirely unimportant. She had met Keith by pure chance, she had accepted his challenge because it couldn't harm her, she'd had a bit of fun. That was how she had realistically seen it at the time; that was what she had told Keith, in fact, thus avoiding any misunderstanding. Yes, it had been like that. And now it was over, and she could forget about it.

But she couldn't forget about it. She thought of Keith at the most unexpected moments ... thought of him while she was at work, as in the past she had thought of Brian. She thought most of all of his extraordinary confidence, his belief that by one act of love (act of sex, but to him it was an act of love) he had absolutely regained her, just as he had regained her by a kiss at Victoria Station. It wasn't over so far as he was concerned, she had to reckon.

She had the feeling that Keith was pursuing her – not exactly that, but keeping an eye on her. Ridiculous, of course, since he didn't know where she lived or where she worked. But as she walked along the street, she half-expected to see his big car stop beside her or feel his hand on her arm.

She realized that Brian's question, which she'd found so odd, had been to the point and perceptive. Why had she told him about Keith? There was no reason, if it mattered so little. Suppose she had let Farrell make love to her – would she have told Brian? Perhaps, perhaps not. She wouldn't have felt it imperatively, unquestionably necessary. Well, she hadn't given herself to Farrell; she had been instantly certain that she wouldn't. It wasn't in her nature to give herself to a man in that casual way, even when she liked him as she'd liked Farrell. Or so she had belie-ved. No, she still believed that. But then it followed that making love with Keith was important; that she hadn't begun to grasp either the causes or the consequences; possibly, that nothing could ever be the same.

She became more and more certain that she would see Keith again. One couldn't think of a man so much – want him? fear him? be obsessed by him, at all events – and not see him. It might be by chance, as before, or it might not. She read in one of her newspapers that detective agencies could trace anybody, given time and a handsome enough fee. For this article to catch her eye was chance, perhaps, but it added to her sense of inevitability. Chance, it seemed to her, was merely the word with which one disguised the inevitable. She would see Keith when her nerve had been worn down and she was ready to welcome an end to the suspense. Keith knew that, surely. What he was actually doing or planning wasn't crucial; his knowledge was.

It happened as she had imagined it. She was walking home from the tube station, and he was waiting at the corner of her street. She was so little surprised that she didn't even ask him how he'd got the address. Later, when they were married, the subject of detective agencies cropped up and she asked whether he had used one. No, he had simply told his secretary to ring up Tamsin's parents.

'You're looking lovelier than ever, my sweet.'

'Thank you,' she said calmly, but not so calmly as she intended.

'Shall we have a drink in that pub?' He was holding her arm already, of course. 'Or shall we go somewhere else? That's my car.'

'I don't mind.'

'I have plans. But let's go in the pub just for now. Looks like a nice pub.'

The pub had just opened. Keith bought drinks and steered her to a bench-seat in the corner. As soon as she sat down, he kissed her.

'Brian comes in here sometimes,' she said.

'That'll be fine. We could talk the whole thing over.'

'Arrange the transfer terms, would that be the phrase?'

Keith laughed. 'That's my Tamsin.'

'Not your Tamsin. You may not like it, but I'm Brian's wife.'

'Yes, there does seem to have been some sort of mistake. I clearly remember your deciding to be my wife.'

'A lot's happened since then.'

'Something's happend quite recently, hasn't it? Does Brian know?'

'Yes, I told him.'

'Good girl. I thought you would.'

'I told him because there's nothing I would keep from him. That's what being married to him means to me. Brian is a very special sort of person.'

'I know he is. Look, sweetheart, I'm not going to say a word against Brian. One poem he's written may be worth more than anything I'll ever do in my life. But my life isn't about writing poetry or landing on the moon or being Prime Minister or anything else. All that matters to me is loving you and making you happy.'

Tamsin couldn't help being touched. But she said: 'Do you think you could love me enough to leave me alone? I've become rather fragile, you see.'

'That wouldn't be love.'

'Not your kind of love.'

'It's a pretty good kind. Specially recommended for fragile ladies.'

'What d'you expect to achieve by stopping me in the street, Keith?'

'A lot. But at the moment, a nice evening. I've got two tickets for *The Magic Flute*.'

'If I go with you, that's all it means.'

'I said, a nice evening.'

It was a treat, no doubt of that. The music took gentle command of her and lifted her into a world of dreams, of fantasy – magic indeed – but also of illimitable serenity, of a beauty that for a time dissolved all uncertainties and anxieties. Though she didn't tell Keith this, she had never seen *The Magic Flute* before. She had been to the opera only two or three times, as a student. It didn't appeal to Brian. But she gathered, to her surprise, that Keith often went to Covent Garden. He made some knowledgeable comments on the singing, and he met people he knew in the intervals.

They went to a place that Keith knew and had dinner. Then they went to another place that Keith knew and danced. At both places he introduced her to friends. It was extraordinary to be part of a crowd, wrenched out of her quiet and friendless life. Part of Keith's crowd, part of another life that she was entitled to share: for he didn't behave as though he were giving her a treat, but as though they were living together and having an evening out. Looking at the other women, she was a little embarrassed about her cheap dress, and then ashamed of being embarrassed. Had she started to care about such contemptible things as clothes and jewellery, all of a sudden? She hadn't wanted to buy good clothes when Brian was being overpaid by Bill Fairbairn. Nor (it struck her for the first time) had Brian suggested it.

Keith drove her home at three o'clock. He had kissed and fondled her repeatedly, so she was surprised that he didn't try to take her back to his flat. It wasn't, she supposed, the purpose of this occasion. But this she saw as another sign of his confidence.

'When do I see you again?' he asked.

'I don't know. You could phone me at work.'

'Where do you work, then?'

'The Speedy Press Cuttings Agency.'

'Christ.'

'Well, that's how things are.'

What was to happen next? Presumably, a frank talk with Brian. So she hoped . . . or feared, she didn't know which.

'I suppose you were with Keith last night,' Brian said.

She had gone to work as usual, come home, and cooked a meal. They were eating fish fingers. It was like a scene from some flat realistic play. 'I suppose you were with Keith (Tom, Alan) last night' . . . how many men, she wondered, had said that to how many women?

'Yes,' she said. 'He took me to Covent Garden.'

'Oh, what did you see?'

'*The Magic Flute*.'

'A good move on his part.'

'That's true.'

Brian pushed his plate aside.

'Would you like an apple?' she asked.

'I don't think so, thanks.'

'I'll make coffee.'

He said: 'If you want to go to bed with Keith from time to time, you'll have to.'

'Is that all you've got to say?'

'What's between us is deeper than that, Tam. It doesn't depend on our being in the same bed every night. This can't change you for me. It isn't by what we do that we know each other, but by what we are.'

'And that can't change?'

'Never. You live in me, not with me. I live in you. Even when you're with Keith, that continues. It's beyond your will or mine. It's the final truth.'

'I hope so. I want to believe it. But what would you say if I told you it wasn't true any more?'

'It isn't what you say, or what you think for a time. It's still true.'

'So it doesn't depend on our being married and living together?'

'It was true before that. We got married when we understood it. If we hadn't, we should have arrived at it some other way.'

'You were pretty keen to marry me, all the same.'

'Was I? I suppose I was. At that time, I still saw truth in terms of decisions – choices.'

'Are you saying you married me to stop me marrying Keith?'

'Ah yes, come to think of it, that's how it happened.'

'I see. I never knew that.'

'For you to have married Keith would have been a denial of what you are. But to deny the truth isn't to change it.'

Tamsin poured the coffee.

'It's funny, isn't it? Keith refuses to recognize that I'm married to you. And if I'd married him, you would have refused to recognize that. It doesn't seem to matter whom I'm actually married to.'

'It matters what we know about ourselves.'

'Yes. I'll try to remember that.'

'Is Keith married, by the way?'

'No, he says he couldn't marry anybody except me.'

'He's an obstinate fellow.'

'So are you.'

'I'm not obstinate. I'm right.'

This conversation left Tamsin in a state of confusion; everyone seemed to know what to think, except her. But at least there was no question of secrets and lies. When Keith phoned, she made a date. They had dinner at a restaurant near his flat and she stayed the night with him. Brian made no comment.

So she had become Keith's mistress, while remaining Brian's wife. She could hardly believe it. It was a pattern into which she had never imagined fitting her life. Certainly it gave her very little satisfaction, and nothing remotely like happiness. She felt continually guilty, not so much toward Brian as toward herself. She was doing something that was unnatural for her; she no longer had any point of balance.

In practical terms, it was rather like being Keith's girl-friend during the few months after her return from Tangier, with similar difficulties

184

and inconveniences. Keith phoned her; or, disappointingly, he didn't phone her; or she phoned him, having to go through his office switchboard and more often than not wait because he was on another line; or he was out and she couldn't reach him. Sometimes they went out together and didn't make love, sometimes they made love in the early evening and got dressed again, sometimes they spent the night together. He had aroused in her a desire which was as passionate as in that earlier period, and yet spasmodic – a matter of moods. On the whole, the nights when they made love were not the nights when she most wanted to.

She tried at times to convince herself that she was a woman who needed a husband and a lover. She had inclinations toward loyalty and inclinations toward sexual adventure. So she had arrived at a reasonable arrangement, and she was lucky that Brian was sensible about it. The trouble was that she couldn't make herself believe this.

Was she, then, a woman who couldn't make up her mind, who enjoyed the luxuries of indecision, who wandered capriciously from one bed to another while she delayed her choice? Like Louise? No, she couldn't believe that either.

She could find in herself – recalling the simple certainties of being Keith's girl-friend – a Tamsin who belonged with Keith. And she could find in herself, in quiet evenings of regained and precious tranquillity, a Tamsin who belonged with Brian. But which was the real Tamsin?

She was in fear of these men: Brian with his calm certainty, his silent and irreducible patience; Keith with his forceful, insistent confidence. They were not rivals – that would have been simple – but each so sure of her that they declined rivalry. Like selective historians, they confronted her with alternative versions of her life. According to Brian, her yielding to Keith was an accidental impulse which he would passively observe until it was exhausted, now as he had once before. According to Keith, her marriage was a temporary aberration. Each asserted his own truth. And each truth was drawn from the man's long and intimate knowledge of her, from deep within her indeed. Yet the final truth might be what neither of them could believe.

Night after night, she quivered under their hands, their eyes searched her, they penetrated her body. She felt herself infused with two streams, coursing relentlessly through her, both by now an ineradicable part of her being.

She said to Brian: 'You're wrong if you think I'm sleeping with Keith for a spot of excitement. I did think that myself, but it's a lot more serious.'

'You're a serious person, Tam. You wouldn't be doing this if you didn't make yourself think it was serious.'

'I'm in love with him, that's what I think.'

'All right, that's what you think.'

'I want you to listen to me, Brian. Keith is able to make me love him. He always has been. He's got a hold on me.'

'It's true he's not doing you any good. Or rather, you're not doing yourself any good. You've looked miserable since this started. Let's go and live in Scotland again, how about that?'

'You know I've got to have a job. Anyway, this is happening because Keith exists. This hold he has on me . . . I can see now that it's never really been broken. Something came back to me the other day. It was when we were students. We were walking over to the Union together, you on one side of me and Keith on the other – this was before I'd even kissed either of you – and suddenly I thought to myself: I'm caught between these two men, I'll never get right away from either of them. It wasn't exactly a thought – I'm only putting it into words now I remember it – it was like feeling two forces coming at me, entering me to stay in me. And I think when I wanted you so much . . . that night . . . you remember . . . it was partly because the Keith force was there too. Now it's coming at me again. It's dangerous, Brian. Do you see that?'

'I see that when you sleep with a man it's got to be justified by . . . no, that's not fair, connected with . . . this idea of a hold on you. I mean, you didn't sleep with Farrell, did you?'

'No, I didn't.'

'I thought not. Perhaps it's a pity. You would have been able to get Keith into perspective.'

'Brian, you've got to believe what I say.'

'I do more than that. I believe in you.'

'Too much.'

'It can't be too much.'

'I need your help, Brian.' He kissed her. She clung to him, demanding more and more kisses. 'Make love to me.'

'Yes, sure.'

But afterwards she thought: she had never before wanted him to make love to her as a rescue.

By this time Tamsin knew that she would soon have to make a decision. Brian said that one shouldn't think in terms of decisions, but life had to be lived, and she saw no other way. Keith was putting on the heat. He considered that he had already won the contest (so far as he recognized a contest) – that he possessed her because she was virtually at home in his flat. It contained a number of things which he had made her buy with his credit cards, or bought for her: a bath-robe, the perfume and the shampoo that he recommended, new clothes into which she changed when they went out together, jewellery. But of course he wanted to possess her entirely. He seldom mentioned Brian. When he did, he implied that she had some tedious and unreasonable attachment which she would do well to drop for the sake of her own peace of mind. He expected her to be with him unless she could give some reason like being tired or unwell. Thus, he had managed to recreate the time when she was his girl-friend, and then his fiancée. It followed that she would soon be living with him. Why not now, indeed, since they had a place?

However, it wasn't Keith's pressure that was wearing her down so much as the need to put an end to this impossible phase of her life. She wasn't made for it, she hated it, she couldn't bear it much longer. She was ashamed of her weakness, too. Always, before, she had been able to make a clean break and go forward with no regrets. She had been sure of herself. The decision was needed so that she could be sure of herself again, and yet she had no confidence that this would ever be possible.

That she was being unfaithful to Brian – simply, vulgarly unfaithful, like any flighty wife bored with her husband – still seemed incredible to her. Curiously, it occurred to her that if she'd been married to Keith all these years it would have been easier to be unfaithful to him, although of course he would have taken it much harder. Being Keith's wife might be a means to contentment or happiness, a good way of living – even a necessity. But being Brian's wife was a dedication, a total absorption. Either that, or it was nothing.

Well . . . it wasn't an absorption now, or she wouldn't be sleeping with Keith. So it was nothing? That she couldn't believe. The idea of leaving Brian was a horror to her. A darkness, a void, not a separation but a dissolution. She would be abandoning herself, as she had understood and accepted herself. Perhaps she was wearing out this self and becoming someone else. But she didn't want to.

If she left Brian, an informed observer (she had to imagine such a person, now that they had scarcely any friends) would find it easy to explain. She was disappointed in him – he wasn't the man she had married. And it was true that she had been grievously hurt when he ceased to write. Something vital in him . . . therefore in her, in their joint self . . . had wasted away. Yet had his promise, his creative gift, been the ultimate essential that had united her to him? At times she thought so, or wanted to think so; at times she thought not. Hadn't she seen, without admitting it to herself, the failure in him too, and united herself also to that? The truth might be that she wasn't brave enough, or strong enough, to keep the pledge. That was why she would leave Brian. And she would know it.

'You'll have to make the break, sweetie,' Keith said. 'You're just making yourself wretched. I hate to see it. Screw up your courage and take the plunge.'

'I haven't got much courage. I can't leave Brian. I can't make myself do it.'

'You know, love, if you're hanging on just because you don't want to hurt him it's a bad reason. And if he knows it, which he must, then it won't even make him happy. It means it's finished, really.'

'I'll know when it's finished. If it ever is.'

'Time's a-wasting, my darling.'

'Well, I do know I've got to do something. I could stop seeing you, of course.'

'Try it,' Keith said, laughing.

And indeed, though this was the obvious alternative, it wouldn't be easy. She and Brian could move to another flat, or even another town; she could change her job, although she couldn't be sure of finding another one and she couldn't afford to be unemployed for long. But Keith wouldn't let her slip away – not this time. And, in a deeper sense, she no longer believed that she could escape from him. He had a hold on her, truly.

Then something alarming happened: she missed her period. She hurried to have herself tested and waited for the result in terror. She didn't see how she could possibly be pregnant, but if she was, she wouldn't know who was the father – it was the ultimate degradation.

No, she wasn't pregnant, but she was unwell. There had to be a reason for an irregularity, given that she'd always been regular. She ought to see a doctor, she was told.

That night – she was with Keith – she couldn't sleep. The room seemed to be unbearably hot; true, she had found the central heating excessive ever since she'd been coming here. She woke Keith and asked him to open a window, because she hadn't the energy to get out of bed herself.

In the morning, there was no doubt that she was ill. Keith competently took her pulse and her temperature.

'You just stay in bed, honey. I'll phone your office.'

It was a fact that she couldn't have got up and dressed, or at all events she couldn't have managed the stairs in the antiquated building where she worked. She was sweating and shivering, and her arms and legs were weak. Keith helped her to walk to the bathroom. When she got back into bed she lay quite still, exhausted.

Keith went down to his office. She was glad to be alone and in peace. She hadn't been left alone for a long time.

At eleven o'clock, Keith came back with a doctor. He was a young man with shoulder-length hair and a patterned cravat, evidently a personal friend of Keith's and just as evidently nothing to do with the Health Service.

'Been leading a busy life, dear?'

'I've got a job.'

'Regular job, have you? When did you last have a holiday?'

'I've no idea.'

'Well, when people don't get holidays they go on strike, and that's what your nice little body's doing. Could give you a lot of Latin words, but it comes down to that. I'll let you have some tonics and things. Main thing is, don't lift a finger. Don't let her lift a finger, Keith, got that? You're a thoughtless bugger, you haven't been treating her right.' Naturally, the doctor assumed that Tamsin was living with Keith.

It was strange to be ill. Tamsin had never been ill before except in Tangier, and then the reason – the food bug – had been straightforward once she knew about it. This illness, she reflected, was about as psychosomatic as an illness could be. It was a glaring proof of her weakness.

When Keith came up to the flat again, to encourage her to eat and boil an egg, she said: 'I want to write to Brian.'

'Sure. I'll have it sent round by messenger.'

He engaged a nurse, although she didn't want one. To her relief, the nurse was a quiet girl from Devonshire, new to London and somewhat overawed by the signs of wealth in the flat. She was earnest and attentive, her hands were gentle, she spoke in a low voice and with a softly slurred accent. When Tamsin didn't need anything she sat and read, usually a textbook for some exam she hoped to pass. Her presence didn't conflict with but supported Tamsin's desire to get through the illness without fuss.

Keith appeared several times a day, bringing grapes, mangoes imported by air, and Fortnum and Mason patés. He stayed in every evening, refusing several invitations, and sat beside her holding her hand. To ensure that she got a good night's rest, he slept on the couch in the living-room. The illness worried him – 'you're very precious to me, sweetheart,' he said. It was a bonus for him too, but although this thought came to Tamsin's mind she didn't believe that it crossed his. She couldn't choose not to be grateful for the clear sincerity of his love.

When he wasn't there, and when the nurse was quietly reading, Tamsin drifted into a state of unresisting resignation. She knew that the longer she stayed with Keith, the longer she was likely to stay. She was making her surrender in the most cowardly way. But she felt that she was capable of nothing more. Her unknown inner self was finding this path to shelter.

The illness didn't last long. It didn't need to, she thought as she began to recover, to make its point. She sat up and read, she watched television, she rewarded Keith by eating hearty meals. She phoned her office and ensured that her wages would be sent to Brian. Then her overdue period set in, and although it was more copious and annoying than usual it made her feel that things were getting back to normal. One night she slept for twelve hours, and woke up convinced that it was all over.

The doctor, however, said that she mustn't dream of going back to work and advised a convalescent holiday. This she couldn't resist; it was beautiful spring weather and she hadn't been in the real country for a long time. So she allowed Keith to shepherd her to the car and drive her to the New Forest. They stayed in an extremely comfortable hotel, of course owned by a friend of Keith's. Keith did most of his work on the phone. Once he went to London for the afternoon, and once he had to hear a new pop group play in the evening and stayed the night in the flat. As she ate dinner at a table by herself, and then as she went to bed alone, Tamsin was intrigued to find that she missed him. But the car came roaring up the drive of the hotel before she was downstairs for breakfast.

Had she made the break already, painlessly and without drama, practically without knowing it? She had never imagined that it would be like this. It was untidy; her life so far had been marked by blunders but not by loose ends. Keith said nothing definite about where they stood, perhaps deliberately, more likely because from his point of view there was no need. The manager and the other guests treated her as Keith's wife – a modern brand of politeness.

One morning, while she was sitting in the lounge and turning the pages of magazines, she was overcome by a sudden feeling of shame. She was living in a dream, surely. It was time to return to hard realities.

Keith was in London for the day. She hurried upstairs and packed her suitcase. She thought of leaving a note, but there was nothing he needed to know except that she had gone. As she walked briskly out of the hotel and down the drive to the road, she felt everything that she had lost coming back to her – her full health, her energy, her power of decision and action. She caught a bus to Winchester and then a train to London.

Brian was sitting at the table. He had a writing-pad and a pen on it, and she had a momentary illusion that nothing had changed since the days when she was working at Paterson's and he was striving with his poems. But the pad was blank.

She put her suitcase down and said: 'Hello, Brian.'

'Hello, Tam.'

He stood up, and they kissed. At once, she felt herself losing what she had gained. The kiss was like a handshake, an acknowledgement of friendship.

'What are you writing?'

'I was trying to write a letter to you. I didn't know what to say, though. Anyway, I wouldn't know where to send it.'

'I was at Keith's place. I told you. Then he took me to a hotel in the country. I'm supposed to convalesce. Fresh air, and all that.'

'Have you really been ill, Tam?'

'Pretty ill. It was sort of a collapse. I couldn't move – for the first few days I literally couldn't move. I'm all right now.'

'You look all right.'

'Yes . . . Brian?'

'What?'

'What did you mean, have I really been ill? D'you think I'd pretend?'

'I thought it might be difficult for you to tell me that you wanted to stay with Keith.'

'Oh. Well, if you could think that, it's bad, isn't it?' There was a silence. Tamsin couldn't take her eyes from the blank page of the writing-pad. 'Did you miss me?' she asked.

'I'll always miss you.'

'But you can do without me. Deep down, I mean. Very deep down, you're independent of me. You know how to be alone, and I don't.'

He didn't answer. The silence gathered round them again; it had become a power, stronger than any possible words.

'You know,' she said, 'I packed all my things this morning, just as if I was coming back to you.'

'And how did it feel, to be coming back to me?'

'I don't know. I don't think I feel anything these days. I don't dare to feel anything.'

She raised her eyes at last and looked straight at him.

'Brian, I'm leaving you.'

They both stood quite motionless now, hardly breathing. She felt unsteady, as she had during her illness.

'Go at once, Tam,' he said.

She made a small irresolute movement with one hand – for help or merely for physical support, she wasn't sure. He didn't move. She turned away swiftly but clumsily, picked up her case, and went down the stairs.

After taking a taxi to Waterloo, she found that she had only just enough money for a ticket to Winchester and the bus fare. I should have taken a cheap day return, she thought. One can always laugh – Christ, one can always laugh. There was almost an hour to wait until the next train. She couldn't afford lunch, so she bought a bar of chocolate.

The train wasn't full, but for most of the way there were two or three other people in her compartment. She tried to resort to the game of

191

making up stories about them. They all looked unhappy . . . who could tell, indeed, what miseries they secreted? This woman might have a husband in prison, that man a wife dying of cancer. But no, she was only seeking a grief crueller than her own. Probably they were merely bored. They carried nothing but lives without experience, which she need neither envy nor pity.

For the last part of the train journey she was alone. She allowed herself to think of what had happened. It couldn't have been otherwise, she understood that; she had found a measure of courage when it was needed; and yet she didn't know where to find the courage to live through the rest of her diminished and dismembered life . . . to live without Brian. She began to weep, crouching in a corner, hiding herself from the sunlight that poured with senseless lavishness through the window.

The train stopped at Winchester. She hunted in her bag and found that she hadn't got a tissue. She had to open her case on the platform, get out a fresh packet, and wipe her face. 'Cheer up, love, it's a beautiful day,' said the ticket-collector. One can always laugh.

She was back before Keith, to her relief. She washed her eyes carefully and put on eye-shadow, which she had begun to wear for the first time in her life. Then she changed into her prettiest new dress.

'Have a nice day, darling?' Keith asked.

'Oh yes. I didn't do much.'

'I won't leave you again.'

She smiled at him. 'Never ever?'

'Absolutely never absolutely ever cross my heart never will.'

'I love you,' she said. It was the truth. Now, it was the only truth that she could afford.

7

Keith must have drunk a hell of a lot last night. I watched him coming towards me across the great empty spaces of the house with his peculiar stiff walk, the walk I'm getting to know from nights like this, as though he were propelled by some kind of remote control. It would be a new twist if Keith became an alcoholic – succeeding where Brian failed, so to speak. Can you be an alcoholic without ever getting drunk, without escaping from the oppressive clarity of thought? It doesn't seem worth it. However, I don't think he will. Nothing is going to change.

'Hello, sweetie,' he said, as usual.

'Hello, darling,' I said, as usual.

'Not in bed yet?' he asked, as usual.

'I wasn't sleepy,' I said, as usual.

He kissed me, as usual.

I pushed my tongue into his mouth, as usual.

Daphne came and asked: 'Shall I make coffee? Anything you wish?' I can never decide whether she sleeps in her dress and apron or whether she can put them on in record time.

'Oh, get out,' Keith said. She got out, not at all discomposed, just a bit disappointed at not being allowed to make coffee. Keith talks to her brusquely nowadays, which would seem to indicate that he's screwing her. I wonder if she'd take off her dress and apron. He might prefer just to lift them. I imagine him giving it to her brusquely, punitively, with a mixture of bad temper and absent-mindedness. Of course it might not be like that at all; perhaps she soothes him and the relief of her unqualified submission makes him tender with her. I'd like to think so.

But I don't really believe he's screwing her. Why should he take the pressure off me? Nothing changes.

He sat down, and I could see that we were going to talk. We have these talks late at night, when we can't do anything else; we're like two people stranded by fog at an airport.

'You could have seen Brian today,' he said. He had told me in the morning that he would be away all day, going to the Isle of Wight to inspect a site for a festival, and getting back to town just in time for whatever he had to go to in the evening.

I said: 'I could have.' I've no idea how he knew that I didn't, but he did know.

'Why didn't you?'

'Your being away isn't a reason for me to see Brian.'

'He'd like you to take the opportunity, surely.'

'Maybe. I don't have any obligations to Brian.'

'Nor to me, do you?'

'Yes, I do have obligations to you, Keith. You've tried to make me happy. I'm grateful. If I'm not happy it isn't your fault.'

'You were, before this Brian thing started.'

'It didn't start. It's always been in my life. You know that.'

'I believe you could be happy if you didn't see him.'

'I believe you'd be happy if you divorced me.'

'That isn't true.'

'It is true. But if you can't, you can't.'

'Are you trying to make me divorce you?'

'Oh no. That isn't how it works nowadays, is it? Besides, I don't believe in divorce any more. I think the Pope's really got something – marriage is indissoluble. Both my marriages have turned out to be indissoluble.'

'You wouldn't ever leave me, Tam? Say you wouldn't. I couldn't bear it if you were to leave me.'

'No, of course not,' I said. 'What difference would that make?'

And I meant it, I mean it. I've left Keith once . . . how final it seemed, writing that clear definitive letter in Brian's little room. I've left Brian once . . . how final it seemed, in that train clattering down to Winchester. But it didn't work, so why should it work now?

We went on talking, pushing the treadmill round and round. Eventually Keith went to sleep on a couch and I went to sleep on another couch. There was no point in going to bed since we weren't going to make love. We either talk or make love, but not both. The next thing I knew was Daphne bringing in the post and the paper.

Keith at once jumped up – he never has hangovers – and put on his track-suit to go for a run on Hampstead Heath. After that he had a shower, shaved, and appeared in his smart pop version of the office suit, ready for another Keithish day. We had breakfast. He had cornflakes, bacon and eggs, toast and Swiss cherry jam, and coffee, as usual, and I had coffee, as usual. I don't think he remembered anything we'd said last night. He was his bright and chirpy self: 'What are you going to do today, honey-bunch? How about taking in that exhibition you were talking about? You don't want to go the day after it's closed. I might be able to come with you if I'm not too pushed. I'll call you from the office.'

He kissed me fondly, and a minute later the Jaguar roared away.

I had a bath. I could hear Daphne pattering about the house, which by this time has become her house more than mine; at least, she does far more of the upkeep and I'm sure she feels more at home in it. She knows I spend a long time in the bath. She can't disturb me, and I don't interrupt her in her programme of maintenance. She can have the house while I'm content with the bathroom.

If I stayed in the bathroom and never came out, I wonder how long it would be before Daphne started to worry. I've been thinking of cutting my veins. It occurred to me a while back, after I saw Amabel, and now I think about it almost every time I have a bath. I would never poison myself, nor take pills which are another form of poison; death should leave the body clean and empty, not fouled with chemicals. And I'd certainly never end my life with the abrupt, vulgar noise of a shot. But the Roman method appeals to me as highly civilised. You could say it was the Romans' great contribution to civilization. There'd be no mess for anyone to clean up. There'd be no pain, only a dreamy fading away – the blood pouring easily and silently into the water, quite a beautiful sight I should think – and a grand final sense of the irrevocable.

But I know I'll never do it. It isn't necessary. It would be an excessive gesture – why not let my life drain away at its own pace? I have obligations, too. I've promised Keith that I won't leave him. I don't claim the right to so easy an evasion. I know what my life has to be, and if I have nothing else I have the patience to continue on my way through it.

I topped up the hot water three or four times, but my spine started to ache and I got out of the bath. I put on a simple woollen dress. Then I remembered that Keith hadn't chosen it and didn't like it much, and probably I was going to the exhibition with him, so I changed into something more elegant.

I had yoghourt and nuts for lunch. Daphne gazed at me reproachfully; she considers that I don't eat enough, and so does Keith. Actually, although it bores me to eat a full meal by myself, I tuck in quite heartily at restaurants or when we're with friends. It doesn't make any difference. I'm still thin.

Keith rang up to say that he couldn't get away for the exhibition after all. I was really disappointed. He urged me to go anyway, and I said I might, but I didn't want to. I used to enjoy going to exhibitions and galleries alone, but nowadays I can't – it's like eating alone. I find that I see more when Keith is with me. The freshness of his enthusiasm sharpens my perception. We often meet people we know, too, and somehow when I'm alone I don't, or perhaps I don't recognize them. I depend on Keith, altogether, to put me in touch with the outside world. In its public aspect, our marriage is very much alive.

So I changed back into the woollen dress and went to see Brian. I walked up the stairs, past one landing after another and one door after another, as one would walk through the streets of a strange town. There are people here, but they're nothing to do with me. I'll come here again and again and remain a stranger. This time there was a woman coming down from the top floor. The stairs are narrow, so I waited for her. It's dark up here near Brian's room and I couldn't really see what she looked like; in any case, I don't peer at people who don't peer at me. I had a dim impression of a small, slight figure and a face as pale as mine. She didn't glance at me and went on her way shyly – not at all nervously, though, but with a kind of solemn delicacy, maintaining the convention of treating me as though I were invisible.

I asked Brian: 'Who's the woman I met on the stairs?'

'She lives in the room opposite,' he said.

'Sure.' The possibility that she'd come out of Brian's room hadn't occurred to me. 'Who is she?'

'Ah. She's the great-granddaughter of the last Emperor of Brazil. She wears a locket round her neck with a picture of the Emperor on one side and a picture of the Empress on the other. In between the pictures there's a folded map which shows where the imperial jewels are buried, deep in the jungle. There are rubies and diamonds and emeralds and the yellow stones that have no name and shine like leopards' eyes. One day she's going to give me the map and I'll find the jewels. I hope you'll come with me.'

'Yes, I'll come,' I said. 'What shall we do with the jewels?'

'We'll move them five miles so the map won't be any use, and bury them again.'

'But hasn't she got anybody she ought to pass the map on to?'

'She has three daughters. An air hostess, a skating champion, and a literary critic. But you see, they all want the jewels, so obviously they mustn't have them.'

I stared up at the stain on the ceiling, which began to look like a map – a map that only Brian and I could read. I was lying with my head on his arm, as usual, and I was wonderfully relaxed and comfortable, with no ache in my spine at all, but my feet were a little cold. Autumn is coming on. I began to look forward to the winter, when we lie under a blanket. I thought of the winter in Scotland when we used to huddle in our sleeping-bags, or both in the same sleeping-bag. It could have been a good winter if we'd known how to make use of it in the right way.

I asked Brian: 'Do you think it's ever possible to understand things when they're actually happening?'

'No, it isn't,' he said. 'It's only when nothing is happening that you understand.'

'Understand what, Brian?'

'You understand that your life isn't what you do or what's done to you. You get up in the morning, you dress, you eat, you drive here in your car, you walk up the stairs – all that's unimportant. Now you're here. We are here together. This is our real life. We don't do anything – we don't need to. It isn't even that we don't need to. If we did anything, we'd spoil it all.'

I'm glad Brian says these things. It's what I come here for. And I believe there's a truth in what he says, a truth that I could never find without him. Yet I'm aware that there's an illusion tangled up with the truth.

I said: 'There isn't really such a thing as nothing happening. I'm lying down. My feet are cold. I'm listening to you. By what you say, you're doing something to me.'

'Don't argue,' he said. 'Don't talk.'

I might have continued: if we don't talk, you're still doing something by your thoughts, by transmitting to me your belief. What this means is that there's always an imperfection, and he knows that although he tries not to know it. Perhaps if we were far away, if we were deep in the jungle . . . But this little room is as remote as any jungle. Perhaps if we were jungle animals, or fish as he imagines sometimes, or plants . . . But we're not, we can't be.

I didn't talk any more. It's best when we don't talk. The slow, grey autumn darkness came on. I found what I needed: a release from the power of time, and silence, and peace. But in finding it, I knew that I must lose it.

I kissed him and said: 'I must go.'

'So long, Tam.'

'So long, Brian.'

I went down the stairs, holding on to the creaky banister. I got into the car and inflicted on myself the ugly, peremptory noise of the engine. When I drove off, an *Evening Standard* van shot past me. It took away all that remained of my peace.

I reckoned that I could just get home before Keith and change into a dress that he likes. I have obligations. So I overtook the van in third gear and beat it to the lights.

It surprises me that I find my way in London. The streets, nowadays, all look the same to me. I am crossing a desert: crossing it or just wandering about in it, going over my tracks.

I go from here to there in order to go from there to here again. I don't know why, but it's always necessary. Things have happened, not as I expected or wanted them to happen, but as they had to. It wasn't possible to keep control, maintain direction, achieve a destination. Not for me, not for Brian, not for Keith. We have struggled with one another without victory, only to remain locked together. We did what we had to do. We are where we must be.

I suppose it will always be like this.